Doctor of Sports

Men of Mercy Series

A Novel

by:
Grace Maxwell

Copyright 2023 Blind Date Publishing

All rights reserved. No part of this publication may be reproduced, distributed or transmitted in any form or by any means, including photocopying, recording or other electronic or mechanical methods, without the prior written permission of the author, except in the case of brief quotations embodied in critical reviews and certain other noncommercial uses permitted by copyright law.

This is a work of fiction. Names, characters, places and incidents are a production of the author's imagination. Locations and public names are sometimes used for atmospheric purposes. Any resemblance to actual people, living or dead, or to businesses, companies, events, institutions or locations is completely coincidental.

Men of Mercy: Doctor of Sports/Grace Maxwell — 1st edition

Dedication and Thank You

Thank you, my readers, for taking a chance on me. I hope you enjoy Eliza and Steve.

To my husband who supports me and reads all I write. You are my muse. (And no we can't do what my characters do — we have a door and young children).

To my boys who hate that I write about sex. I love you!

Thank you to my typo hunters, Courtnay, Linda, Iris, and Nancy and to my editors Jessica Royer Ocken and Diana Loifton. Any typo that are here are stubborn SOBs and determine d to stay.

Chapter 1

Steve

The private room at the Pan Pacific is crowded. Most of the Vancouver Tigers football team has arrived through the back doors, here to celebrate the start of a new season. As the team doctor, my job is to make sure everyone is healthy and able to play. Well, tonight my job is to have a good time, but those are the *official* duties of my position.

I like these parties because there are always a lot of women—the wives and girlfriends, or the WAGs as we call them, and also cheerleaders. But my favorite are the women who are here to meet a player.

I'm not a player, but I get more attention than the assistant coaches because I always drop that I'm the team doctor. It's one of the perks of the job, and tonight, I have a room upstairs at the hotel, just in case.

With a drink in my hand, I wander over to the coaching staff. They're surrounded by women. Jimmy always has the most, which is hilarious. He's married and faithful, but a magnet for ladies.

Then I see her across the room. She has a long mane of chestnut hair. We lock eyes, and she smiles. I smile back.

She's talking to Tanya Wei, the head of our marketing group, and after a moment, Tanya looks over at me. Then the woman whispers something and laughs.

I like what I see in that red dress with lots of cleavage. With a dress like that, she has to be here for the same reason I am — to scratch that itch.

Without breaking eye contact, she makes her way across the room to me.

"Hello," she says. "I'm Eliza."

I reach for her hand and bring it to my lips. "Nice to meet you, Eliza. I'm Steve."

She giggles. "Does that work with women?"

"I don't know. You tell me. I have a room upstairs if you're interested."

She smirks. "You're very sure of yourself."

"I know what I like when I see it."

"And you like me?"

"Most certainly."

"Why don't we slow things down a bit, Prince Charming."

"I'm a doctor if your heart is beating too fast."

She smiles and shakes her head. "Tell me something about yourself."

There's something about her I can't quite put my finger on, but I like her. I don't mind working this a little bit, and even if she turns me down tonight, I think it might be fun to connect with her later. "I grew up here in Vancouver."

She straightens her back. "Really? That's rare."

I nod and take a sip of my whiskey. "I did. We moved a few times, though. I was born at Mercy Hospital and lived in Burnaby, and then we lived in several different houses around Vancouver while my dad fixed them up and sold them."

"Your dad flipped houses before it was popular."

I've never thought of it that way. "I guess he did." I'm mesmerized by her caramel-colored eyes for a moment. "What about you?"

Her brow furrows. "I grew up in West Van."

West Van tends to be old-money Vancouver. "Very nice. Did you attend Bowden?"

"How did you know? Is that where you went?"

I laugh. "No way. My parents went to public schools and believe Canada has one of the best school systems in the world, so I graduated from King George."

"Wow, the downtown high school. I'm impressed."

"I was on the football team, but they were known for hockey. I played both sports until they made me choose."

She curls a strand of hair around her finger. "Why did you have to choose?"

"Because I knew I'd never be in this room as an athlete."

"And what brings you here this evening?"

"Didn't Tanya tell you?"

Her lips curl. "No. She warned me away from you. She said you were a sheep in wolf's clothing."

My hands go to my heart as if she had shot me. "She didn't say that."

Eliza nods.

"I'm the team doctor. I work half the year for the team, and the other half I work at Mercy Hospital."

"Oh! Where you were born."

I nod. "I like it. I'm an orthopedic surgeon."

"So, you're telling me you're good with your hands?"

I nod. "When you're ready to find out, you let me know, and we'll head upstairs."

"I'll keep that in mind."

Her hands are empty, and it dawns on me that I should change that. "Can I get you a drink?"

"What are you drinking?"

"Irish whiskey."

"That's my dad's drink."

"I can get you anything you want. What sounds good?"

"Hmm... How about Stoli with a lemon twist on the rocks?"

I nod. "Okay. Don't move. I'll be right back." I head to the bar and order her drink and a second for myself. When I turn around, she's talking with the owner of the team, Tom Rourke. She's laughing, and I realize she must work in the front office. I don't think I've seen her before.

Tom is pulled away before I return with her drink. When I hand it to her, we toast. "Cheers."

"What do you do for the team?" I ask. I want to be careful, because if she's Tom's assistant, I need to back away. I don't date women for long, and I certainly don't want to rock the boat with the head office.

"I float around wherever they need me." She takes a sip of her drink.

She's just the perfect package—bright and engaging with a stunning body and legs that go on forever. "You're not Tom's assistant or second assistant or something?"

"Tom?" Her head tilts to the side.

I give an internal sigh of relief. "Tom Rourke."

"Oh. Mr. Rourke. No. I'm definitely not his assistant. I work in marketing mostly."

We talk for a while longer, and she nurses the vodka.

"Did you choose vodka so you wouldn't get drunk?"

She smiles. "You're very observant. I need to keep my wits about me with you around."

"I would never make you do anything you didn't want to do."

"So, if I told you I wanted to go to your hotel room, you'd take me up there and do what?"

"What do you want me to do?"

She smiles. "I don't know. What are you good at?"

"Oh honey, I could make you come three times without even penetrating you."

"Really? How can you be so sure?"

"I've never left a woman unsatisfied."

She snorts. "Are you sure they're not faking it?"

I tilt my head to the side. "Positive."

"Then I guess you need to show me."

"Do you need to let anyone know you're heading out?"

"No. We're good."

The party is in full swing as I place my hand at the small of her back and lead her to the elevator. I don't know where tonight is going to take us, but I'm excited.

After stepping into the elevator, the tension is thick. I'm used to women making the next move. I know she's committed to coming to my room, but I don't want to overstep.

"Did you plan on bringing someone upstairs tonight?" she asks.

"Would that bother you?"

"No. I'm betting it would mean you're pretty much a Boy Scout and always prepared."

"If you're asking if I have condoms, I do."

She smiles and steps close to me. Her soft mounds pillow against my chest. She licks her lips, and my cock is already straining against my zipper. Her kiss is assertive and erotic, and I quickly take over, showing her how our evening is going to go.

The elevator pings at our floor, and we break apart.

I reach for her hand and lace our fingers together. The sizzle of chemistry is strong. We stroll down the hall, and a swipe of my phone over the lock opens the door. I lead her into my suite.

I pull two bottles of water from the minibar in the corner. I need to cool down a half-minute, or I'm going to explode in my pants. I haven't been with a woman who turned me on like this in a long time.

Eliza takes a bottle of water from me and sits in a big leather chair. She looks at me as if waiting for me to perform.

"Show me the color of your panties," I say in a low voice.

She smiles as she hikes up her dress. She sits with her legs wide and gives me an amazing view of dark blue silk.

Fuck.

Eliza runs her index finger over to the damp fabric, stroking the cleft where moisture has collected. Her eyes drift down at the sensation of her own touch. She's turned on. I'm mesmerized, watching her take her pleasure. She doesn't need me for that. But I can't just sit and watch.

I grab the ankle closest to me and hook her leg over the arm of the chair. "I'm pretty sure I can do that to your utmost satisfaction." Corny as it sounds, she's so hot I would do anything at this point to get inside her.

Dropping to my knees, I take her other ankle and place that leg over the other chair arm. Her thighs are spread wide open, those blue silk panties turning almost black with her wetness. With a flip of my wrist, I rip the panties from her, tucking them into my pocket.

"Those were real silk," she says breathlessly.

"I'll buy you a new pair."

Her pussy is completely bare, and it pulls me to her like a magnet, my dick hard.

We don't bother with any more play. I lean close, and her slim, pink-tipped fingers bury themselves in my hair as my mouth nears her swollen pussy. I can't wait to taste her, but I want this to be good too.

She whimpers when I move up and kiss her mouth instead. Our tongues dance, but when her hand wanders to her center, I stop her. "No. I'm in control here."

She stands, and I reach for her dress, pulling it over her head in one deft movement. She's wearing a blue silk bra to match. She reaches behind herself and frees her tits. They're glorious. They sit high and full with small, rose-pink nipples that have hardened into points.

I unbuckle my pants, letting them drop to the floor. Then I pull off my tie and shirt, tossing them close to her dress. I reach for her and turn her around, leaning her bare back against my chest. Her skin is hot, almost feverish against mine.

I kneel and lick from the base of her spine all the way up to her neck. She gives a deep shiver, assuring me that she's extremely responsive. I already know she's intelligent and witty. I can only hope she's as confident during sex as she seemed to be before. There's nothing more attractive than a confident woman who knows what she wants from a man and knows how to get it.

Once again, I spin her around to face me. I ease her back into the chair and drop to my knees to taste her rosy nipples. I flick at the tips with my tongue, her body jerking in reaction. I let my teeth scrape down from the top of her full breast, capturing the nipple in my mouth. Alternating from hard and fast to slow and easy seems to drive her crazy. Her hips push toward me, trying to find some relief from my relentless teasing. Every inch of her skin tastes and smells of honey. She's delicious.

My mouth trails down her flat stomach, my tongue finding her belly button before reaching the top of her mound. I pause there, lightly biting her skin before plunging my tongue between her thighs.

I don't want to do the typical male thing and start right in on her clit. I've taken too many risks already to have this be just a routine one-night stand. Deciding on my plan of action, I point my tongue and plunge it into her, darting in and out like a small cock fucking her. Her body bucks up off the chair, a gasp bursting from her chest. She props herself up on her arms and watches as I assault her pussy this way. Her eager moans assure me she likes what I'm doing.

I lightly strum her clit, now out of its hood and throbbing visibly. The rose shade of her pussy grows darker as she becomes more and more aroused. I keep up the tongue fucking for a little while longer, bringing her close to the edge but not quite over it. I have other plans and can't wait to see how she'll react.

With two fingers inside, I find her magic button. I keep

up a light pressure, watching her body flush and twitch. Then I press harder and lean down, flicking her clit just a few times to send her over the edge. She stands, pushing her mound into my hand for more friction. She comes hard, gripping my hand inside her with each convulsion of her inner muscles.

"Steve, fuck, I can't wait any longer. Don't you want to be inside me?" Her voice breaks through my mental wanderings. I can hear the strain of the tension building between us.

I roll a condom on and sit in the leather chair, I pull her down to my lap, her back to my chest. She takes hold of my cock in one hand, guiding it into her slick, hot passage. I silently name all the bones in the human hand to keep from shooting off, to get myself under control so I can give her a good ride.

She takes her time getting seated. Inch by inch, she eases onto me, sighing deeply when she hits bottom. Damn, she feels so good—tight without being painful, hot, and so wet that some of her liquid leaks down onto my balls. Placing her hands on the arms of the chair, she lifts herself until just the head of my cock is inside her before letting her body fall back down onto me. She grunts as my cock bottoms out and immediately rises back up. She does this several times, each time falling faster than the last.

I dig my fingers into her lush hips, amazed at how strong and limber she is while still feeling so soft. When she leans forward, I hold on, wondering what she will do next. Her thighs do all the work, raising her body up and down to ride me, and the feeling is truly incredible. It makes me feel like I have a huge cock with each stroke tapping against her cervix. She's loving it, moaning and arching her back, practically growling on the downstroke.

It isn't enough, though. I love how it feels to have her in control, but I want a turn. Grabbing her under the knees, I lift and turn her, placing her in the chair, her hands holding onto the back for support. Somehow, I manage to keep my cock inside her the entire time. Something about this woman makes me feel like a superhero — or a god.

My hips piston my cock into her, hard, fast, and deep. I can feel my balls tighten, a deep electricity churning inside them, signaling that my finish is close. Her insides pulse, and I know she isn't far behind me, but I'm not about to let myself come first. I want to feel her spasming around my cock, milking me. Reaching down, I use two of my fingers to circle her clit, making sure I don't rub too hard. My other hand cups her left breast, tweaking the nipple firmly enough to draw a gasp from her.

When her body shakes, I know she's close. I rub her clit faster, pounding into her with everything I have. Sweat pools at the small of her back, a bit of hers, a bit of mine. She's moaning and begging me to fuck her harder, faster, each word bringing me closer and closer to the fall.

Her body clenches, and a small scream rips out of her, telling me she's tumbling over the edge of the cliff as she squeezes me tight. With one final push, stream after stream fills the condom. I don't think I've ever come this hard in my life.

After a minute, my breathing slows enough to allow me to pull back and flop down on the bed. She remains still for a moment before she sits down in the seat of the chair, her eyes half closed. The satisfied look on her face makes my cock twitch for a second round. She licks her lips and sits up a bit, stretching in the most seductive way, letting her breasts jut forward as her back arches.

"Come on over here." I motion.

She gets up from the chair and glides over to join me on the bed. I pull her in tight and don't wake until the next morning.

Next thing I know, daylight streams through the curtains and falls on my clothes, now neatly folded in the leather chair. I listen, but there's no noise.

She's gone.

I'm disappointed.

I dress and walk downstairs to grab a cup of coffee. In

line, I see Marty Holloway, quarterback for the Vancouver Tigers. He slaps me on the shoulder. "Guess I'm not the only one who stayed the night."

I smile. I'm not one to brag.

"I saw you having a good time with the owner's daughter last night," he says, raising his cup to me. "Smart move to butter her up. Rumor has it old man Rourke is going to give her the team later this year."

"His daughter?" I ask.

"Yeah, the hot brunette in the red dress."

I school my face. *Did I just fuck the owner's daughter?* I close my eyes. I already know the answer.

Chapter 2

Eliza

I stretch like a cat in my bed. Damn, there are muscles it seems I hadn't used in far too long. I had fun with Steve last night—more fun than I should have. It was nice being anonymous and not kept at arm's length because I'm Tom Rourke's daughter.

"Are you listening to me?" Tanya yells from the bathroom.

"I am now. What do you need?"

"Where is your aspirin, ibuprofen—Tylenol, Advil, anything that will help with this hangover?"

"It's called water. Drink lots of water. There's aspirin in the right-hand drawer of the left sink."

I hear her slide a drawer open and shut, and then she slides out another.

"As you face the sinks—"

"I'm facing the sinks. Who has two sinks, anyway?"

"The sink on the left has drawers beneath it on the right and left. Look at the top left drawer."

"Gaad, finally. This is way too hard. In my hovel, I have one bathroom with one sink, a shower that is also a bathtub, a toilet, and a bathroom cabinet. That's it. It is too crowded with one person, let alone two. In fact, I think my whole apartment fits into your living room."

I rest my arm over my eyes. "It's my mother's house. She's in Italy or India or wherever she needs to be to find herself this month."

"Must be nice to have Daddy Warbucks to foot that bill."

"Don't be fooled. She earned all of it. My dad is great, but he was no picnic to live with."

"He's been married to his current wife for how long?"

"Since I was nineteen." I sit up. "Bring me some Advil too, please."

"Did you go home with Steve McCormick?"

"No, I didn't go home with him. But he's nice. He probably told me three times he was the team doctor, though. That must really impress people."

"Did you tell him your name?"

"Of course I did." I bristle. I didn't tell him my last name. I become a pariah or the best friend when I tell people my last name. *Nope*. I want to like people for who they are and them to like me for the same.

"Hmm." Tanya appears, wearing her dark sunglasses. "Really? He went to medical school, so I'm betting he's pretty smart. He would know not to mess with the owner's daughter."

"Who said we messed around?"

"That hickey I spotted on the side of your boob."

"What?" I look over in the mirror, and damn if there isn't a big magenta bruise on the side of my right breast. I look at the other side and fuck, I have one there too.

Tanya snickers. "That's what I thought. Steve's not the kind of guy to call a lady after a good roll in the hay."

"And you know that because…"

"Oh no. It was never me. But I've had more than one heartbroken intern or staff member in my office, all blubbery because he got in their pants and didn't want any repeats."

"You don't have to worry about me being upset. I could tell he was a one-and-done type of guy. It was fun."

"I've heard he's pretty well endowed."

I smile. My eyes nearly popped out of my head last night when I saw his dick. Not only was it longer than I've ever had, it was fat too. Boy, was it a tight fit—or maybe my virginity had returned since it'd been so long since I'd had sex with another human being. "I'd say he's bigger than average."

"So, you didn't exchange numbers when he left?"

I chuckle. "No. He fell asleep, and I got out of there. I didn't want Charles to rat me out to my dad."

Charles Wentworth is my dad's fixer. He has assistants, but Charles is the guy he calls when he needs something handled. Sometimes, that could be my mother, or maybe it's someone at one of his companies who needs to be looked into. But Charles is always telling Dad what he finds out about people.

"I'm impressed. You got away before he did. That must have his head spinning."

"Well, once he figures out I'm not a lowly intern, he'll probably tuck his tail and run."

Tanya laughs. "I'm going to buy popcorn for this."

"You don't even like popcorn," I yell as she leaves me in my room.

"I like popcorn just fine. I just prefer candy at movies."

I spend the weekend going through our current marketing plan for the Vancouver Tigers, and I make a lot of changes. Turns out, I have the time. Other than Tanya, most of my friends have moved out of Vancouver. The cost of living is off the rails here, and they're also probably enjoying living somewhere where it doesn't rain nine months of the year. So I don't mind working. It's better than shopping all day or having lunch plans to talk about nothing with someone I barely know.

And it means that I've hit the ground running this morning. It's barely eight o'clock, and I'm already settling into my office at the stadium.

I've been back here less than two months. I just finished a graduate degree at the London School of Economics. I've been working for the last six years to take over this business from my dad. He owns probably nineteen different companies, but this is the only one I want.

The Vancouver Tigers are an underrated professional football team in the Canadian football league. I want to change that, and I have the skills to do it. I went to Columbia University in New York City and studied sports management. I interned with the National Football League for two years. After graduating, I worked in the back office for the San Diego Pelicans, an NFL team, before spending two years at grad school in London.

I'm ready to take over the team as soon as my dad is ready to give it to me. I have a meeting on his calendar today to discuss his future and get a feel for his plans for me.

"Knock, knock," Darius says as he enters my office. Darius Johnson heads up professional player recruitment for the Tigers. He doesn't look at the college players; he has the dream job. For his paycheck, he watches professional football games. He also creates reports on every player in the league and a few in the NFL. His job is to be prepared if we need a position filled at the last minute for any reason, like an injury. He's also become a friend.

"What's up?" I shoot him a grin.

"I want to go to lunch. I met a guy who's a waiter at Crimson Rose last night while I was out, and I want to see him in his element."

"Is that why you're looking so dapper today?" He's dressed in salmon-colored slacks, a white shirt, and beige suede loafers, something only he could pull off.

"I'm not telling." But he smiles, and I know that's why. "Pretty please? I don't want to go there on my own."

I shrug. "As long as I'm back in time for my two o'clock with my dad."

"Girl, I still have a job. We'll be back long before that."

"You say that now, but just know, I'll leave by one thirty."

"No problem. Let's go before the lunch rush. How does eleven thirty work?"

"I'll meet you downstairs."

I wave as he exits and return my attention to my screen in front of me. I go through the numbers again, and I still can't see why things aren't adding up. I pick up my phone. "Tanya, do you know why the numbers for the new design are off on our spreadsheet?"

"Which numbers?"

We talk it through, and after a minute, I realize the numbers in the spreadsheet I was given by accounting have two digits inverted. I roll my eyes. People are human, but accounting should have checked what they were sending out. If they get this wrong, what else are they getting wrong?

"Thanks," I tell her once everything is sorted. "I'm going to lunch with Darius. There's a new guy he's interested in. You want to join? That way I won't feel like an idiot while he's flirting."

"Sure."

I give her the details, and when the time arrives, she meets us downstairs.

We walk together over to the restaurant, and Darius cranes his neck all over for the first five minutes we're there.

But eventually we conclude that the guy he met is not working today. He pouts a little, and instead of him flirting through lunch, we talk about work.

"The kickoff party was a lot of fun Friday night," Tanya says, trying to be sly.

"It was nerve-wracking for me," Darius says.

"Why? You can't be held accountable for how these guys perform," Tanya says.

Darius looks at me.

I hold my hands up. "I don't own the team yet. But you have the best data out there. You can't help it if someone breaks an ankle or has a bad year because of something going on in their personal life. If that happens, we cut them from the team and move on to your next recommendation."

"We've acquired three players I didn't recommend," he says. "I got overridden by someone on the coaching staff, but I don't know who."

"Which three?" I ask.

"Sean Rhymes, Nathan Cotton, and Mattieu Pelletier." Darius takes a deep pull on his ice water.

My ears perk up. "Why didn't you recommend them?"

"Sean Rhymes is a good player, but he created a lot of problems at the Montreal Columbes."

"But wasn't that because he didn't speak French?" I challenge.

"More than half the team isn't bilingual," Darius counters.

"And why Cotton and Pelletier?" I ask.

"I don't want to tattle too much," he says, looking away. "But know this. My information is accurate. I keep lists of players by position across the CFL and NFL. I watch social media sites, and I have Google alerts for these players so that whenever they're in the news, I see it. Sometimes, it's also what you don't see—pictures of teams without certain players in them. I know enough about the three players I didn't recommend to say we shouldn't have hired them."

That is not what I want to hear. The team needs chemistry when it comes to winning championships, and having bad apples in the mix is not going to get us there. Canada's premier sport is hockey, and I want more eyes on football. I know I can do that, but not if I have problem players. I'll find out who went against his research and why. The list of options is pretty short, but I won't necessarily know who the influencer is. It could be someone outside the team.

We finish lunch with plenty of time for me to return to the office. I don't know if I'll mention what Darius said to Dad before I know who the other two players are, because it could have been part of a deal with another owner. The request could have come from him. I need all the information I can get before I make my case.

When it's time for our meeting, I touch up my lipstick and head upstairs to my dad's office. "Hello, Marlene," I announce as I enter.

Marlene Dennison is dad's secretary. And she is exactly that. She takes shorthand as he dictates things to her, and she controls his calendar. During work hours, no one has the ability to show up without an appointment, even me.

"He's just finishing a call," she tells me. "If he's not off in three minutes, I'll ping him and let him know you're here."

I sit down in the seating area and wait. I look through the marketing report I'm prepared to give him. We've updated the Tiger logo, which we like to do so we can sell more products and create more revenue. We're not part of a big-league powerhouse like the NFL, with tons of money coming in from media deals. But I have a plan to make that happen.

"He'll see you now," Marlene says after a minute.

I stand. "Thank you."

Walking into my dad's office, I'm surrounded by pictures of me and my half siblings. There's a large picture of my little brother and sister with my dad's fourth and current wife, Laura, and Dad on the wall. I always hate that I wasn't included, but that may have been more my mother's choice than my father's. Anyway, it's not worth the jealousy.

"Hello, sweetheart. What brings you here today?" Dad asks.

"I've been busy down in marketing, and I have a few things to show you. We just did a revamp of the Tiger logo." I slip out a copy of the new rendering and hand it to him.

"He looks meaner," Dad says.

I nod. "Research showed that the other was too cuddly."

He sits back. "It's expensive to redo everything."

"Dad, we were asked by the league to do an update. Our colors, orange and black, will remain the same."

We spend my allotted time talking about the league requirements. I know they bother my dad, which is why he appointed me as the liaison. He prefers hanging out with the other owners and smoking cigars to hearing about changes the governing body requires.

When I stand to leave, Dad clears his throat. "I was on the phone with Donnie Cochran."

I stop and slowly turn around. Donnie has been trying for years to get Dad to sell the team. "What is he offering this time?"

Dad shakes his head. "You are the smartest girl I know. You're wasting your talents on this team. You should be running the paper mills or the fisheries."

I internally groan. Those businesses gross me out. I'm not interested in those industries at all. "I've worked hard to be here," I remind him.

He holds up his hands. "And for what? You're twenty-eight without a life. Trust me, I wasted a lot of time building up my businesses so you and your brother and sister —"

"Half," I interrupt. Minni and Logan are just little kids.

He looks at me, annoyed. "So you wouldn't have to slave away at a job."

"I love this job. I love this team. I want to do it," I tell him for probably the thousandth time. "What did Donnie offer?"

"Well, Toronto just brought in an investor at a forty-percent share for twenty million."

I already know this. "Yes. They valued the team at sixty million. They won the Grey Cup last year."

"Donnie offered me forty million."

I snort. "That's not worth it." I breathe a sigh of relief.

Dad looks out at the cargo ships lined up to unload their goods in the port. "I'm seriously considering it."

I rush back over to his desk. "Why would you do that? With the stadium expansion, it's worth so much more."

Dad turns his gaze back to me. "Because I don't want you to waste your youth working ninety-hour weeks for nothing. You can work for Rourke Paper, and I'll pay you a half-million a year. That job you'll work thirty hours a week."

My blood pressure shoots through the roof. "The paper industry is dying, and I love football. You know all I've done to get here."

He shakes his head. "But what you don't realize is that you need more than the team or a job to make you a whole person. I loved your mother, and I don't blame her for our breakup, but if I'd been around more, maybe we would have been able to make it work."

I take a few deep breaths. "Dad, please. I want the team. Please don't make me beg. I don't care about a life outside of work. I don't need a man to take care of me."

He slaps his desk. "I know you don't need to be taken care of. But you need to have some sort of life. There is nothing more boring than listening to people drone on and on about their work at a dinner party. You need to get married, have kids, do things that aren't related to the team."

My shoulders fall. "Dad, please don't sell to Donnie. I will do what you want, but please."

He takes a deep breath. "I'll think about it. Come over for dinner on Sunday night. We'll come up with a plan."

I nod, and I turn and walk out of his office because there's nothing else I can do right now. I know my dad when he's like this. His mind is made up. I'm going to have to play ball with him because I don't know what I'll do if he sells even a fraction of the ownership to Donnie.

Chapter 3

Steve

I sigh as I slide into my regular seat at Joe Fortes, across from my friends Davis Martin and Michael Khalili, who beat me here this evening. I motion to Nancy at the bar. We're around often enough that she knows what I'm drinking, and she soon walks over a highball glass with two fingers of Johnnie Walker Blue.

I take a sip and thank her. It's so smooth, my favorite.

"What has you all worked up?" Davis asks.

I sigh again.

"Uh-oh. Does Stevie have girlie problems?" Michael teases.

"Just because you talked Nadine into marrying you doesn't make you special," I snap at Michael.

Davis turns to Michael. "He's cranky. He must have had a woman shut him down. It's hard when that happens. Of course I wouldn't know." He makes a face.

I can't help but smile at that. "Shiiiit. You followed

Paisley around like a lost puppy dog. You don't fool me. But yes, it is a girl." I take another drink for courage. "She's Tom Rourke's daughter."

Davis snorts. "Well, there goes your job with the Tigers."

I sit up straight. "Says who?"

"You're peeing in the executive-level sandbox," Michael notes helpfully. "You can't fling your typical shit there."

Griffin and Jack arrive and settle in.

"Stevie here is having girlie problems," Michael says, catching them up.

"Stop it already." He knows I hate when he calls me Stevie, but that's why he's doing it.

"He's taken the bite of forbidden fruit and wants to go back for more," Davis adds.

Griffin's eyes go wide. "I have to report you to the police if she's underage."

"She's not underage," I whine.

"How do you know? Did you ask for ID?" Michael asks.

I slap my hand on the table. "Look, she's my boss's daughter. She's over the age of consent. The problem is, rumor has it old man Rourke is giving her the team. She's worked for the NFL and for one of the NFL franchises. She was living somewhere abroad and is back to take over—or so I've learned."

"You learned this after you slept with her?" Jack asks as Nancy places a drink in front of him. "Thank you," he tells her.

"I asked around," I say without answering the question.

"She must be hot," Griffin says, smiling as Nancy sets a glass in front of him as well.

I roll my eyes. "How's it going with that nurse you've been seeing?"

"She got a little too clingy. I've moved on." Griffin takes a deep pull on his Macallan. "But don't change the subject. Tell us more about this woman."

I look at my glass and debate what I want to say about her. These guys are my closest friends. We've known each other since we were kids. Our fathers are friends. I take a deep breath. "She left while I was asleep."

Jack claps me on the back. "She ran away before you could?"

I nod. "Yep. And I think the only reason I'm hung up is because I wanted another round in the morning."

"Since when do you spend the night?" Jack asks.

"I spend the night," I protest. "Sometimes, I spend the weekend. I just don't do repeats. And Friday night, I knew I'd be drinking at the team party, so I had a room at the Pan Pacific."

"You could have taken a rideshare home if you didn't want to drive," Griffin points out.

"I know, but I thought it would be a nice change. Plus, Denise is in town, and I didn't want to see her." I can't look at the guys. Denise is not one of my prouder conquests.

"Which one is Denise?" Michael asks, knowing full well who she is.

"She's the flight attendant for British Airways," I mumble.

"Right," he snarks. "The one that likes you to spank her and asked you for a threesome for her twenty-fifth birthday."

"We had fun, but she's not someone I want to explore anything further with."

"What's her number?" Griffin teases.

"I have no problem giving it to you if you want it. She's up for just about anything. She'll particularly like the number of dollars in your bank account."

Griffin shakes his head. "No. No sloppy seconds for me."

"Says the guy who had a woman show up at our parents' house." Davis snorts.

"Wait," Griffin says. "I had never met that woman before in my life." He shakes his head. "Mom read me the riot act. She was not happy to have that woman sneaking around the property, setting off alarms. That brought the police with full sirens and really irritated their neighbors."

"Did that make the papers?" I ask innocently. *Yes, it did.* "And didn't she tell everyone she was pregnant with your baby?"

"Yes, which also pissed our mom off." Davis smiles over his glass at Griffin.

"You're for sure the favorite these days because you married Paisley," Griffin laments.

Davis bounces his eyebrows. "Well, what can I say? I've always been the favorite."

I am happy to watch these two spar as I think about Eliza. I like all women. I don't care about the color of their hair or skin, if they're chubby or thin, if they're short or tall, or their religion. I just like them smart. Eliza was smart.

And she was fucking hot.

I think about what she looked like when she reached her pinnacle, and I quickly have to change course and think about my mom and my sister, so I don't grow a giant woody. These guys would never let that slide. *Going shopping with my mom and sister while they look through hordes of clothes at The Bay.*

Yep, that did it.

"I don't know what to do," I tell the guys when I notice their attention has returned to me. "I'm sure if I had one more time with her, that would get her out of my system."

"Then just ask her," Michael says. "Did you exchange contact information?"

"No. But I looked her up on the company intranet and got her cell number."

"I would track her down at work, rather than call her," Davis warns.

Steve and Griffin nod in agreement.

"I'd text her the address of the Pan Pacific with your hotel room number, and then you can get your clean getaway after you're done," Michael says.

I think I like that idea.

"If you value your job, you won't treat her like a quick

lay," Jack adds.

I let my head roll back and look at the ceiling. "I love my job with the Tigers. I don't want to put that in jeopardy."

"Go see her at the office and make sure she's good with everything that went down," Jack suggests. "Maybe invite her to lunch and see where it leads." He drains the last of his drink.

I nod. "We have practice tomorrow before we fly out to Winnipeg for the game this weekend. I'll be back in the office early next week."

"Where is the team practicing?" Davis asks.

"The same place as always—in Surrey at the practice facility. The guys should be working out all morning."

We talk about the team and their prospects this year until Paisley, Davis's wife, and Nadine, Michael's wife, join us.

"What's the hot gossip today?" Nadine asks as she joins Paisley with an Italian soda.

"Steve is hung up on a girl." Davis smirks at me.

"Does that mean Paisley and I will have someone new to pal around with?" Nadine smiles.

"No," I'm quick to tell her. "She's not going to be a long-term thing."

"I don't know," Michael offers. "She's beautiful, and you work with her. There might be no escape."

I roll my eyes.

"Didn't you sleep with Amber Jensen when she was head of your department at the hospital?" Griffin asks.

I did, and I don't want to talk about it. She was thinking wedding bells from the minute I got inside her, and that made for a miserable two years with her as head of the department. She's the reason I stopped using the hospital as my dating pool.

Nancy walks over from the bar, and several of us order a second round of drinks.

"What's different about this one?" Paisley asks.

"Honestly?" I ask.

She nods.

"I don't know."

"I do," Davis volunteers. "She snuck out on him, taking all the control away."

"Has she reached out to you?" Paisley asks.

"We didn't exchange numbers."

Paisley's eyes go wide. "So she's playing it cool with you instead of the other way around. You're the chaser, not the runner."

"I don't run," I say, almost indignantly.

"Sure you do," Nadine counters. "There's nothing wrong with that. Michael was the same. He was used to women returning his calls right away, or more often, initiating the calls. I wasn't doing either. He had to work it."

I sit back and think about what Nadine and Paisley are saying. They're dropping truth bombs. I can't believe it, but they could be on to something.

Now, what am I going to do about it?

Chapter 4

Eliza

Before I left work on Friday, Marlene sent me a calendar invite for dinner with my family today. I'm not sure I understand why my father thinks I need a reminder. I'm quite motivated. He got an offer on the business, and it's my job to make sure he doesn't take it.

The alarm on my phone rings, telling me it's time to head over to Laura and Dad's house in West Vancouver. See? Motivated.

I make the drive across town. Their home sits high on the cliffs above the Pacific Ocean, with views of the Burrard Inlet, which stretches out before the house, its calm, blue waters reflecting the sky above. In the distance, the majestic peaks of the North Shore Mountains rise.

To the left is the busy port of Vancouver, with its towering cranes and cargo ships coming and going. The hustle and bustle of the port is a stark contrast to the serene beauty of the inlet, but somehow, it all seems to fit together perfectly.

From their front door, you can see the Lions Gate Bridge with its towering green pillars and suspension cables. It's a stunning feat of engineering and design, and I always feel a sense of awe as I drive over it to get out of downtown and over the rocky shores of Stanley Park. With its lush forest and sandy beaches, the park is a haven of natural beauty in the midst of the city.

Mom and I lived above the Lions Gate Bridge when I grew up. Dad had a fancy apartment downtown. Now it's the reverse. When I arrive, I plug in the code to the gate and park out front. As I ring the bell, Minni flings the door open and catapults herself into my arms.

"You're finally here!"

"Were you waiting for me?" I ask. She nods and smiles, and immediately I see she's lost her front tooth. "What is that in your mouth?"

Her eyes twinkle. "I lost my tooth."

"Holy cow. It's not possible. What did the Tooth Fairy give you?"

"A hundred dollars."

My jaw drops. *Wow, I used to think I was doing well with a Loonie – one whole dollar coin.*

Before I can respond beyond that, I'm enveloped by my little brother's arms around my leg, and my dad and Laura are right behind him. It's a lot of people.

Dad comes over and squeezes me tight. "My oldest daughter has returned."

"Hey, Dad."

"What is this hey stuff? Hay is for horses." He chortles.

Dad and I go through this all the time. Such the jokester, that one.

I take a deep breath and inhale the aroma of dinner. "Shrimp and scallops?" I ask Laura, my dad's wife, as we walk into the kitchen.

She nods, and I find the table is already set. Minni starts telling me all about the day she's spent helping her mommy get dinner ready.

"It wasn't all day," Laura whispers, giving me a warm hug. "I'm so glad you're back from London. I love having you close."

"Me too! Me too!" Minni bounces up and down.

My brother, Logan, fusses at Laura's feet, begging to be picked up. I try to help out by keeping him entertained, and he plays hide and seek with me for a few minutes, not realizing I can see him when he covers his eyes. His mother laughs, and eventually, she sweeps him into his highchair.

Laura and I struggled when she and my dad got together. We were too close in age for my comfort, but she's good for Dad, and she and I have found a way to be friendly. Laura and my mom are friendly as well. Remarkably so. Dad had two marriages between my mom and Laura, and they were really bad fits. I guess everyone is grateful this one finally worked out. At the very least, I can always remind myself of what's worse than this.

Minni entertains us during dinner, and as we finish the last of the shrimp and scallops, we all lean back in our chairs, satisfied and content. Laura has Minni take our plates into the kitchen, and I help her clear the other items from the table.

When Laura picks up Logan and tells Minni it's time to go upstairs, Dad stands. "Elizabeth, why don't you join me in my office for an after-dinner drink?"

"Of course," I answer. Butterflies flutter in my stomach. *This is it.* I'm ready to show him how prepared I am to take over the team. I have a business plan that I even had bound for him. He's going to love it.

In his office, he points me to the couch near a gas fireplace. It takes the humidity out of the air. "Port or brandy?" he asks.

"Port would be fine," I tell him.

He pulls out two glasses, which seem to be a cross between a water glass and a pilsner glass, and pours us each about three fingers. It's going to be that kind of meeting.

"What did you bring with you?" He groans as he sits down in the chair next to me.

"I have my strategic plan for the team, which includes the reasons you shouldn't sell to Donnie Cochran, and I have some notes about other things that will bring in more income."

He holds out his palm, and I hand him the book.

He weighs it in his hand and flips through it. "There's a lot here. Did you just do this this week?"

My shoulders relax. "No way. A part of this came from my graduate thesis. I've continued to update it and play with it since I've returned."

He sets the book down on the table next to him and takes a sip of his drink. "You are so much like me."

The corners of my mouth turn up. "Thank you. That is quite the compliment."

"But it's also a criticism."

I tilt my head. "How so?"

"I broke your mother's heart."

I blanch. She and dad are still close, but mostly so they can deal with me. "She's never shared that, and I've never asked."

"She did enjoy my growing bank account as I worked my way through multiple mergers and acquisitions."

"I can't disagree with that. She's spending some of it now in Italy."

He smiles ruefully. "I wasn't really home when we were married. I was off meeting with CEOs of companies I was buying or selling to. I didn't have time for her or for you."

"But I always knew you loved me," I say, not sure where he's going with this.

"The team needs more financing than I'm willing to put into it. I—"

"If you look at my plan, you'll see I have all sorts of revenue-producing ideas for that."

He places his drink on the bound plan, and I know immediately I'm not going to like this conversation.

"Donnie made a good offer. I'm going to take it."

I jump up. "*You can't.* I've worked my entire life to prepare to run the team. You promised me when I was sixteen that I could have it."

"Are you sure?"

I nod. "Absolutely."

"What I'm trying to tell you is that until I met Laura and she insisted I stick around, I didn't realize everything I was missing. I don't want you to be like me and look back on your life and realize this dream team you want will never be there and you have nothing to show for all the work you've put into plans and focus groups. The team is a bottomless pit. Every year the salary cap increases, but the revenue has been flat."

"I'm not ready to give up. The team is something I want. I want to show you it can be the most profitable business you have in your portfolio."

"You're not understanding what I'm saying."

"Because you're not saying it well," Laura says from behind me. She walks in and sits next to me. "What your dad and I want you to see is that there is life outside of work. If you want to work, work in one of the family businesses, but don't kill yourself working weekends and late into the night."

"I like my job. Working those kinds of hours doesn't bother me."

"That's my point," Dad says. "If you had a husband and a few kids, you'd change your mind."

"Daddy, I do want the house with a white picket fence. I just don't want it now."

"You're going to have to force her," Laura says to my father, as if I'm not standing right here.

"Force me to do what?"

He holds up his hand to stop what is sure to be a major bickering contest. "I'll meet you in the middle. We all know Donnie is patient. He'll wait six months."

"I can show you how we can double our revenue in that time."

He sighs, shaking his head. "In exchange for that delay, you will need to find someone to marry. Before I consent to giving you the team, I want to know you have someone to support you at home, someone to force you to find some balance, rather than working twenty-hour days."

"I don't work twenty-hour days," I say indignantly.

He tilts his head to the side and raises his brow. "I sent you the invite at the office, and I have the security logs."

"Dad, I have a personal life."

"Not enough. If you can find someone to settle down with that you truly love, I'll let you have your way. But I don't want you to jump into this with just anyone. I want to see that you're in love."

This is crazy. "In six months?"

"When I met your father, we knew within three dates," Laura informs me.

That's because you knew he was loaded. Fortunately, I'm able to keep that thought to myself. I shouldn't be that way. Laura is a nice person, and I know she loves my father. I just wish she didn't think of me and my mother as mistakes he made earlier in life.

"I've been seeing someone," I tell them. "I like him." Okay, I'm exaggerating, but maybe that's enough to get him to back off on this. "I have a social life."

"Well, if you're not wild and crazy about him after you've been out a few times, he's not the guy for you," Laura says.

"Are you serious? I need to find someone and get engaged in six months or else you're selling my team to that slimeball Donnie Cochran?"

"He's not a slimeball," Dad protests.

"He has an orange furry thing on his head that he combs over a bald spot," I say dryly.

Laura giggles. "She isn't wrong."

My dad sits straight up in his chair. "Six months, and Charles and I will be checking up on you."

"I just need to have a life and be engaged?"

"Yes. And the fine print states that it needs to be someone I approve of," Dad adds.

I sit back down. "You won't like anyone. That will be your out."

He holds up his hand. "Okay then. You'll have to pass Laura's sniff test."

"Oh, I'm going to love this." Laura claps her hands. "Lizzie, when I met your dad, he'd been three times divorced, and he had a long line of women looking to be the next Mrs. Rourke. He was dipping his fishing pole in a lot of ponds. I showed him what he's trying to get you to see—a reason to come home. At some point you have enough money. You don't need to be able to buy the world."

I don't have a good example of what she's talking about. My parents never had that kind of relationship, and by the time Dad got together with Laura, I was at university. I sigh. "Fine. Tell Donnie to back off. Read my business plan, and we can talk again about this in six months."

"I would expect that if you're serious about someone, you'll be coming here for dinner so we can meet him, and he can meet your brother and sister."

"Half," I say.

Laura waves that away. "Minni's just like you. You may have different mothers, but your dad's DNA is heavy in both of you. She'll want approval on this guy."

She's six years old. Really? "Great." I finish my glass of port. "I want all the expectations written down so we both agree. I don't want Donnie to sweeten the pot in another month and you sell the team without my consent."

"Fine. I can have my lawyer draw up a contract."

"That's not necessary. We can just put it in writing, and we should both sign it."

"I'll work on it this week." Dad pulls out his phone and opens the calendar app. "That means by the start of the new year, you need to be engaged."

Laura claps. "I love spring weddings."

I close my eyes a moment. "I'd rather elope."

"That's going to be a requirement," Dad says. "A big, splashy wedding. That will weed out the scammers—and make sure they know there will be a prenup."

"Fine. Start writing this all down, and we'll figure out how to move forward." I stand. "I'll see you at work tomorrow." I know not to argue with him.

"Arnold will drive you home," Dad says.

"I have my car."

I walk out, and Minni is waiting in the hallway. "You're going to get married? Can I be in your wedding?"

I ruffle her hair. "Of course. You're a little big to be the flower girl. Maybe you could be a junior bridesmaid?"

"I want my dress to be purple."

"Like Barney the Dinosaur?"

"Yes, but shiny."

As she walks with me to the car, I reach for her hand. "I'll see you again soon."

I open the door to my car and pull her close.

"I can't wait to meet your fiancé," she says in a dreamy voice as I release her.

Too many Disney princess movies. I snicker to myself. "I can't either."

The entire ride back to my apartment, I think about what my dad said. Having a life is easy. I go out with Tanya all the time. But the other part may be more difficult. I either get engaged or he's going to sell *my* team? Maybe I can find a nice-enough guy I can pay a million or so to get engaged to me. The question is, where do I find him?

He must be believable. Maybe I can call Thomas Klein from grad school? We had fun together, though admittedly, I have no idea what he's up to now. And I think he's still in London.

Still, I text him a simple "Hi" before I go to bed, but when I check in the morning, I haven't gotten anything back.

I need to figure out my options.

Chapter 5

Steve

We lost the season opener against the Winnipeg Express this past weekend—actually they wiped the floor with us—so that wasn't the best way to kick things off. And as a result, behind the scenes, it's chaos. A few of our new-to-us players are not really turning out to be team players. The problems in the locker room are spilling out onto the field.

Everyone managed okay when we lost during the preseason. But the season opener wasn't even close. The *Vancouver Sun* is full of commentary, and no one seems optimistic about our season. I want to believe they're wrong, but this opening loss doesn't help. I think the local high school would have played better than we did.

Today is the day I work out of the team's offices in the stadium. We call them the *back office*, which is the operations side of things. While it may only be a game, we are a business. Normally, I like to be out with the players, doing hands-on work, but today, I'm looking forward to this. I've been thinking a lot about Eliza, and I've figured out my plan. It's going to start with an invitation to lunch. Lunch is low key and has time constraints, so it's not as if we can sneak off and have a quickie.

But maybe I should reserve a room just in case she's up for that?

No, that would be presumptuous. This needs to be conversation over food as we get to know one another. Then we'll make plans for dinner, maybe Published on Main or Cioppino would be a nice, romantic lead-in to a night of gymnastics.

I'm feeling confident. I rarely chase women, so this is a little out of my comfort zone, but I'm back in control of things now. Nothing to worry about.

By ten, I'm making my way through the things I have to do, but I haven't seen Eliza arrive. I decide to walk down to the marketing department and ask the group admin if she's working from home or something today.

When I walk into the marketing department, everyone's in a meeting, and Eliza standing in front of a whiteboard as she addresses them. I turn right around and try to sneak out, but then I hear my name. "Dr. McCormick? Did you need something?"

When I turn back around, the entire meeting has stopped, and the marketing team is staring at me. I clear my throat. "Uh, I was looking for some new Tiger gear for my team for this weekend's game against the Colombes. I can come back."

Marianne Lee, a marketing team member, stands. "I just restocked the closet. Did someone take it all already? I swear there's someone selling our team stuff on eBay or something."

I shake my head. "N-no. I'm sorry. I forgot to look there." I sound like a complete idiot.

She follows me down the hall and opens up the metal closet door. It's filled to the brim with all the Tigers swag I could ever want.

"It's all right here," she says, turning to look at me.

"Since it's a home game, you're wearing white, right?"

I nod. "Yes."

"Okay, I'll pull everyone's sizes after our meeting and get them to you."

"Oh, I don't want you to go out of your way for me."

"I don't mind, but I'm sure a drink after work would make it up to me." She winks.

I smile, but nope, I'm not going there. "Oh, I can't tonight. But I can do this. I don't want to put you out."

"It's my job, Dr. McCormick." She runs her hand up my arm, and I look away to find Eliza looking out the doorway with a raised brow.

I step back and retreat to the stairwell. "I'll just get out of your way for now. When's your meeting over?"

"Three o'clock."

"I'll be back then."

Marianne smiles. "I can't wait."

She turns and walks back down the hall, and I practically run upstairs to my office. *That didn't go as planned.* I looked like an idiot.

I force myself to sit down and return to the medical charts the physical, massage, and occupational therapists, as well as a half dozen trainers and the neurologist on my team have produced.

The therapists have the most contact with the team, but as the chief medical officer, I review all the charts to make sure everyone is healthy and nothing slips by us. I give a report to the coaches before each game about which players should be on medical reserve.

Shortly after three o'clock, before I can find a stopping point to return to the marketing department, there's a knock at my door, and Marianne walks in with team shirts for this weekend's game.

"As promised," she announces.

"Oh, thank you. I was going to come up to you."

Janna, one of the three massage therapists, looks at me

funny from her seat across the room. We just got shirts and haven't even worn them.

"So, about that drink tonight?" Marianne twists a strand of hair around her finger and licks her lips.

Janna rolls her eyes as she steps out.

"I wish I could, but I still need to do rounds at the hospital tonight. Maybe we can get the group together for drinks sometime next week?"

"Sure, that would be fun."

I can tell she's disappointed, but I'm not interested. At least not right now. She isn't Eliza.

Shortly after she leaves, Janna returns. Makes me wonder if she was hiding out somewhere. "Did you ask for the shirts, or was that her reason to come down and get a date out of you?" she asks.

"I wanted to ask Eliza Rourke something, and I walked in on the middle of their marketing meeting. Shirts were the only thing I could think of that would make any sense."

Janna shakes her head. "You're playing with fire…"

I spend the rest of the afternoon going through all the physicals and making notes about blood work that needs to be watched and a few injuries that seem like they should be areas of concern for the coaching staff. Currently on our roster are forty-six players, but we have a practice team with an additional eighteen.

When I finally get through all the medical information, I look up, and the office is silent. In June, the sun doesn't set until well after nine, so it's hard to tell what time of day it is. I poke my head out to look around, and I don't see any other lights on. Then my stomach growls. My watch tells me it's nearly eight thirty.

This is a typical Monday in the office, so I'm not that surprised. I gather up my things to head out and decide to take the internal stairs down to the marketing department so I can put back the shirts Marianne brought me. We don't need them, and maybe this way I won't have to explain that to anyone.

As I enter the department, I see a light on in one office. *Could I be that lucky?*

I walk over and find Eliza at her computer. I watch her for a few seconds before I knock on the glass outside her door.

She jumps straight up in the air. "You scared me to death." She clutches her heart.

"Sorry. I didn't mean to startle you."

"Are you stalking me?"

That sends a jolt through me, but this time, I'm able to cover. "No." I chuckle. "Mondays are just my ugly day. I go through the entire roster and practice team's medical records here in the main office and make notes. Why are you here so late?"

"I'm working on something for my dad."

"Yeah, you failed to mention you were his daughter when we met."

She shrugs. "Would it have mattered?"

I look at her and decide being honest is best. "Maybe."

Her shoulders fall. "That's why I didn't tell you. Everyone treats me differently once they know who my father is."

I can relate to that. "It's late. Have you had dinner? Maybe we can go out and get a bite and see where the night takes us."

She looks up at me. "I'll go to dinner, but I'm not going to sleep with you tonight."

I reach for my heart like she's shot me with an arrow. "I know it isn't because you left unsatisfied."

She laughs. "I'm very good at faking it."

I narrow my eyes. "You didn't fake it. You taste very good."

She blushes. Then after a moment, she shuts her laptop and puts her computer away.

"What sounds good for dinner?" I ask. "Anything—other than me, of course—that you're craving?"

"Very funny." She slings her bag over her shoulder. "I had half a bagel this morning, so I'm starved."

"You want to try Gotham Steakhouse in Gastown?"

"Oh!" Eliza's eyes twinkle. "That's perfect. They have the best ribeye and a great oyster selection."

"I have my car downstairs. Did you drive or get a ride in today?"

"I got a ride," she says as we descend to the parking garage.

"Great. I'll drive." There are a handful of cars left as we exit the elevator and walk toward mine. With the expense of parking and the shortage in many neighborhoods, employees often leave their cars here and race around the city in a rideshare. Free overnight parking is a good company benefit.

When we reach my Audi R8 I open the wing doors with the key fob and pop the small trunk. "You can put your bag back here. That way it's locked away from the valets while we're at dinner."

"Good thinking." Eliza slides into her seat. "If I didn't know better, I'd say you were compensating for a small penis."

"But you do know better. I just like to drive fast. This is a fun car for the Ski to Sky Highway—in the summer, of course." That's the winding road to Whistler. It hugs the water on one side and the cliffs on the other.

She shifts in her seat, and her skirt rides up her bare thigh. I remember her dark blue panties and wonder what she's wearing tonight.

"Do you put snow chains on this car?"

"This car drives like shit in the snow. And it's not the best in the rain, so when it's dry, I like to drive it, even if it's only the few blocks to the stadium."

We pull out of the garage and turn down the street. Gotham isn't that far, and the one time I wouldn't mind hitting every traffic light, I don't. We arrive in what seems like mere moments.

I pull up in front of the valet stand, and they have a spot for me right out front. That's one advantage of driving a two-hundred-thousand-dollar car, even in this town.

I open both doors from the inside with the push of a button, and I watch the valet look at Eliza. I know he's hoping for a peep show, but she manages just fine. Good thing because I'm ready to clock the guy. I leave him the valet key, which doesn't allow him to go very far from the fob in my pocket.

Eliza waits for me on the sidewalk while I walk around. I extend my hand for her, and we walk into Gotham. It has dark, wood-paneled walls with deep red velvet drapes and an art déco feel. The ceilings are high, so it's not too loud, and the hostess seats us in an intimate corner.

"Thank you," Eliza says as she fills our glasses with bottled water.

A moment later, the server arrives and gives us menus before taking our drink orders.

"I'll have a bee sting," Eliza says.

"I'll have a negroni," I add.

The server nods and walks away.

"Is Eliza your name when you're out meeting men and Elizabeth what you go by?" I ask.

She laughs. "Eliza is what my friends call me. My father, coworkers, and strangers call me Elizabeth." She gives me a look. "Do people really use fake names?"

"My friends and I, when we were younger, used to go out and use fake names and fake jobs with the women we met so they wouldn't know who we were."

Her brow wrinkles. "That's right. You hang out with Jack Drake and the Martin men. I had such crushes on them when I was in high school."

I try not to bristle at the idea that she had crushes on my friends. They've been tabloid darlings for a long time. "Yes, those are some of my closest friends."

"Why do you work? You don't have to. Doesn't your dad build buildings all over the city?"

She's done some research on me. Rather than confirm or deny, I push her question back to her. "Why do *you* work?"

Eliza shrugs. "I love the game. It's what I've wanted to

do since I was seven years old."

The server returns with our drinks, and we order dinner. Eliza goes for a steak, a half dozen oysters, a baked potato with everything, and sides of sauteed mushrooms and asparagus with hollandaise sauce. There's no way she won't have three meals left over after she's done. My order of bacon-rimmed filet mignon and twice baked potatoes seems almost pitiful by comparison.

When the server leaves, we hold our glasses up and toast to a successful season for the Tigers.

"What made you decide you loved football?" I ask. For some reason I want to know all about her.

"It was something I could do with my dad," she explains. "He and my mom divorced when I was young, and I spent weekends with him, which meant I was at the games during the football season."

"Wow. My love of football was driven from playing."

"Yet you're considered one of the best orthopedists in all of Canada, even all of North America," she notes.

"It helps to be doctor to the Vancouver Tigers and the Canadian Olympic teams."

"What do you think about the league's new insistence on a neurologist as the chief medical officer?" She's asking because that's my job. I've been CMO of the team for more than five years.

I shake my head. This is a tricky one. "The league is finally admitting to the long-term damage that can come from playing football, and that's a good thing. But it's only a small fraction of what I look for. Neurologists are a must in our toolbox as we serve the team, but it's a mistake to insist on that for the CMO. I know it sounds self-serving, but I believe it's true. We need a wholistic approach. I won't lie, though, I'll be crushed if I lose this job. I have plenty of patients out of Mercy Hospital, so I won't be out of work, but I love football, and I love working with players at their fittest."

Eliza smiles as the server approaches with her oysters.

She places them in the center of the table, but I don't think Eliza plans on sharing.

"You didn't get an appetizer?" Eliza looks confused.

"I had a smoothie for breakfast, and I had lunch today. Go ahead."

"Would you like one?" She holds up a giant oyster.

"No, but I'm going to enjoy watching you swallow all six of those."

She has an oyster close to her mouth, ready to slide it down her throat, and I can't help but remember our night together.

"Does eating oysters do something for you?" she asks.

I nod slowly. "We had a good night. I was a little disappointed that you left. It would have been fun to try a few more things in the morning."

Her caramel-colored eyes look back at me as she tips the oyster and swallows it. My dick is so hard right now it could pound nails.

Over dinner we talk some more about the various people we know in common. She went to a fancy prep school, just like many of my friends.

Following our delightful dinner, we walk out to my car. "Would you like to come to my place?" I offer.

"I would, but I shouldn't."

"Why not?" I sound like a teenager whose parents won't let him borrow the car.

She sighs. "Because you know it's a bad idea."

I school my features. I'm not desperate, I remind myself. I have a cadre of women who are more than willing to be in my bed. I'm not going to beg. "Okay," I tell her. "I'll drive you home."

We get my car keys from the valet, and she directs me to her house.

"Thank you for dinner," she says when we arrive. "I don't have many friends here anymore. I'm glad you're one of them."

A plastic smile freezes on my face. I've been moved to the friend zone. *God, kill me now.*

Chapter 6

Eliza

I kick off my shoes and fall back onto my bed, looking up at the ceiling of the guest room at Mom's house. Why did I turn down going home with Steve? Or I could have easily invited him up. I enjoyed the last time we were together, so what could be holding me back? Maybe I'm smarter than I give myself credit for. I need to work on this boyfriend-to-fiancé thing my dad is looking for, not anything else. And I don't think Steve is going to be up for that.

I call Tanya.

"Are you just getting home from work?" she asks when she answers. "It's nearly ten thirty."

"No. I went out to dinner with Steve McCormick. He was leaving when I was, and we were both hungry."

"You were hungry for his dick again, weren't you?"

"Well, I did order six oysters on the half-shell and stare at him while I swallowed them."

"You're cruel. It's amazing he didn't throw you down on the table."

"He invited me home with him."

Tanya gasps. "What? His home? Not a hotel?"

"He said his home."

"Where does he live? I bet it's in Shaughnessy Heights."

I chuckle at the thought. Shaughnessy Heights is the most expensive neighborhood in all of Vancouver. "No, I got the feeling he doesn't live the life of a trust-fund baby."

Tanya snorts. "Have you seen his car collection?"

"I know what he gets paid working for the team, and I can imagine roughly what his salary at the hospital is. He can afford those cars."

"Have you considered him for this thing your dad wants?"

"Not even for a second," I respond immediately. If only that were true. It's an impossible option, but it did cross my mind several times during dinner. And then I didn't go home with him. "What would be the benefit of that for him?"

"Girl, having you on his arm."

"He could have a lot of women on his arm."

Tanya huffs. "Can't you come up with something that will appeal to him? Something he needs?"

"The man doesn't need anything."

"He needs you."

It's useless to try to convince Tanya of anything when she's like this. She's so headstrong. Instead, I bring up the strategic plan I'm working on.

"I hope it includes details about you capturing a man, making wild monkey love, and having a boatload of kids," she says.

She's not listening to me at all. "Monkey love?" I clarify.

"You know…monkeys are rarely still, so it means lots of positions, lots of touching."

"I thought maybe you meant we'd be grooming one another."

"That could be fun. Or having him brush your hair for hours."

"Your kinks are definitely different than mine."

"Oh, do tell," she says eagerly.

"Goodnight, Tanya."

She laughs. "See you in the morning."

I lie in bed and wonder where Steve might live. There are plenty of condos downtown, and if he lives in an actual house, there are lots of those too. When my mind tires of thinking on that, I go back over the night we spent together. He was a generous lover. I left because I didn't want the awkward morning. Now, I'm wishing I had stayed.

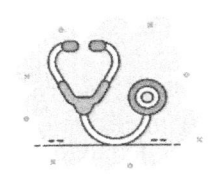

My alarm goes off at five, and I drag myself into Mom's home gym. It's well equipped with a lot of Pilates equipment. I would love a treadmill, but the stretching and resistance is good for me. It mixes things up.

I'm just finishing my workout when my phone pings.

Steve: Good morning. How do you like your coffee?

Me: I like it to taste like Earl Grey tea.

Steve: With milk and sugar?

Me: Yes. Why? Did we make plans this morning that I forgot about?

Steve: I'll be by to pick you up at 7:30 to drive you into work. That way you don't have to take a rideshare.

Me: You don't have to do that. I can get myself to work.

Steve: I'm sure you can, but I'm offering, and I'll have your beverage of choice.

Me: People may talk...

Steve: If we get there before 8, most won't even know, and the ones that do will be too worried about their jobs to say anything.

He's right, but I still think this is a mistake. Yet for some reason, I agree.

Me: I'll be downstairs at seven thirty. What should I bring to our morning gathering?

Steve: Since you're asking, I can't get those sexy panties I peeled off of you that night we were together out of my mind. Maybe today's pair?

My eyes nearly pop out of my head.

Me: You're funny. You want people to see us together.

Steve: Why does it matter? You won't be renewing my contract because of the new CFL requirements. I'm not a neurologist.

I sit back and reread his comment. He knows the bind we're in. If I had control of the team, I'd fight it. Steve is an asset to the team.

Me: I'll be downstairs at 7:30.

Steve: With my favorite panties, I hope.

Me: We'll see.

I race to the bathroom and shower. After, I lather up with my favorite lotion before I dress. The panties he referred to came from Agent Provocateur. They're sexy, but not the only sexy pair I own.

I love sexy underwear, and I often wear it just for me. I love the way silk feels against my skin, the power it gives me, and the way it energizes me.

Today, I slip into another favorite set, but Steve will never know.

When seven thirty arrives, I'm downstairs, wrapped tight in my raincoat as I watch a Toyota 4Runner drive up to the door. The window rolls down, and I can see it's Steve.

I rush out through the rain and into the car. "Another car?"

"This is the car I use the most, particularly if it's going to rain or snow."

I pull on my seatbelt, and he hands me my tea. When I take a sip, it's perfect. "Thank you. This is just what I needed this morning."

"Did you bring what I asked for?"

I roll my eyes. "I thought you were kidding."

He shakes his head and grins. "I was just curious whether you'd do as I asked."

He has no idea. I'm enjoying his game. "And what is my punishment for not complying?" His dick has started to tent beneath his pants.

"I imagine a spanking would be in order."

I stiffen in my seat. But two can play this game. We've already arrived at the stadium. He pulls into the parking garage and then into his assigned spot.

Once he's parked, I look over at him. "I guess I need a firm hand."

He shakes his head. "I can't believe you said that *now*."

I reach into my bag and hand him a pair of panties. They're favorites of mine. "Enjoy." I give him a wink.

His eyes grow wide. "You're such a dick tease."

"Only with you."

"I'm taking you to dinner again tonight."

"We'll see how the day goes. It's a busy one."

"No. You be ready at seven, or I will take you over my knee right there in your office and spank your ass so hard you'll feel it for a week."

I shiver. "We'll see."

I get out of his vehicle and head toward the building, leaving him with a giant hard-on and my panties in his hand.

I have a day full of meetings. And I soon realize I'm completely distracted. I must check my phone a dozen times, but he doesn't make any contact. I should be relieved, but I find I'm disappointed.

When seven o'clock rolls around, I look up from my computer and stretch my neck from side to side to release the tension.

"I know other ways to relax you," I hear from the doorway.

I have to smile as I look over. "I know you do, and there's a line of women willing, ready, and waiting."

"Like there isn't a line of men waiting to do the same for you."

I smirk. "In my experience, there are two types of men attracted to me. One sees my money and thinks of all the things they could buy if they got their hands on it."

"Same with the women you described."

"And the other kind want me for the doors I can open."

Steve looks at me thoughtfully. "We have a lot in common."

"That doesn't mean we need to repeat our close encounter. I didn't think that was your thing anyway."

He shrugs. "We're two adults. We can enjoy some mutually beneficial workouts."

"That's what you call it?"

"Hey, I'm not doing my job if both of us aren't breathing hard — at least three times."

"Oh, that's what this is about? You didn't get your third time?"

He smirks. "I thought we both had fun."

"I definitely had fun, but right now, with the season underway, I don't have time to have fun."

"I'm keeping the panties you gave me."

"I figured you would."

"Do you need a ride home?" He holds up his hands. "Just a ride in the car. Nothing more."

"Thanks. I've got a few more hours of work, and then I'll drive home. I have a car downstairs."

He looks at me, his eyes wide.

"It was easier to take one car than two."

"Will I see you at the game on Sunday?"

"I should be there."

He smiles and disappears down the hall.

I need a cold shower. Damn, what he does to me.

Chapter 7

Eliza

"Will Hudson be on the starting roster on Sunday?" George Bennett asks as soon as I answer the phone.

He's the agent for Hudson Meecher, our star cornerback. But Hudson's been plagued with injuries, and if he can't play, that affects his salary and the ten percent George gets. "That's up to the coaches," I tell him. "I don't have any say with that. He's been performing well, and he played last week in the opener, so I'd think so…"

Agents. What a racket for a player like Hudson. He rarely gets in trouble, and he works hard. Agents negotiate their player's salary, but there are salary caps, so there's only so much they can do. Hudson was a rockstar four years ago, but this is probably his last year in the league. He's twenty-nine and slowing down.

"Will you be at the game?" George asks.

"Why would I be anywhere else?" I tease. "This is my

family's team, and we're always at the game."

"Do you have plans after?"

I know what he's asking, but I'm not interested. Not even a little bit. I smile politely, hoping it comes through in my voice. "Thank you for thinking of me. I have plans."

Those plans should be going out on dates and trying to find someone who will get engaged to me in the next six months, but my only plan is to go back to my mom's and sleep until Monday morning.

After hanging up, my phone rings several more times, and each time, I end up dealing with agents. I also realize all these calls are coming from my dad's office. When did I become the head of player relations?

When I finally have a break, I call Marlene.

"Hi, Marlene. I was just wondering why you were sending agent calls to me and not player relations?"

"Your father typically takes those when they come in, but he's out of town," she explains. "He asked me to send them to you."

My brows reach my hairline. Dad didn't mention he was going out of town. "Do you know why player relations is sending them to us?"

"Usually because they can only promise so much. Your dad is where the buck stops."

I guess I understand. Ultimately, we hold the purse strings. "Thanks, Marlene."

The calls continue intermittently, and before I know it, it's after two. I want to stretch my legs and get a change in scenery.

I call Tanya. "I'm heading to the Surrey practice facility," I tell her. "I'll be back a little later."

"Going to check out a particular doctor?" she teases.

I am, but I also want to see what practices are like under this coaching staff. "I've been on the phone all morning with agents. They're nervous, and I want to see why."

"Why do you think they're nervous?"

"I'm not sure. I'm going to arrive unannounced and check it out."

"Have fun. Call me tonight after you're done. I'm having dinner with Jun."

That surprises me. Jun is her ex-husband, and she's not had a lot of great things to say about him. "I want to hear all about that, including why you agreed in the first place."

"Talk later," she says quickly, and then she's gone.

I walk downstairs and get into my Audi RS 5. It's a four-door sedan, but still nice and sporty. The hardest part of my trip is getting to the highway from downtown, and I enjoy the way the car handles as I finally make my way down Highway One to our facility.

As I drive, my mind returns again to this ridiculous position my dad has put me in. How am I going to find a decent guy to get engaged to by January? No one can force me to fall in love, so I just need to make this look the way Dad wants it to. But even so, I don't want just anyone. I won't compromise who I am to fit with some guy.

I'm going to have to share space, and most men I know are slobs. My last boyfriend left his clothes on the bathroom floor all the time. Drove me crazy.

And maybe even more important than what I want is what will Dad accept? This guy is going to need to have his own money. Dad's already mentioned a prenup, and I don't want to risk that someone will sell the story and cause all kinds of problems.

The perfect man will have a job. As silly as it sounds, many of my friends from school don't really work. They hang their "consulting" shingle and really just poke around. That isn't going to work for me.

He also needs to live in Vancouver. I don't want some guy who lives on one of the islands or up in Whistler or across the country. To make it believable, he needs to be local.

And then there's the flip side of this perfect guy. If he has money, a job, and lives local, why would he want to do this for me? What do I have to offer?

I take a deep breath. I mean, Steve McCormick *is* all of those things. On paper, he's ideal. He has a lot more money than I do. He's a doctor, and working for the team is just something he enjoys. And he lives in a house, so that means he's responsible. That's an extra plus on my list.

As I exit the highway, a calm resolve washes over me. Dad has presented me with a test. I always excel at taking tests. I can do this.

I park and walk into the practice facility, where I'm greeted by the smell of sweat, dirty socks, athletic tape, and Axe aftershave. It's a strange combination, but it's always here.

I wander up to the coaches' box and find several assistant coaches there, glued to what's going on on the field. I find myself a seat, but they don't seem to realize I've come in. I finally catch my buddy Darius' eye and go to stand by him in the back of the box. As the head recruiter, he attends all the practices and games. That way, if something happens, he can be on the phone talking to a backup.

"How's it going?"

He shakes his head.

I raise my brow.

"They're going to scrimmage with the practice team," he tells me. "You'll see."

I wish he would just tell me, but a few minutes later, the scrimmage gets underway, and I quickly see the dysfunction on the field. Seems our loss to open the season wasn't a fluke. This looks like a pee-wee game when it should be more like a finely tuned orchestra. I'm even more shocked when a fight breaks out.

What. The. Hell?

Darius gives me an I-told-you-so look.

This is ridiculous. If the team isn't cohesive now, what are they going to be like when playoffs are on the line or, more likely, when they're losing every game and even the fans are rooting against them?

Everything I've been working toward is going to go out the window. Hot anger races through my body. How did we get here?

I watch the players break from a huddle. When the play begins, the ball is not hiked to the quarterback well. Still, he manages to toss it to Hudson, who juggles the ball and barely has it under control when he's hit. He goes down hard, still cradling the ball, but he's not getting up.

The player who hit him, number fifty-one, Sean Rhymes, now has a coach in his face screaming. I don't know what he's saying, but Rhymes rips his helmet off, throws it on the ground, and walks toward the locker room. I'm happy with that decision.

Hudson is still lying on his back. Steve is out there with him now, as well as a few others. After a minute, they've got him sitting up and, with two of the trainers for support, they take him back to the locker room as well.

It feels like my head is going to shoot off the top of my body as rage surges through me. "Is this how it is every day?" I ask aloud.

One of the coaches turns and looks at me. His eyes grow big as he realizes who I am. "Ms. Rourke. I'm sorry. We didn't know you were coming today."

"Why would that matter?" I snap.

"Well, uh, that is, uh..."

"Don't announce me to the coaches," I tell him. "I'm heading down to the field."

"Yes, ma'am."

The practice field is more like an American high school field with about two dozen or so rows of seats around it. We do some exhibition things here, but it's walled in and covered so we can practice without prying eyes.

Despite my three-inch stilettos, I'm down the stairs quickly and walking across the field. My heels are going to be a mess on the spongy turf, but right now, I'm too angry to slow down. When I finally realize I could damage the field, I stop and pull my shoes off before I finish stomping over to the coaches.

There are some catcalls, and the head coach, Michael Roy, turns, ready to scream at whomever is on his field, but then he shrinks back.

I take a deep breath. Being the dragon lady won't work.

"You lookin' for a ride, lady?" one player yells. "I'll show you a ride." He undulates his hips and grabs his dick.

"Jackass, that's Rourke's daughter," another player says. "She's your boss."

He disappears into the crowd, and they snicker at his stupidity.

I paint a smile on my face. "Hey, Coach. How's it going today?"

"We didn't know you'd be coming out." He bristles.

"As a team owner, I didn't realize I needed to run that by you."

"Does your daddy know you're here?" He stares down at me, but I'm not intimidated.

I tilt my head to the side. "Does your mama know you talk to your female boss that way?" I growl.

There's some scoffing from the other coaches, which only seems to make him angrier.

"Why don't we step into your office, Coach Roy? Let's have a chat." My voice is saccharine sweet.

His arms are crossed, nose flared, and his stance wide. His pupils are pinpoints. If looks could kill, I'd be a pile of ash right now. But he's missing the point entirely. The issue is his shambles of a team, not whether or not I was here to see them.

"Would you like to get my dad on the phone?" I ask after a moment. "He's on vacation in the South of France." *I mean, maybe he is. Who knows?* I look at my watch and do some quick math. "It's eleven thirty his time. He's usually in bed, but I'm sure he won't mind getting you all straightened out on my role."

The coach turns and storms off.

I don't feel like he's inviting me to come with him, so I look over at Jimmy Majors, the assistant coach. "I don't like what I saw. Make sure everyone understands that this isn't going to be tolerated."

"Yes, ma'am." Jimmy salutes me.

I roll my eyes. We're not in the military.

I cross the field and head for the locker room. As I enter, there's a ripped jersey on the floor. I find half of a shoulder pad set on one side of the room and the other half on the floor by the showers. The towel bin is upturned, and towels are everywhere, and the frosted-glass window to the toilets is shattered. The player who was sent off the field seems to be long gone, and he's likely the one who destroyed things in his wake. I will work that out with Darius later.

For now, I walk down the hall to the medical bays where Steve is working with Hudson.

Hudson is crying. It wrenches my heart to see him like this.

"You may have torn the ligaments," Steve tells him.

"Doc, I need to play this season," Hudson pleads. "Shoot it up with steroids and let me play through."

The hair on the back of my neck stands up. Many teams treat their players like a commodity, and maybe they are, but that doesn't mean they're not humans. We can't just wreck them and throw them in the trash.

"Let's see what the MRI says," Steve tells him. "But I won't give you steroids if it's torn. In that case, I'll schedule you for surgery, and I have a great physical therapist who will work with you so that you're not crippled for the rest of your life."

"I've got to play," Hudson insists.

Steve's shoulders fall. "I get it. I know why you feel that way. And you can hate me for the rest of your life as you walk around that farm in Alberta. But one day you'll be grateful you can still walk."

Hudson cries harder, and Steve embraces him.

I step away from their private moment, floored by

Steve's sensitivity. I'm not happy that Hudson's career might be ending more quickly than he wants—and particularly after something that happened in a practice—but I'm grateful that Steve puts the health of the player first. What would a neurologist know about a torn ligament? This new CFL requirement needs to be fixed.

I take a deep breath and continue my walk to Coach Roy's office. He's been with the team for five years, and in my estimation, he's an *okay* coach. We've been in the middle of the pack every year he's been here, and that isn't good enough. He's quick to blame the players, but when I worked with the Pelicans in San Diego, they had a lackluster roster. The coaching staff made them shine.

As soon as he sees me in the doorway, he starts in. "If you ever do that to me again in front of my team, I'm going to—"

"What? Fire me?" I place my hands on his desk and lean in. "Last I looked, my last name is on your paycheck."

"You don't run this team. You're a marketing bunny."

"Really? You think that's all I do?" I stare him down, and he blinks. He comes off all blustery, but he's a pussycat inside.

He stares over at the whiteboard in his office. "Today's practice went to shit."

I sit down in the chair opposite his desk.

He stands and starts to pace. "I don't know what the fuck is happening. I don't even know what's going on with Meecher."

"I saw him talking to Dr. McCormick, and he thinks he tore a ligament."

He takes off his hat and throws it against the wall. "Damn it!" he screams. "This is his last season. He was positioned to make the all-star team."

All I can do is nod. Everything he's saying is true. This is a travesty, but it happened on his watch, in conditions he allowed to take hold.

"The player who hit him stormed out of here after

dumping the locker room," I tell him, keeping my voice calm and even. "You need to fire him. If his agent gives you grief, send him to me. His leaving is quitting, and I'm holding him to that."

Roy's eyes narrow. "Are you sure your daddy's going to be okay with that?"

"He left me in charge."

He sighs. "Okay. I can bring up an offensive tackle from the practice team and get Darius to start putting out feelers for a replacement."

I turn and see a man in a suit pacing in the hallway. "I'm guessing that's the player's agent?"

Coach looks up. "Yeah."

"I've got this," I tell him.

"You really are stepping in for your dad."

"Yes. I've loved this team since I was a little girl. I'm ready to bring the Grey Cup home and get a television deal in the process."

"I like the way you think."

I nod as I stand. "Work with your coaches to figure out the problem with the team. We can't go on this way."

He opens his mouth to say something, but then closes it and slumps behind the desk.

I step out and approach the agent, but he brushes right past me and into Coach Roy's office. He dives into an explanation of how Rhymes is feeling, taking zero responsibility for the illegal hit or the destruction of the locker room.

Coach holds up his hand. "She's the owner. You need to talk to her."

"Oh, I'm so sorry," he says, turning to me. "I thought you were one of the WAGs."

I smile sweetly. "I noticed that. Since Sean Rhymes walked off after injuring another player, we'll take that as his resignation."

"No, that's not at all what happened." The agent runs his

hands through his gelled hair.

I can tell this is the kind of guy who thinks he can sweet talk his way into anyone's panties. Problem is, I've known assholes like him my whole life. I don't play that way.

"But it is," I counter. "I saw it. *And* he's destroyed the locker room and left the building."

"He's on his way back."

"That's okay. We've already accepted his resignation." I turn to leave it there.

He grabs my arm, and I look down at his fingers and then up at him. He releases me. "He has a contract."

I nod. "He did, but he violated section three, which means he voluntarily resigned from the team."

"Where is Tom Rourke? I want to talk to him."

I smile. "Feel free to call his office. He's in the south of France right now. Marlene will put you through to his daughter, Elizabeth Rourke." I lean in. "And that's me."

I walk out, leaving him standing there.

I don't like agents much. I've watched them be smooth as butter with the players they represent and then throw them under the bus in a heartbeat. My guess is that he'll have a conversation with his player tonight, and I'll see him and Rhymes in the office tomorrow. But they'll have to have an escort. Rhymes' key card to the practice parking lot and facility will be shut off, and security won't allow him free access to the building.

Steve is standing at the end of the hallway. "Wow, that was impressive."

I shrug. "I'll tell you what's impressive, the way you handled Hudson Meecher."

His brow furrows.

"I heard what you said to him. When will you have the results from the MRI?"

He sighs. "I don't need them to know, but I'll have them later tonight. I've scheduled him for surgery, and I've already moved him to injured reserve."

"Perfect." I look around, and there's no one. "Do you want to grab a bite tonight?"

Steve's eyes gleam. "Have you changed your mind?"

I snort. "Hardly. I want to talk about what I saw today."

He nods. "There's a place on the other side of the bridge as you head into town in Port Moody. I think we can talk freely there without anyone overhearing us."

"Perfect. When are you done?"

"I'm done now."

"I'll follow you. What are you driving today?"

He tilts his head to the side. "The Toyota 4Runner. What did you expect?"

"The SPC."

"What's an SPC?"

The corners of my mouth turn up. "The small-penis compensator."

He rolls his eyes. "You're funny. I'm ready to show you again what I can do with my magic wand."

"Puhleeze." I roll my eyes. "Anyway, I need to check in with someone before I leave. Text me when you're walking out."

I go in search of Darius, but he's already driving back to the city. I'll have to get his take later.

I head out to my car and decide to wait for Steve out of the way while I work through my email on my phone. I leave a message on Dad's cell phone, so he knows what happened at practice and how I've handled it.

He left without telling me, and I'm irritated, but I try not to be aggressive.

My phone pings.

Steve: I'm heading out now.

Me: I'm in my car. I'll follow you.

A minute later, I watch him walk out with a young

female trainer. She's giggling and playing with her hair, flirting with him. My gut tenses, and I realize I don't like that at all. Where is this coming from?

I start my car and watch as he gets into the 4Runner and pulls out. I follow him back to the highway and across the bridge over the river. The traffic is slow, and I'm tempted to call him and talk as we drive. But if I ask him all the questions I want to ask, going to dinner won't be necessary, and I want to spend time with him.

Because he's a valuable resource for the team, and I value his perspective on what I saw today, I remind myself. Not because he'd have any interest in getting engaged.

Chapter 8

Steve

Looking in my rearview mirror as I drive toward Port Moody, I can see Eliza. She's singing along to something and dancing in her seat. She seems carefree, and I like seeing her that way. She was certainly buttoned up tight back in the locker rooms.

Not that I blame her. Today's practice was a clusterfuck, and they've been that way on and off since practices began. I'm surprised we haven't had more "friendly fire" injuries. I don't even know why management brought on Sean Rhymes. He's a dirty player and couldn't get along with a wall.

My mind goes back to Hudson Meecher. Poor guy, he deserves better than this ending to his career. That hit was wrong. Maybe that's why I was so moved as I watched Eliza stare down Rhymes' asshole agent. It was totally hot, and it only made me want her more.

I pull into the parking lot and leave my car for the valet as Eliza pulls up behind me. I wave off the attendant who rushes to open her door. "I've got this."

He nods and steps aside.

Eliza smirks and places her hand in mine as she gets out of the car. I don't let go until we're inside the restaurant and being seated. It's early, and the crowd at the Boathouse is easily twice our age.

"Do they have an early-bird senior special?" she teases.

"I think it's the view," I tell her, gesturing toward the window. Across the inlet, the water is like glass. A sailboat comes in and glides to the dock.

"You could be right," she says as she picks up her menu.

When the server arrives, we order dinner. Just like last time, Eliza orders a hearty meal. Most of the women I've gone on dates with recently order salad and barely pick at it. That drives me insane.

"Are you going to get a drink?" Eliza asks.

"No, I have a surgery in the morning, and I don't drink the twenty-four hours before. But help yourself. It doesn't bother me."

She orders a glass of wine, and after the server leaves, we sit quietly, watching the paddle boarders come in.

"It's beautiful," Eliza breathes. "But that's not why we're here."

I nod. "Today's practice was a shitshow."

Eliza smooths the napkin on her lap. "This conversation is confidential. I'm trying to understand what's going on with the team. Do you know who made the decision to hire Sean Rhymes?"

I shake my head as the server delivers Eliza's wine and my lemonade. I take a drink before I respond. "Practices have been going like that lately. But Rhymes isn't the only problem. There's a lot of pressure on Coach to win, and I guess he thought he could manage a few difficult players if it got him toward that goal."

"Tell me what you've observed."

I look away. This is probably my last year with the team

anyway, so it's not like the politics are going to get me fired. "I can't quite pinpoint it, or I would have gone to your dad."

Eliza sits forward.

"But I can tell you the team isn't gelling. They're divided into groups, but not by position. Or sometimes you can see a team become two units—offense and defense and maybe a third for special teams. But our team breaks down in clusters of maybe two or three guys."

"Why do you think that is?"

"Honestly?"

She nods.

"They've hired several guys who think the team is all about them, and they each have a few acolytes—or they're battling to have them." I shrug. "I can see how it happens. Professional football players have been the best in their leagues from pee-wee ball through university, but someone has to remind them that they're always part of a team."

Her brow furrows.

"Okay, after the season opener, did you see Mathieu Pelletier during the press conference?"

She nods, and her eyes hold a hint of understanding.

"He blamed everyone but himself for that loss. It was always someone else's fault. And when he wins, it's all about him. I remember him from last season. *He* did this. *He* did that. The guys who'd helped to make it happen didn't even exist. He was a one-man team."

"Why can't the coaches and handlers advise him on how to talk to the media?"

"It's not just about what he says; it's about what he believes. He's been around long enough that I'm sure he's been corrected many times, but he doesn't hear it."

"But that bravado is part of being a professional football player."

"I agree. And teams can manage maybe one of those, but we have *three* guys right now who are all the same. So not only do they behave the same, they're all competing for the same thing."

"That makes sense. But why would Coach override Darius Johnson's recommendations?"

"Good question. It may not have been him. It could have been your dad."

She shakes her head. "I've thought about that, but this is our investment. That would sabotage the value."

I shrug. "Maybe, but maybe your dad wants to move the team. Maybe he's ready to sell and he wants the loss."

Her eyes grow big, and she takes a deep breath. "He's never done that in any of his businesses."

Our meals arrive. She has some kind of white fish with a delicate sauce. She takes a bite and moans, which reminds me of our night together.

"What did you order?" I ask.

"The sablefish. This butter and wine sauce is amazing. What did you order?"

"The mixed seafood grill—salmon, prawns, scallops, and crab-stuffed prawns. Would you like a bite? It's pretty good."

"Only if you'll have a bite of mine."

She picks up a generous bite, and I lean in and take it right from her fork. I groan at the taste. Her eyes heat.

I fork a portion of the crab-stuffed prawn and hold it out to her. She takes the bite, closes her eyes, and sits back. "That's amazing."

"I can't decide who got the better dish."

We talk a bit more football, but for most of the rest of dinner, we flirt and get to know one another. She's just returned from London and misses the good tea. "North American teas all have orange pekoe, which becomes bitter when steeped for too long. That's not true of teas you find in the UK or India."

"I have no opinion on this, so I'll just nod and agree."

She giggles, and I feel my smile widen. "What is your plan now that you're back?" I ask her.

"I've set my life up to run the team. That's my plan."

"What's your dad's plan?"

She sighs. "We're working on a deal for me to take it over."

When we finish dinner, I reach for the check, but she stops me. "I asked you here to get your opinion on the team — well, really to confirm what I was seeing."

"I'm not used to women picking up the check."

She raises an eyebrow. "Are you used to women signing your paycheck?"

"Yes. The head of Mercy Hospital is a woman. That doesn't bother me in the least. I'm not intimidated by a woman with an opinion."

"Good. Because there's nothing wrong with having an opinion."

"Would you like to come back to my place?"

She snorts and shakes her head, but she's smiling. "You're relentless."

"You've seen that up close and personal."

"Maybe another night."

"At least you haven't shut the door on that prospect."

"No. But my life is going to become very hectic."

"What are you trying to tell me?" I ask. "Is your dad arranging your marriage to a Saudi prince?"

"No way. He would *not* like a woman with opinions."

"The Saudi prince wouldn't care as long as you didn't *express* your opinion." I rise from the table to help her with her coat.

"What's the use of that?" She grins as we walk out to the valet stand, and I don't want to let this go. I want to see her again.

They bring up her car first. "Okay, I know you'll be busy this weekend and through the week, but how about next Sunday? The team isn't working, and you get a day of rest, don't you?"

She huffs out a sharp breath. "Don't you have some arm candy to bother?"

I roll my eyes. "No arm candy. I only have you."

"I'll think about it."

She walks around to her car as mine pulls up behind her.

"I'll see you at the game this Sunday."

"And good luck tomorrow. Is Hudson your surgery?"

"No, he's slotted in early next week."

"Okay, let me know how it goes."

I nod my agreement and watch her drive off. At the end of the parking lot, she turns the wrong way. That's my opening! I quickly call her, and she answers on the first ring.

"You're going the wrong way if you're trying to get home."

"Crap. Thanks. My car is new, and I don't know how to use the map function. I don't need it around town, so I haven't bothered with it."

"Turn around, and I'll wait for you to pull in behind me. I'll get you as far as Mercy Hospital."

"Sounds good. I know how to get home from there." She's quiet a few moments as I wait to see her turn the corner.

"The light's red. I'll be there in a few."

"Don't worry about it. This gives me the opportunity to convince you to go out with me."

"What do you think are your selling attributes?"

I see her and pull out. "You're right behind me?"

"Yep."

"Okay, my selling attributes are… I'm a nice guy."

She snorts.

"I'm stable. I grew up all over the metro area, and I can't imagine living anywhere else."

"Me too. I love it here. It's never too hot or too cold."

"I have a tight group of friends, and we all look after each other."

"I have Tanya, and she's been my best friend since elementary school."

"And I'm good with my hands."

"Keep it PG, please."

"I am. Just because you've experienced some of the things my hands can do, doesn't mean those are the only things they can do."

"Fine."

"I walked away from my family's business, and my sister runs it," I continue. "And I'm not sorry. She does a great job, and I have a life. There's room for more than work."

She's quiet a moment. "Really?"

"Yep. My dad was seriously pissed that I didn't want to take over, but he worked so much when we were growing up that we hardly knew him. With the job I have, I'm on call twice a month, but for the most part, when I'm done at the end of the day, I'm done. I can do what I want, and I don't have to worry about working late."

"I've seen you work late."

"You have. But that's rare, a product of the team's schedule on occasion. Mostly, I like meeting my friends for drinks and spending the long evenings playing golf until ten at night during the summer."

"That makes up for the winter days that have less than eight hours of daylight, I suppose."

"Here we are at Mercy. Have a good night, and I'll see you soon."

"Sounds good." She hangs up.

A few minutes later, I'm home and pulling into my driveway. I think about what I should do to make an impression, to keep whatever this is with Eliza going. Julia Martin once shared her personal florist's contact info with me, so when I get inside, I reach out and tell her generally what I'm looking for and where to send it. She agrees to pull something together and asks what I'd like the card to say.

"Please say yes," I tell her. "And then sign my name."

I have to be at the hospital by six tomorrow morning, so I get to bed early and dream of Eliza.

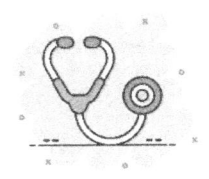

"How did the game go this weekend?" Colton Caulfield, the anesthesiologist on my surgery, asks as we're cleaning our hands in prep on Wednesday morning.

I sigh. "They got creamed—again."

"That doesn't sound fun." He turns the water off with the foot pedal and prepares to walk into the surgery bay where Hudson awaits.

The game this weekend was awful. At times, I was sure some of our players forgot what team they were playing for. I've already seen a few memes on the sports channels, even in the U.S., that are highlighting one particular play where the quarterback threw the ball and hit a tackle square in the back. He went down hard. The worst part is I didn't even get to see Eliza. Not one of my better weekends.

I follow Colton in, and Hudson's surgery goes relatively well. His tendon isn't torn as severely as I expected, and it doesn't take too long to do the repair. He should definitely be able to continue walking normally, but beyond that is yet to be seen. He's an athlete, so he could bounce back, but he'll have to decide if it's worth fighting back to playing form. But if anyone can get through the rehab, he will.

After he's settled and comfortable in a room, I go back to my office and pull my cell phone out of my pocket. I heard it sound during surgery, but there was nothing I could do about it while I was busy fixing the torn tendon.

Before I can get to my messages, there's a knock at my door, and I look up to find my friend Davis Martin. I wave him in.

"Hey. What's up?" he asks as he enters.

"I just got out of surgery. What's going on with you?"

"My mom asked me to remind you that you agreed to attend her fundraiser next weekend...and be part of the bachelor auction."

I sit back and roll my eyes. "I forgot. Do you think I can get out of it?"

He shakes his head. "It's still almost two weeks away. You can adjust your schedule if you need to. You told her the team had a bye week and you'd do this for her."

"I'll be there. Maybe I can get someone I like to bid on me."

"A petite brunette who runs your team?"

I look down, certain I'm blushing. "I don't kiss and tell."

"Since when?"

"Get lost. But you can assure Julia I'll be there."

I return to my phone, and I'm disappointed to find nothing from Eliza. I'd hoped she might thank me for the flowers. *Crap.* There's a message from my sister reminding me of Dad's seventieth birthday later this year. She's organizing a party she wants my help with.

I'll deal with that later.

I pull up Eliza's number and call.

She answers on the third ring. "How did he do?"

I'm taken aback by her briskness until she laughs.

"I really hope this is Steve McCormick."

My heart slows. "Yes, it is. Hudson's doing well. The tear wasn't as bad as we thought. He's in great shape, and if he decides he wants to hit rehab like I think he will, he might be back for the all-star game and the end of the season. We'll have to see how he does. But he's definitely out for at least six weeks."

"That's great news."

"It is. I just hope he doesn't push so hard that he ends up hurting himself all over again."

"How long will he be at Mercy?"

"I won't release him for at least two days. He needs to

learn how to get around on crutches without putting too much pressure on his knee."

"Makes sense. I'll have the team send something over."

"I'm sure he'd like that. His manager and his wife and son are with him now."

"Oh, thank you. I'll send something to entertain the little guy."

"I'm sure that will go over well." There's a pause in the conversation. I guess this is my opening. "Have you thought about my offer for getting together on Sunday night?"

"I have..." she says after a moment. "What were you thinking?"

"There's no pressure, but given our work relationship and my tendency to be linked to women in the tabloids, I'd like to be low key. What if we were to have dinner at my place? No sex required. I just thought we'd stay under the radar."

"I didn't think about why you knew of a quiet restaurant in the suburbs."

"You've found me out."

"Okay. I guess I'll have dinner with you Sunday night, but let's meet at my place. Well, it's actually my mother's, but she's out of town."

"That works."

"Do you remember where I live?"

"I do. See you then." I'm about to hang up, disappointed that she hasn't mentioned the flowers. *Were they delivered?*

"Oh, Steve?"

"Yes?"

"The flowers were stunning. I love pink calla lilies. I'm the envy of every woman in the office."

"Who did you tell them they were from?"

"They only know the name starts with S, but Tanya knows."

"I'm glad you liked them."

"I decided after the game on Sunday that I was going to agree to dinner. You didn't have to send flowers."

I smile. "But I did. You bought dinner last time."

"Do you do this for all the women who buy your dinner?"

"I don't know. The only other women who've bought my meals are my sister and my mother."

"Really?"

"Yep. Come to think of it, I haven't sent many women flowers, either. I don't usually do the pursuing. Women chase me."

"So, are you telling me I'm doing this wrong and should chase you?"

I laugh. "You can do whatever you want. I have a feeling no matter what you do, I'll follow along."

"I'll see you Sunday night."

"What do you want me to bring?" I ask. "Maybe an overnight bag?"

"We've agreed that sex is off the table."

"We didn't agree to anything yet, and besides, that doesn't mean we can't spend the night together."

She sighs. "You're impossible. I'll see you on Sunday."

We hang up, and I think I'll have a smile on my face until Sunday. Then my phone pings, and she's sent me a picture of the round, clear vase with at least three dozen pink calla lilies. *Thank you*, she's written.

I can't wait to see her again.

Chapter 9

Eliza

I've been nervous about meeting Steve for dinner all week. The calla lilies he sent were stunning, and they just got prettier every day. Tanya was thrilled for me, so I left the flowers in her office so she could enjoy them. The dinner with her ex didn't go well. He wants to do some sort of friends-with-benefits thing, and she just wants to move on, so it left her a little depressed.

In contrast, I've been on a high since we won our first game of the season yesterday, though I'm trying to temper my excitement. We beat the worst team in the league, the Yukon Polar Bears. But I'll take a win wherever we can get one and hope we get some momentum to make this a trend that continues.

And now my dinner date has finally arrived. I spent today getting a pedicure and full wax. I have no plans to spend the night with Steve, but I wanted to feel prepared, sexy, and confident. I've thought about it all week, and I'm going to ask him to be my fake fiancé.

Or at least I was. Now that he's actually here at my mom's place, I'm doubting whether this is a good idea. There are about five different ways this could devolve into a giant mess. But it's a mess of my father's creation, I remind myself. He's the one who put me in this outrageous position. Plus, he's gone off the grid and is not returning my calls, which is further pissing me off.

I take a deep pull on my red wine and look over at Steve. "I have something to run by you."

"Now I'm curious."

I smile but look down at my hands. I'm still struggling with how to ask. Nothing I've thought of makes it sound like a good deal for him.

"I'm totally up for under-the-radar friends with benefits if that's what you're going to ask."

When I look up, he gives me his panty-melting smile, and my stomach fills with butterflies. *What is going on with me?*

I clear my throat and then steer the conversation a different direction. My mouth has a mind of its own, it seems. "I bought a condo in The Butterfly. I'm planning to live there once it's finished." The Butterfly is a fifty-story building not far from here that's going up with lots of concrete and glass, and it's all rounded corners. It's been very popular in the media.

"My dad—well, my sister—is building The Butterfly." He takes a pull on his beer. "I looked at the penthouse when they first opened for sales six years ago, but I wanted a house, a house nothing like my dad's. He lives in something way too big for my taste. As a builder, he was mortified when I bought a home and refurbished it."

I sit up straight. "Are you kidding? I bet it's beautiful."

"It was a large home when it was built, but at some point, it had been broken up into four apartments. I gave the two tenants who were left a year's notice and cash to move out. Then I worked with an architect, and we tore it down to the studs and created a nice five-bedroom single-family home again. The design keeps with the age of the house but has some modern touches."

"That's what I want to do one day. If I find a house, I may need your contacts for the architect and contractor."

"Those are the hardest part, so I used some of my dad's people. He may not have liked that I wasn't moving into a shiny new condo building, but he works with good people, and he was still willing to help me out."

"With your love of building, why are you in medicine?"

"Well, there's the part about having a life that I told you before, and also, as I'm sure you know, a family business is often no picnic."

I nod. "I'm the oldest, so I'm taking first pick of my father's holdings. And that's good because I only want the team. My dad wants me to take over the paper company or the fisheries."

"Your dad has pretty diverse holdings."

"Doesn't your dad?"

"Nope. Just real estate. He builds the buildings — or his company does; my sister is in charge now — sells off the units and moves on. They tend to hang on to a few units in most of the buildings they build, and then the real estate group manages them. I think they have property in about eight buildings right now. Most are here downtown, but they built a high-rise at the base of Whistler, and they're also building a resort in Tofino."

I'm impressed. "I love Tofino. Being on the west side of Vancouver Island, it's totally different from here. There's nothing to see for miles but the Pacific Ocean. "

He nods. "It's a great area. My favorite thing my dad built are these low-rise buildings he did early in his career. They're in West Vancouver on the waterfront."

"I think I know what you're talking about — the floor-to-ceiling windows and the round rooms with the curved glass are incredible."

"Yes, those are the ones. They're called turrets."

"My dad lives up the cliffs north of there, beyond the beaches. I remember when they built those condos. Everyone was so sure the first storm was going to break those windows."

He shakes his head with a laugh. "Those things were so thick and heavy. They weighed like five hundred pounds."

When I finish my wine, I suggest we sit down to dinner. My mom's personal chef has made chicken and pasta carbonara.

We make small talk as we eat, and I'm pretty sure I'm getting farther from being able to ask my question, rather than closer to the target. But I don't know what to do.

"So, what did you want to run by me?" Steve finally asks.

I guess he's not letting me off the hook. I tell him again about my love for the team and how I've wanted to own it since I was a little girl and all the work I've done to prepare.

He listens patiently, but I can tell he's confused. I need to cut to the chase.

"Do you know who Donnie Cochran is?" I ask.

Steve nods. "Yes. I believe he's made his money in less-than-respectable ways."

I agree. "He's been sued multiple times, and somehow, all the cases go away. He's also been after my dad for years to sell him the team."

Steve seems surprised. "Is your dad tempted?"

I nod. "Unfortunately, yes. He believes his first marriage, to my mom, was ruined by his priorities. He was more about making money than being home. I think my mom would say the issue was more than that, but I don't ask. Anyway, my dad had two marriages after that, which also went bust, and then he finally married a woman just a few years older than me. They've been together a while now, and they have kids, and he's very happy being a husband and father and not so work focused."

"Cochrane's offer is why he wants you to take over the

fisheries or paper business instead?"

I nod. "Maybe. Probably. He also says those are jobs that don't require a monstrous amount of hours and are pretty self-contained."

"He'd sell the team so you couldn't have it?" Steve asks.

"Well, it seems he might. I'm negotiating with him about the team, but he wants what he thinks is best for me, which in this case is what was best for him. He's decided being married with kids is essential to happiness."

Steve shakes his head. "I'm so sorry. You seem to have the team heading in a good direction. You're strengthening the brand. I can only imagine what you could do as owner."

"That's what I think." I fight back tears.

"So, what are you going to do?"

I look out over Coal Harbor and see the Second Narrow Bridge and the lights twinkling over North Vancouver. "My dad has told me that if I have a social life and a serious boyfriend within six months, he won't sell to Donnie. He'll let me run the team once he's sure I have a support system and other things in my life."

If Steve is shocked by this, he doesn't show it. "What does he define as serious?" he asks.

"Engaged."

"I see."

He's still ice cold. But suddenly I have an idea. "You have an interest in my taking control of the team," I explain quickly. "I'm prepared to argue with the league about the requirement that we make a neurologist our chief medical officer. We need a neurologist on the payroll for sure, but I'm glad it was you managing the situation with Hudson."

Steve looks at me, and finally, a little surprise shows on his face. "Wait. You want to get engaged to me?"

I shrug. "We get along well, and we both want me to take over the team, right?"

Steve pushes his chair back and walks over to the window. "I don't know about this. It seems pretty drastic for a job."

Tears form in my eyes. I knew this was crazy, but I can't think of any other way. Still, I won't beg. "I understand."

"There isn't anyone else who could pose as your fake fiancé?"

"No one my dad would believe."

He turns back from the window. "Why would your dad believe me?"

"You're less of a threat."

Steve tilts his head.

"You have money. It's reasonable that we met at work."

Steve returns to looking out at the water.

"Look, you probably have a guest room in your house. I could move in there. We'd parade around like we're a loving couple, going out and doing things together. After some time, I'll buy the engagement ring, and we can do a fake proposal. We'll be roommates. You won't have to worry about me turning into some sort of fatal attraction."

He whirls around, and I can't be sure what he's thinking.

"This is about securing our futures. We need to stay focused on getting us both something we want. Then in the end, we can remain friends."

He shakes his head. "I'll be disappointed if I'm not able to work for the team anymore, but I still have plenty to do at the hospital. I can take the extra time I'll have and work for something like Doctors Without Borders if I'm not going to be with the team."

I sit back. "I see." We're not on equal footing after all.

"It's not that I wouldn't enjoy playing house for a while, but I'm not sure I'm prepared to have you as a roommate. I'm not made that way."

"I get it. No need to explain. We're good."

He returns to the table, and we manage some polite conversation while we finish our dinner. Then I take our plates to the sink, rinse them, and place them in the dishwasher.

He stands. "I guess I'm going to head out."

I wipe my hands on my back pockets. "All I ask is that you think about it."

He shakes his head. "I will, but I'm just not sure how it would work."

I take a piece of paper from my purse. "These are the rules my dad has outlined. I'm trusting you not to broadcast this to the world. But at least you'll know what he's expecting."

Steve takes the paper from me, but he doesn't even look at it.

Chapter 10

Steve

My mind is going a thousand directions at once, and I'm not even sure I said a proper goodbye to Eliza. *What the hell?* I mean, this is the twenty-first century. Who tells a woman she needs to be married to take over a business? I'm angry for Eliza, and I want to help her, but playing this game does not seem wise.

After pacing around my living room for a while, I text Davis, Michael, Jack, and Griffin. It's not late, so maybe I can get them to come over for an emergency drink.

Me: It's an emergency.

Davis: I'm on call so I can't drink.

Michael: I need to hide. Count me in.

Griffin: I'm on my way.

Jack: Be there as soon as I can. I'm on a date.

Jack's statement sparks several comments about at least letting her finish before he leaves her stranded. This is a classy bunch.

I finally sit down and read the list of things Eliza's father says she needs to do.

> *By the 1st of January, you need to have a thriving social life and be in a serious relationship, engaged to be married.*
> *We need to have spent time with your fiancé.*
> *He needs to pass muster with Laura, Minni, Charles, and me.*
> *I love you, and there is more to life than work. This is designed to show you that.*
> *Love,*
> *Dad*

This is bigger than she indicated. This means at least six months. I can't do this. This is ridiculous. No way.

I'm literally shaking my head when Michael walks in, and I can hear Jack's motorcycle out front.

I get out a stack of glasses and set them on the coffee table, along with a full bottle each of Johnnie Walker Blue and Woodford Reserve. I have this crowd covered.

I leave Michael in the living room and go to the kitchen for ice. From there, I hear Davis. "What's going on?"

"I don't know yet," Michael replies.

I'll tell everyone at the same time.

"I like the living room furniture. It's new, isn't it?" Davis says when I return.

I nod. "My mother insisted I have this place professionally designed."

Davis laughs. "I love that. When Paisley and her sister

moved in, they redecorated my place. It seems someone else is always in charge."

I nod. "It took some time to get the couch in. It was on back order forever."

Before too long, everyone has arrived. We're sitting in the living room, and all eyes shift to me.

I clear my throat. I tell them about my dinner tonight with Eliza, and then I read the email she printed for me.

There's a stunned silence when I finish.

"Are you thinking about it?" Griffin finally asks.

"I guess so..."

"Is the job with the Tigers that important to you?" Jack asks.

I shake my head. "It's not that at all. I want to help her. Her dad is dictating that she needs to be getting married to inherit a business he's known, since she was little, that she wanted. I get that he wants her to be happy, but his approach is just crazy. She's worked hard for this, and I want her to reach her goal."

"Sounds to me like you feel more for her than the usual women you meet." Davis stares down at his water.

I shrug it off. "I don't know her well enough to know that. I like hanging out with her."

"What do you want to do?" Michael asks.

"I think I need to date her a little first."

"Are you going to introduce her to John and Mary?" Davis asks.

John and Mary are my very dysfunctional parents. I think for a moment. What would that feel like? "If I could guarantee they'd behave, I would."

Jack pours himself a carbonated water. "You know being serious means she'll have to meet your parents, who, by the way, will want a huge Catholic wedding, Mass and all."

I groan because I know Jack's right.

Griffin's beeper goes off. "Sounds like you know what you're going to do," he says as he stands. "I've gotta jet. Catch up with you guys for golf this week."

He waves goodbye, and Jack turns the television on.

I guess that's settled then. Or we're not talking about it anymore, at least. "How was your date?" I ask Jack.

He shrugs. "I met her in India last year. We've been talking, and she's in town from Australia."

"Wait..." I sit up and look at him. "She flew in all the way from Australia and you're here?"

"You needed me, and she's hoping for more than I can provide."

"Wow," Davis says. "She spent a lot of cash to get here, and that's sixteen hours in the air."

"She has some friends she's traveling with. They're going to the States to hit San Francisco and New York City. She's good."

The guys stay and chat for an hour or so while we watch the Blue Jays game. I find I'm adjusting to the idea of exploring things with Eliza. I'm just not sure how she actually feels about me. Am I just a means to an end? It kind of feels that way. But I do want to help her.

When the guys finally head out, it's after midnight. I text Eliza.

Me: Let's have dinner at my place and talk tomorrow night.

Eliza: Are you sure?

Me: I'm not committing to anything. I said we could talk. You didn't even show me your panties today.

Eliza: This is what I wore today.

She sends a picture of a black lace bra and thong.

Me: It's hard to tell exactly what that looks like. Can

you put it on?

Eliza: I'm already dressed for bed. Plus, isn't it unfair to try to bribe you with sex?

Me: Dinner my house tomorrow night, 7 p.m. — panties optional

Me: I'm at the Surrey training facility tomorrow.

I send her my address.

My phone pings again, but it's not Eliza. It's Chloe, someone I'm definitely not interested in seeing.

Chloe: The cheerleaders are having a fundraiser on Saturday night. Hope to see you there.

Nope. No way.

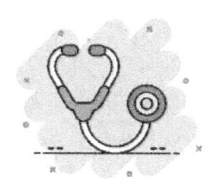

After a long day on Monday, I'm running behind, but I make it home before Eliza arrives, and that's all that matters.

I change into jeans and start my oven. Thank God for my mother and her frozen meals. Every few months, she shows up with a batch of freezer dinners for me — her home-cooked food she's put in foil pans and frozen. I pull out a lasagna casserole, which has small shell pasta instead of lasagna noodles. All I need to do is pop it in the oven with the garlic bread.

I slide it in just as Eliza rings the bell.

When I open the door, she's in tight jeans and a red furry

sweater that I immediately want to touch. She looks fantastic, and despite what she's told me, my lower head still seems to think this fake-engagement thing could be a lot of fun.

"Come in," I say.

She walks in and stops. "This place is incredible."

"Would you like a tour? We have some time before dinner. I was late getting home tonight, so it's going to be about an hour before everything is ready."

"I'd love a tour. I want to hear everything you did."

I pull a book from my bookshelf. "My sister talked me into doing before and after photos."

Eliza gasps. "She's so smart."

I show her the run-down apartment building this was when I bought it. "See? It had great bones."

"And you know bones."

I grin. "There were two first-floor apartments. I didn't want to play with too much of the plumbing, so the kitchen and bathrooms are still in the back, but you'll see it's better that way."

She flips through the before pictures, and then I walk her around. The concept is mostly open, but the kitchen is more separate. When we walk in, I show her how all the appliances have cabinet covers so they blend in.

She nods her approval. "And I love the sunroom. How perfect is this on a Sunday morning to read the paper over a lazy breakfast?"

"My favorite thing to do." I smile.

I point out that the claw-footed bathtub in the bathroom is original to when the house was built, but I've updated it with a modern shower head. I love this bathroom.

She's very appreciative. My heart always soars when people compliment the work I've put into this place, and it feels especially good when it's Eliza.

I show her the alternate first-floor bedroom, which I use as my home office. It's covered in Tigers paraphernalia.

She studies my collection. "You have something signed

by the whole team each year for over a decade?"

"Actually, I have something from every team since nineteen seventy. I've been watching the online sites to get things that go back to when the team was started in 'fifty-four.'"

She smiles. "Does my dad know this?"

"Probably not. I've never told him."

She pulls her phone out of her back pocket and takes a picture. I hear a *whoosh* as she sends it to someone.

"I just sent it to him and told him you were looking for early stuff. We have tons of things in storage. I bet he can get it for you."

"Wow, that would be great." Then my heart stops. "Did you just slyly tell your dad you're at my house on a date?"

She turns as red as her sweater. "I guess I did."

"What if I'm not interested in the deal you've suggested?"

She shrugs. "It still shows him I'm getting out and having the life he thinks I need to have."

There is a lot I want to say, but I just nod. She's got to navigate this the way she feels is best. "Follow me. We'll go up the front stairs to the second floor."

She follows me as we climb. "Each of the steps is made with a solid piece of maple I got in Quebec," I tell her.

"How did you find such old trees?"

"A maple syrup farm lost a good part of their orchard because of wind and rain, so my sister and I flew out and bought the downed trees. They were expensive, but it was worth it for Canadian maple."

She nods. "That's something my dad would have done."

"I've always liked your dad." I direct her down the hallway. "Upstairs, I now have five large bedrooms, each with their own en suite bath."

"I love the decor."

"You can thank my mother for that. She's been the lead designer in all of Dad's buildings. She does the welcome centers and all the show units."

"She's very talented."

"Well, thank you." I smile, basking in her praise until my gut lurches. "I didn't offer you a drink when you came in. I just showed off my house."

"No worries. I love it. Now, I want to look at the book you made again."

"Well, come on downstairs. I'll check on our dinner and get you a drink." I start us down another hallway. "What would you like? We're having a lasagna dish. I have a pretty full bar and all sorts of wine."

"Were you thinking of wine with dinner?"

"Yes. I have a great merlot if that works for you."

"Perfect. I'll have a glass of that."

"Here's the best part." We walk down the back stairs.

Eliza laughs, and the sound washes over me. "Don't tell me you have a basement?"

"No. Dig two feet and you'd hit water, but this was the entrance for the back apartments, so now it leads out to the backyard and garage."

She nods, but it's dark now, so she can't tell that I have space for four cars back there.

We return to the kitchen, and I pour her wine and seat her at the table while I pull out plates and silverware.

"How much of this did you do yourself?" she asks.

"Not much. I'm pretty scheduled with work, so I didn't have the time to do the labor. I did the tear-down in some places so I could see the quality of the floors, which were terrible, and look at the plumbing, also a patchwork of bad pipes. I paid people to do that part."

"Well, what they did is fantastic. I still can't believe you got all that maple."

"It was a friend of my sister's parents. They were upset about the loss, but we helped ease the blow for them."

"That was kind of you."

The timer dings on the stove, and I open the oven to uncover the dish and put the bread in. "We have another twenty minutes."

"It smells fantastic. You made dinner tonight?"

"I heated it up. Don't think I'm a terrible person, but I don't do nearly enough with my parents, and my mother often has free time, so she does things like make meals to put in my freezer. *She* made our dinner tonight. I couldn't decide between lamb stew or lasagna casserole. I hope you enjoy it."

Eliza is laughing hard. "You are so flippin' spoiled."

I look at the floor. "True. When I went to university down in the States, I missed her cooking so much that she flew in for a week and cooked like a hundred meals for me. She fed me and my roommates for the rest of the year. It was great. And I'm so grateful she still does it."

"Does she do this for your sister?"

"No way. My sister goes to my parents' house to eat. My schedule doesn't allow for that. Plus, my sister has the grandkids."

"I still think you're totally spoiled."

"I never said I wasn't."

Eliza sets her joined hands on the table. "So... After you raced off last night, I didn't think I'd hear from you again."

"To be honest, I wasn't sure you would either. But I'm upset that your dad has pushed this requirement on you. I do want to help."

"He means well, but I think he and Laura are so blinded by their love that they can't see anything else. I mean, my dad has been married four times. It's not like he has all the answers."

"This is a huge commitment for you, even if it's not real. What are you going to do if he actually wants you to get married in the coming year?"

She shakes her head. "I don't think he will. I think I can put that off. He just wants me to prove to him and to myself that I can have a life outside of work." Eliza stares at her glass. "It is a huge commitment. But I really think it's the only way. My dad is stubborn, and he has other options for the team, so he doesn't have to compromise. This will be worth it. If I run the team, you'll have a job. And after that, we can break up and remain friends."

"As I've told you, I like the job with the Tigers, but if I do this, it won't be because of that. I'd be doing it so you can reach your goal. And hopefully, you can show your dad it's not an either-or situation. You can have a family *and* a job you love. Your parents sucked at that, and frankly mine did too, but it is possible."

"I thought you said your parents were still together?"

"They are. They hate each other's guts, and it wouldn't surprise me if my mother didn't spike Dad's food with rat poison every now and again. But they're good Catholics and don't believe in divorce."

"Ewww," she says as she laughs.

I sigh. "I don't feel like we really know each other, so I thought we could start off just by dating."

"Well, I see what you mean. I want to keep our relationship professional. I think being friends at the root of things is our best bet."

"I'd like to revisit that. This Sunday night, there's a fundraiser at Julia Martin's home. It's a bachelor auction. If you're available, we can go together, and maybe you can bid on me for a date. I guarantee there will be press there, and we can make sure our picture makes the newspaper."

She nods slowly. "So, you'll really do this?"

"I think we should date and see how we feel about it after some time together."

"Okay." She looks at me carefully for a moment, and then nods again. "I like that idea."

Chapter 11

Eliza

"You look fabulous!" Tanya says.

I manage a smile. Julia Martin's fundraiser bachelor auction is this evening. I smooth out the front of the dress. It's not really my taste, but I had the personal shopper at Nordstrom pull a dozen options, and this is what Tanya and I agreed on. It's a shiny red silk dress with a keyhole neckline.

And I went back and forth over a diamond necklace, but I like the Mikimoto pearls the best.

"Steve is going to go crazy," Tanya continues. "The front is all conservative, but those slits up the side are pretty high."

"I know. I sat down earlier and realized my panties showed."

Tanya's eyes grow wide. "Does that mean you're going commando?"

I shrug. "Even the clear-band thong showed."

"Steve is going to jump you before you get to the party."

"This is a business arrangement. Sex and business don't mix. I think it would be a mistake if we got involved that way. You need to understand. I can't let my father rule my life. What he's asking for is completely unreasonable."

"Agreed, but why would you take sex off the table? What does Steve think about that?"

"Well, we still need to work out the details, but I'm sure he'll understand."

Tanya's eyes grow enormously. "You gave me every detail of the night you and Steve had together, and I needed a tall glass of ice water. Why would you shut that off? You could have some of the best sex you'll ever have."

"Because I know me. I don't want to confuse things, so I have to stay focused on my goal and keep my personal life separate."

"Okay, but just don't forget about the personal-life part while you're busy putting one over on your dad. Maybe there's a way everyone can win."

"I do like to win," I tell her.

"True that."

We high-five just as Mom's phone rings.

"He's here." Tanya squeals.

I answer. "Hello?"

"Ms. Rourke, there's a Dr. McCormick here?" the doorman says.

"Thank you. Please let him know I'm on my way down."

"I think you'll want him to come up."

"Oh, okay. Send him up, I guess. Thanks." I hang up and turn to Tanya. "That's strange."

"What?"

"He said I should have Steve come upstairs."

"Why?"

I shrug. "Beats me."

I open the front door as the elevator pings and Steve walks out with a dozen long-stemmed roses. My mouth drops to the floor.

"Holy cow!" Tanya blurts. "I was just leaving!" She rushes into the elevator and is gone before I can form a complete thought.

"Too much?" Steve asks when the elevator closes.

I shake my head. "Those are beautiful. Come on in."

I walk into the pantry and pull down a large vase. I don't know if I should cut the stems while he waits or do it later. I don't want to make a mess on my dress, and one splash would do it. I decide to just fill the vase with water and cut them later.

"Are you nervous about the auction?" I ask as I carefully turn on the sink.

"No. I know you'll be bidding. Julia will have all sorts of eligible men from around town. She's had to get creative since two of her sons are off the market and the other one is in trouble."

"Why is he in trouble?" I ask, setting the flowers on the table.

"Some woman Griffin had never met showed up at his parents. She jumped a fence, which set off a dozen alarms, and by the time she was arrested, the press had arrived, so she announced she was pregnant with his child."

"Wow. That's a lot."

Steve offers me his arm, and we take the elevator down. He leads me out to a Land Rover with a driver. I cross my legs, and Steve's hand slides appreciatively over my thigh.

Then he catches the look on my face and removes it. The side of his mouth curls. "Are you nervous?"

"What have you told your friends?"

"They know about the arrangement, but they're not going to say anything."

I roll my eyes. "Great."

"You told your friend."

"I told one friend. How many did you tell?"

He recites each person's full name. "Four people." His eyes find mine. "But they are trustworthy. I don't want you to be concerned."

"I guess I'll just have to trust you on that, right?"

"Right. But you still seem nervous." He eyes me.

"Okay, I'm a little nervous. We haven't really worked out our story."

"You won't need that tonight. Tonight, you're just going to bid on me. I'll pay whatever you bid, so make my donation a big one." He winks. "It's for a good cause — kids with cancer."

"I have money," I tell him. We drive out to the cliffs in front of the University of British Columbia. The homes here sit on substantial pieces of property overlooking the Pacific Ocean. When we arrive at the Martins', we leave the car with the driver and tour the house. The Martins own the two biggest newspapers in the country, several television stations, and the country's largest wireless-phone network. After a moment, Steve moves us toward a group of people about our age. I recognize a few of them.

"Steve!" A woman in a baby blue sheath dress embraces him. On her left hand is a stunning diamond ring with sapphires.

"Paisley, I'd like to introduce you to my date, Elizabeth Rourke."

She turns, and her warm smile disarms me completely. "Paisley Martin. I'm so happy to meet you."

"Please, my friends call me Eliza."

"I'm glad we're friends." She turns to two women who are chatting nearby. "This is Nadine Khalili and my soon-to-be sister-in-law, Allison Pate."

I smile. "Nice to meet you both."

Paisley then turns to the men and introduces Henry, Davis, Griffin, and Phillip Martin, followed by Michael Khalili and Jack Drake.

"Will all of you be in the bachelor auction?" I ask. "I'll have a hard time deciding who to bid on."

Jack picks up my right hand and softly kisses my knuckles. "I would be honored to take you on a romantic date in my private plane to a destination of your choice."

"Back off, asshole," Steve growls.

The group laughs.

"I'm thirsty," Allison announces. "Why don't we leave the guys to talk about us while we go find some drinks?"

I look at Steve. "Could I bring you something?"

"Bourbon is great." He squeezes my hand.

We walk off toward the bar.

As we wait in line, the woman in front of us is looking through the list of men. She stops at Jack Drake and nudges her friend. "Holy hotness. I'm bidding on him. He's a doctor and spends part of his time volunteering in third-world countries. How sexy is that?"

Her friend nods. "There are a few doctors. There's one who spends half the year working for the Vancouver Tigers. He has the most incredible blue eyes. I could stare at him all night."

I look over at Paisley, and she's grinning.

"I think I'm going to have some competition," I whisper, but apparently, not quietly enough.

The woman turns around and looks me up and down. "As if."

I draw myself up straight, but Nadine puts her hand on my arm and shakes her head. Once we have our drinks, we return to where we left the men. As we go, I take in the room's beauty and all the incredible art. When we get back to where we started, the women from the bar line are in the corner gossiping. I walk right up to Steve and lay a big, wet kiss on him.

He's a bit stunned, but it takes all of a half second for him to return the kiss. When we break, I struggle to stay upright.

I look back to where the women were standing.

"They left." Nadine snickers.

"What was that about?" Steve asks.

"I was just scaring off the competition." I take a sip of my drink.

Nadine giggles. "We were behind two women who were

talking about who they were going to bid on, and they insulted Eliza."

"What?" Steve's eyes grow large.

"There's some sort of program with all the bachelors," I explain.

Just then Paisley returns with a stack of programs for the ladies in the group. She passes them out and starts reading about her two brothers-in-law who are taking part.

Soon both Phillip and Griffin are blushing.

"What does it say about me?" Jack asks.

Paisley clears her throat. "Dr. Jackson Drake is one of the top-rated plastic surgeons in Vancouver, with experience in cosmetic and reconstructive procedures. Personalized, high-quality care is the founding principle of Dr. Drake's practice. He spends half the year with his practice here in Vancouver and the other half with Doctors Without Borders, helping those in need of reconstructive surgery for everything from burns to cleft palates. Dr. Drake also has his private pilot's license, so the winner should be ready for a romantic evening on a remote island."

Jack actually blushes a little. "Why did I agree to do this?"

"Ooh, here's a good one," Paisley continues. "Ladies, are you ready for the ultimate catch? We're excited to present one-of-a-kind orthopedic surgeon, Dr. Steve McCormick, who also serves as chief medical officer for the Vancouver Tigers football team. Not only is he an expert at treating injuries and getting players back on their feet, but he's also a charismatic and charming man who knows how to sweep you off your feet. In his free time, he likes to work with his hands as he fixes up his Victorian home. With his dashing looks, impressive intellect, and adventurous spirit, he's the complete package. Get ready to bid on the ultimate bachelor who can provide you with adventure, excitement, and passion. Don't let this doctor slip away."

The group is laughing.

"What's so funny?" Steve asks.

"How much do dates go for?" I ask.

"Davis once got the highest bid ever—before we were dating—which was ten-thousand dollars." Paisley winks at her husband.

My heart clenches. This may be more expensive than I thought.

A glamorous woman approaches us. "What are you all doing hiding here in the sitting room? You have to go see Paisley's latest creation. It's out back."

Paisley lets everyone walk ahead, but then she introduces me. "This is my mother-in-law, Julia Martin." She turns to Julia. "This is Steve's date, Eliza. Don't scare her off. We like her and want to keep her around."

Julia breaks into a glowing smile. "Thank you for coming tonight. Your date is one of our big bachelors this evening."

"He's told me I should bid on him, but I've already met two women who might scratch my eyes out if I get in their way."

Julia laughs. "I'm sure he only has eyes for you."

As we continue out to the back, Julia turns to several who've remained behind. "Go check out Paisley's latest," she tells them. "It's my favorite to date."

When we rejoin him downstairs, Steve leans over. "Since you've not been back in town very long, you may not know that Paisley is a world-famous artist."

Paisley leans in. "I have only fooled a bunch of people into paying absurd amounts of money for my art."

"This is her piece here," Allison says.

In the middle of the room is a piece of gray driftwood that has been partially dipped in silver. It's both natural and ethereal. Simple, yet engaging. She's clearly very talented. "That's beautiful."

"What's your latest piece?" Nadine asks.

"I did it just for Julia," Paisley explains. "It's a cherry

blossom branch made of wood and silver."

"Just wait until you see all the intricate flowers she designed. It's breathtaking," Julia says.

Somehow, she manages to be everywhere at once.

Paisley blushes, and the group begins to walk outside.

"Julia, I'd like you to meet my date, Elizabeth Rourke," Steve calls as Julia passes.

"Paisley kindly introduced us earlier," she says, extending her hand. "You're Nicolette and Tom Rourke's daughter, right?"

My eyes widen. "Yes. How did you know that?"

"I worked with your parents on a few things when you were young, and we still travel in some of the same circles."

"I'm stunned you remember me at all."

"You were quite young the last time I saw you, but I saw your mother before she left for Italy last year. She's so proud of you."

"Ah, yes. Who needs a publicist when you have a devoted parent?"

"I should make sure my children hear that."

"They already know," Steve assures her.

"The bidding for Steve will be fast and furious but don't feel obligated to join in."

"We'll see how high it goes. Steve's agreed to match my donation, so I'm considering how much of his money I want him to give."

"I like this one," she says to Steve.

In the backyard, there are tables set up in front of a large, T-shaped stage. Beyond that is a marvelous view of the ocean and the pink and orange sunset.

"What a beautiful evening," I breathe.

Steve pulls me into his arms. "You don't have to spend any of your money. Just bid whatever it takes to win the date. We'll get our pictures taken, and we'll make sure your dad sees it."

"Thank you."

We're seated with Steve's friends for dinner, and Nadine tells us stories about her job as head of her husband's family business. I remember reading about her and feel silly that I didn't put it together. And Paisley is both humble and so kind.

Steve slips his hand onto my leg again, and this time I let it stay. The warmth of his palm calms me. I feel a little lost with some of the conversation. While they've been great about including me, I don't know everyone they're talking about. "The next time you all decide to get together, you should consider including Eliza," Steve tells them. "She just moved back here from London and is getting to know the city again."

I feel myself blushing. "You don't have to invite me anywhere. I'm not friendless here."

"Oh, we'd love to have you join us," Paisley counters. "These guys get together all the time, so it's only fair. We also include an ex of Jack's sometimes. We loved her so much, we kept her around."

Jack tilts his head. "Who are you referring to?"

"Laine."

He rolls his eyes.

I'm curious about that story. I'll have to remember to ask Steve later.

After dinner, Allison excuses herself to serve as the mistress of ceremonies for the evening.

"You probably recognize Allison. She was a very popular actress, but she quit to marry Davis's oldest brother," Steve whispers. "They're tying the knot next spring. Julia is slowly handing off her community commitments to Allison and Paisley."

I nod. "I thought she looked familiar. My brain isn't quite tuned in yet, it seems. I remembered reading about Nadine while she was talking."

"All right, ladies," Allison's voice booms over the sound system. "Let's start the bidding."

She begins with Davis's brother Phillip. He's quite handsome and works as a senior executive for Martin

Communications. He looks very formal this evening in a suit and tie. The bids start conservatively, but a date with him ends up going for over seven thousand dollars.

The next two go for a little less than that, but still, very respectable donations.

When Jack walks onstage, he's traded his tuxedo for a white T-shirt, well-worn jeans, and a black leather jacket. He looks like a bad boy, and the women eat it up. He blows the lid off of Davis's record and goes for a stunning eighteen thousand dollars.

When Steve takes the stage, he has a bouquet of red roses like the ones he brought me. Women in the audience swoon, but he looks at me and winks.

The bidding starts at two thousand dollars, and there are about eight women in the running. For a little while, I just watch. In no time at all, Allison urges the bid up to eight thousand, and the bidders drop down to two women. One nudges it up to ten thousand, and when there's a pause, Allison begins to close the bidding. "Ten thousand going once —"

"Fifteen thousand," I announce.

"Eliza, good to see your bid," Allison says.

"Eighteen thousand," the woman counters.

I sit back, and the crowd is going crazy. Steve looks like he's going a little crazy too. But there's no reason not to have some fun with this.

"Eighteen thousand going once, going tw —"

Steve looks at me, eyes wide. I smile. "Twenty-five thousand dollars."

The crowd is on their feet, urging the woman to go on.

"Are you just going to up any bid I make?" she asks.

"He's my date this evening," I explain. "I'll do whatever it takes to take him home tonight."

The crowd laughs.

"He's all yours," she says.

I have to grin at that.

Three more bachelors are auctioned off before the

bidding concludes, and the lights come up. As the crowd mingles, the other woman who bid on Steve wanders over to me.

"Patricia Standing." She holds out a dainty hand.

"Elizabeth Rourke," I tell her as we shake.

"He's a handful, you know."

I nod. "Yes, I'm well aware of it. But he's fun."

"He's a lot of fun. Last year, we went to New York City for our date and saw a Broadway show."

"I'll set my expectations high."

She walks off, and Steve arrives with the bouquet of flowers. "I can't believe you bid that up so high."

I shrug. "It was fun."

A photographer comes over and introduces herself, saying she's from the *Vancouver Sun*. Steve and I pose for pictures, and several women stop by and congratulate me. It's actually quite fun.

"I'll go over and pay," Steve says after a little bit.

I put my hand on his arm to stop him. "I've got this. Don't worry about it."

But he insists. "I told you I'd at least match it. It's for a good cause."

We wander over to the cashier's table, and Julia hugs me tightly. "What a night!"

"I assume it was a record breaker," Steve says.

"Oh, and Jack, you were a bad boy. I can't believe you changed." Julia is beaming with pride.

He shrugs. "It's for a good cause."

"Melanie Thompson apparently saw you change and made a ten-thousand-dollar donation just for that."

"I guess that means he's the highest price tag tonight," Steve says with a smile.

"What are you going to do for your date?" she asks, looking between us.

But Steve is giving nothing away. "We'll have to figure that out."

He gives Julia his credit card and makes an additional donation that matches mine. I'm almost sure she's going to burst with happiness.

We talk a short time longer, and it seems every few feet we're stopped by someone who is happy for us.

"It seems like love," one lady says as she pinches Steve's cheeks.

My feet are starting to throb, so I hold on to Steve and slip my shoes off. Four-inch stilettos are a killer in the grass all night.

"Would you like me to carry you?" he asks.

"Don't you dare!" I laugh.

"Are you ready to head out?"

I nod. "Yes, but I don't think I've had this much fun in a long time."

After saying our goodbyes, we climb into the backseat of the Land Rover, and Marco, Steve's driver, takes us back to my place.

"I'm almost positive our picture is going to be in the newspaper's society page on Tuesday," Steve tells me.

"I'm not quite sure where my dad is, but hopefully, he'll see it. If not, I'm sure one of his friends will point it out."

"You didn't have to contribute tonight," Steve tells me again.

"I don't mind," I assure him. "I earn a decent salary. and I'm living rent free until my mother returns from finding herself."

"Would you like to come over to my place tonight?" Steve leans in and kisses me. His tongue enters my mouth and strokes softly.

My stomach flutters, and I consider taking what he's offering. My body would really like to. But I can't. I like Steve, but this is only supposed to get my dad off my back, so he'll give me the team.

"As much as I'd love to, I think it's better that I go home," I tell him.

Dating Steve feels way too natural. I can't lose sight of my ultimate goal.

Chapter 12

Steve

My phone rings, but I'm busy thinking about last night with Eliza, so it takes me a minute to answer. I'm going to end up with a major set of blue balls if I can't get her back into bed with me, so I've been trying to figure out how to make this work.

"Am I interrupting anything?" Mom asks when I finally get there.

"I'm at the stadium downtown doing paperwork. How are you?"

"I'm doing great. I just haven't seen you in a while, and I wanted to make sure you were still coming to dinner tonight."

I look up at the ceiling. The first Monday of every month I go to my parents for dinner, and it's often a painful experience. "Will Olivia and Paul be there with the kids?"

"Probably not Paul. They're not talking right now. But the rest of them should be here as usual." When I don't respond, she adds, "I'm making roast lamb with all your favorites."

My stomach is ready. I love my mom's lamb with roasted potatoes and carrots. I guess I should get the rest of me ready too. "I can't wait," I tell her. "It's exactly what I need. I'll be there."

"Will you be bringing the woman you went to the party with yesterday?"

Wow. The story has only made the tabloids. I figured if Mom saw it, it wouldn't be until it runs in the society page tomorrow. "What woman?" Seems better to play dumb.

"The one that's plastered all over the tabloids and internet. She's a looker. She must really like you if she paid twenty-five thousand dollars to go on a date. I hope you do something very special with her."

I'm going to skip right over mom's inquiring mind. "Do they list her name?"

"Elizabeth Rourke. Did you know her father owns the Tigers?"

This ball is rolling fast. "Yes. She did me a favor and bid on me for the bachelor auction."

"The tabloid says two women were bidding aggressively to win a date with you." Mom sounds giddy with that bit of gossip.

"Mom, Eliza and I work together. We're friendly."

"You know, there's nothing wrong with settling down and having a few grandchildren for me to spoil."

I pinch the bridge of my nose. "Both you and Olivia are terribly unhappy. Why would I want to do that?"

"We're not unhappy." She's quiet a moment because I've been a little too direct.

"I'm sorry, Mom. I don't want you to be upset. I'll be at the house by six for dinner. Would you like me to pick up a brioche bread pudding from the Irish bakery downtown?"

"Oh, I shouldn't…"

I know she's thinking of her constant dieting. "I can get

the chocolate caramel sauce. I'm sure the kids would like that."

"Fine. Just make sure you'll love me with a few extra curves."

My mom is perfect. Her body has given her two children, and it houses the softest heart I know. I sing a few bars of "Just The Way You Are" by Bruno Mars.

She laughs. "I can see why those women paid so much to go on a date with you."

After we hang up, I order the dessert from my phone and request delivery. Bread pudding is Mom's favorite, but she won't come into town for just that, so I often get it for her.

I return to looking at medical files. Hudson is doing physical therapy now, and I want to be sure he's not pushing too hard. If he continues at this rate, he should be able to come back around the tenth week of the season, which is about the halfway point. I send a note to the therapist to find out when Hudson's next appointment is, as I want to be there to see him.

My phone pings, and I smile as I read the message.

Eliza: We made the tabloids, and the Vancouver Sun's pictures come out tomorrow.

Me: Our evil plan is working.

Eliza: Do you want to meet for dinner tonight to discuss the next part of our plan?

Me: I can't. I'm having dinner with my parents. Would tomorrow work?

Eliza: I'm flying out to Toronto for an owners meeting, but I'll be back for Friday's game with the Calgary Oilers. How about Saturday night?

Me: That works. I'll make a reservation. Are you craving anything?

Eliza: I'm pretty open.

Me: Anything you don't eat?

Eliza: Exotic. I'll have ostrich, but not monkey brains, bugs, or snakes.

Me: Who took you out for that kind of meal?

Eliza: That's a fun conversation to have over dinner.

Me: I'll look forward to it. No monkey brains, bugs, or snakes. I'll send you the reservation once I figure it out.

Eliza: Thank you!

I keep my head down, and before I know it, I've worked through lunch and the brioche bread pudding has been delivered.

When it's time to leave, I turn the lights out and head down to the garage. On the way I see one of the women from accounting who always flirts with me.

"Hi, Dr. McCormick."

"Good evening, Danielle."

She smiles. "I saw you in the paper."

I place the bread pudding in my car and try not to cringe. "Julia Martin is a good friend."

"You got the highest bid. It must be nice to have women fighting over you."

I chuckle. "They weren't fighting over me. I asked Ms. Rourke to drive up the bid so we could donate as much as possible to the kids with cancer Julia's fundraiser was supporting."

"So, you're not dating Elizabeth Rourke?" she asks, moving a bit closer.

"We're friends." I sit down in my car. "I've gotta run. I'm having dinner with my family."

"Oh! Have fun."

I wave and drive out of the parking garage. That was a little creepy. I've had true stalkers in the past. But nothing a good old restraining order won't fix.

The drive to my parents' is not an easy one. They live in the hills in a giant home, though for the most part they occupy about four rooms. My father's goal was to have one of the most expensive homes in all of Vancouver. It's in a gated community where several very famous Canadians live, including Michael Bublé and his family.

When I arrive, my five-year-old niece, Emma, races out, and before I can even turn off the engine, she's opening my door. "Uncle Steve! You made it."

I love her enthusiasm. She's a perpetually happy kid, and I pray she never changes.

"Hey, munchkin. What's going on?"

"Dylan upset Mommy. He pooped in his pants."

"Well, sometimes three-year-olds will do that."

Emma puts her hand in mine as we walk through the door.

The house is in its typical chaos. Dad is sitting in the sunroom with the evening news on very loud. Mom and my sister, Olivia, are working on dinner in the kitchen and gossiping.

I catch their eyes and throw my thumb toward Dad. It's how we judge his mood. If I get a thumbs up, he's good to talk to. Otherwise, I'll be stuck with Mom and Olivia prying into my relationship with Eliza.

"He's good," Mom says as she chops vegetables.

Olivia shakes her head, but I decide to chance it anyway. I walk into the sunroom and sit down. "Hey, Dad."

"Hey, Doc. What's up?" Dad yells over the television.

I reach for the remote and turn the volume to almost nothing. "I'm good. What's going on with you? Have you guys figured out your winter plans?"

"I'm going back to Hawaii. Your mother isn't talking to me, so I don't know what she plans on doing."

Oh good, they're not talking to each other. This is so much fun. Just after Christmas, my parents go toward sunnier weather. They've done Mexico, all over the U.S., Spain, and Greece.

"I told your father I was going to visit my sister in Dublin," Mom calls from the kitchen.

"She didn't tell me that," he retorts.

I will my blood pressure to go down. "Is that why you had the television so loud? So you can't hear her when she yells at you?"

He rolls his eyes. "I don't care what she does. I get tired of hearing her yammer on about a bunch of nonsense. Tell me what's going on with you. Olivia says you have a new girlfriend. Did you bring her here tonight?" He sits up in his chair and looks around.

There's no way in hell I'd subject Eliza to this, even if she was my girlfriend. But I guess I may not have a choice if we do this thing. "I don't have a girlfriend. Julia Martin did her annual bachelor auction, and I asked Tom Rourke's daughter to bid on me and make sure she won. Another woman probably knew that and drove the price up. I didn't mind. The charity helps kids with cancer."

"So, you're not dating her?"

I shake my head.

"What's wrong with her?" Mom calls from the kitchen.

"Absolutely nothing. She's beautiful, smart, loves football more than I do, and she knows better than to get involved with me."

Mom stops mid-chop. "You're handsome, smart, you make good money, and you're great with kids. You're a prize."

"Mom, you remain the president of my fan club."

"You should think about this Rourke woman," she insists. "She might be the one for you."

"She's probably going to be my boss soon. That is, if I

have a job next year."

"What does that mean?" Dad asks.

"Come eat," Mom insists as she puts the salad on the table.

We corral the kids and get them in their seats. Then we finally sit down and say the Catholic grace.

When I look up, Dylan is staring at me, and I can tell he's got a bit of the devil in him. I make a face at him, and Olivia scowls. She *is* the devil. She tortured me when we were growing up, needling me until I'd react and then acting all innocent, so I was the one who got in trouble.

As we pass potatoes, carrots, lamb, and salad, we talk.

"Anyway, why wouldn't you have a job with the team next year?" Dad asks again.

I explain the league's new rule about the teams' chief medical officers.

Dad stabs his slab of lamb. "That's ridiculous."

I take a bite and savor the glorious taste. But everyone's eyes at the table are waiting for me to reply. "I agree. And Eliza does too, but she doesn't have a lot of sway with the league. She might have more once she takes over operations. If her dad gives her the team, she'll be the first female owner."

"Why would she want to work in such a masculine field?" Mom asks.

Olivia looks at Mom like she's grown horns and a tail. "I don't know, maybe because there are no feminine or masculine fields? It's a job. Maybe women aren't players, but the Tigers' front and back office are mostly comprised of women."

I sit back and listen as Olivia schools my mother.

Mom finally has enough and holds up her hand. "I just grew up differently."

She did. She was raised to be a wife, mother, and a good Catholic.

"Eliza told me she bought a place in The Butterfly. How's that going?" I ask Olivia.

That fills the rest of our evening with a discussion of how

architects really don't understand structural building and their incessant desire to push boundaries beyond what manufacturers can provide. I listen and nod. Dad's the one who chose the design. The building is going to be an architectural treasure for the city, and it's difficult and groundbreaking, but they'll make a lot of money. Once they're on to the next building, they won't remember how difficult this was, as long as they can avoid a mutiny among those waiting to move in.

The kids are getting antsy. Dad flings a carrot at Dylan, and he giggles, but Dad pretends not to notice.

"Dad, don't teach him that," Olivia warns.

"I'm the grandparent. I can do whatever I want," he chirps.

Olivia gives me a look, but I just shake my head. He wouldn't have allowed us to do that, but the rules are different for Emma and Dylan.

"What do you think Dad would have done to us if we started throwing food?" she asks.

Dylan picks up a spoonful of potatoes and carrots he's mashed together.

"Oh, don't do that," I cajole.

Dylan's eyes sparkle, and without even looking at Dad, he flings the potatoes.

I can't control my laugh, and he flings more at me.

Olivia freaks out, screaming at me as if I'm the person who taught or encouraged her kid to do this.

"What about Dad?"

"I didn't do anything," Dad quips.

Olivia looks like she's about to have a coronary.

Evidently Emma is feeling left out of the fun, so she throws a piece of meat at her brother.

I stand up and call a halt to the food fight.

Olivia kneels to wipe food off the floor. Mom has a housekeeper, so whatever she doesn't get will be found by Helga.

"Come on, little guy." I lift Dylan out of his seat. "Let's

get you cleaned up."

We walk upstairs, and I strip him down in the bathroom. He points to his junk. "I have a big penis."

"Man, you'll be trying to convince women of that your entire life. But let me let you in on a secret. It's not the size; it's how you use it."

"Don't be teaching my three-year-old son that crap," Olivia says over my shoulder.

"He's the one who brought it up." I send him to the potty while I turn the shower on.

Dylan steps in, and Olivia directs him while we watch from the hallway. He loves the low extra shower heads.

I can tell my sister is not her usual self. "Where's Paul?"

"I'm assuming he's with his girlfriend."

I knew they were having trouble, but what? My fists clench. "I'll kill him."

She shakes her head. "We decided to have him move out last March. He met a twenty-two-year-old college coed, and they have lots of sex and he doesn't have to worry about food fights and a wife who makes about eight times what he does."

"Okay, there's a lot to break down there. Why am I just hearing about this now and it's been almost four months?"

"Because Mom and Dad don't know."

"You haven't told them?"

She shakes her head. "And you'd better not tell them, either."

"Oh, I'm not getting into that mess."

"According to him, I work too hard, and I never want to have sex with him, which isn't far from the truth. It's hard working full time, and then he leaves everything else to me too. And before you start in on us having a nanny that cooks and lightly cleans, I don't want her raising my kids. That's our job."

"I know how to kill him at least a dozen ways that will never show up in an autopsy."

Olivia smiles. "Thanks. I'll let you know."

"I'm really sorry."

She shrugs and goes back into the bathroom to get Dylan out of the shower.

"What do you want me to do with these?" I pick up his dirty clothes.

"Throw them in the hamper. He'll need them the next time he's over."

She gets him dressed in his pajamas, and I give her a tight hug. "If you want to get out of town when Paul takes the kids, let me know."

"I want to meet Elizabeth."

I wouldn't mind that. They actually would get along great... "I'll see what I can arrange. I think it would be great for you to start a female CEO group for Vancouver."

Her eyes dance. "That would be awesome."

After we go back downstairs, Mom helps me get Olivia out to her car. After she drives away, I head back in to help Mom clean up and do the dishes.

"Do you like women?" she asks as we wash.

I nearly drop a plate. "Yes, of course I do. I just don't see myself settling down."

"You're so good with children, and you have a good job. What would stop you?"

I look up at the ceiling. "Mom, it's not like I had a great example growing up."

She looks at me, her eyes wide.

"Look, I love you and Dad. And I know you love me and Olivia. But you don't love each other."

"Of course, we do," she insists.

"You go out of your way to irritate each other."

"If we didn't care, we wouldn't do that."

"You live separate lives."

"So what? We do things together too."

"If the church didn't frown on divorce, you'd have kicked Dad to the curb a long time ago."

She waves that away. "You grew up in a house where we were together. That's what was best."

"It was," I concede. "But it didn't teach Olivia and me how to love, how to be in a real partnership relationship, and Olivia is repeating what she learned with Paul."

Mom scrubs at her dish. I've hit a nerve. My lack of desire to marry comes up about once a year, and she somehow thinks something is going to change. It hasn't. The real question is going to be how I manage their expectations after they eventually meet Eliza.

"I love you, Mom." I drape my arm over her shoulder and pull her in for a side hug. "You are an incredible mother and grandmother. You've set the bar so high that no one will ever be able to reach it."

She looks at me with tears in her eyes. "Thank you."

"And Eliza loved the lasagna casserole."

She lights up. "Maybe next month you'll bring her to dinner?"

I look at her. "Why are you fighting with Dad?"

"We're not fighting."

"When was the last time you talked to him?"

"We talk all the time."

"I'm not talking about the way he got upset that you put tomatoes in the salad just to irritate him tonight."

"Just because he doesn't like tomatoes, doesn't mean the rest of us can't have them. He can pick them out."

This is how they barb each other, and this is not what I want.

After we're done with the dishes, she walks me out to my car. "Do you need more freezer meals?"

"I'm doing okay right now," I assure her. "I still have two or three left."

"Bring Elizabeth to dinner. I promise your dad and I will behave."

"I know, Mom. You always do." I kiss her on the forehead and drive back to my place, thinking about Eliza and what I'm getting myself into.

Chapter 13

Eliza

"I like the jeans and pink sweater better," Tanya says from the kitchen.

I shoot daggers at her from my eyes. I've already changed three times, and right now, I'm wearing black dress pants with a white T-shirt and a silk multicolored jacket with a ribbon tie. "Too much?"

"I know your plan is to negotiate the terms of this fake arrangement, but you look like you're ready to negotiate for player of the year."

I look down. She's right. I wore this earlier this week for the owners meetings. It was the perfect mix of business and feminine. "Okay. I'll change one more time."

Tanya continues to look through Mom's fridge. "And rather than your boots, wear those strappy Jimmy Choos you have."

"But what if…" It's summer, and it's not raining, but if

we walk too far, I'll be hobbling.

"You're going out for dinner. Your tight jeans and those sexy sandals will get him thinking about getting his dick wet. You want that."

I suppress a growl as I return to my bedroom. "I don't. This is a business relationship." Okay, maybe I do, but that's not the point right now. I'm not doing this Dad's way. I'm doing it mine.

I walk out with my sweater and jeans back on and sit on the couch to put on the sandals.

Tanya shakes her head. "You're high if you think he's doing this for a job he doesn't need."

I sigh. "I know. He's made that clear. He says he wants to help me reach my goal."

She raises an eyebrow. "That should be your first topic of discussion tonight."

I know she's right, but what if I don't like what he says? Or worse, what if I do? I need to focus on faking my way through all of this.

"He's going to be here in five minutes. You better hurry."

I race back to the bathroom and almost fall because these sandals are way too tall. I touch up my lipstick and fluff my hair and rejoin Tanya in the living room.

"Stunning," she says as she takes a generous spoonful of yogurt.

Then the elevator pings, and out steps Steve. His lopsided smile greets us.

"How did you get up here?" I ask.

"The doorman remembered me from last time. Apparently, he saw coverage of the bachelor auction, and after talking to me about the Tigers for a few minutes, he let me up. I asked him not to announce me, so don't be upset with him."

"As long as you don't do that when my mother returns," I warn. "She'll have him fired in a minute. My dad tries to get up here now and then, and she doesn't allow that."

He chuckles. "I bet my parents wish they had someone like that."

"Why?" I ask. "They don't have a doorman?"

"Well, no. They live up in Burnaby Heights in a house."

"Oh. Yeah, I guess a doorman for your house wouldn't have enough to do, especially in a gated community."

He smiles at Tanya. "Good to see you, Wei."

She peels herself off the couch. "You too, McCormick." She turns to me. "I'm out of here."

"Have fun tonight," I call as I look for my handbag.

"Be good to my friend," Tanya tells Steve as she exits. "She just got back from being away, and I want her to stick around."

Steve doesn't flinch or seem alarmed. "I gotcha covered," he says evenly.

I turn with a smile, handbag in hand, and resist looking him up and down. He's wearing jeans, a patterned button-up shirt with contrasting seams, and expensive loafers. "Where are we headed to dinner?"

He smiles. "It's a surprise."

"Okay." I take the arm he's offered. "Let's get out of here."

We ride downstairs, and instead of an ostentatious car, he has the black Toyota 4Runner this evening.

"Wow. Isn't this a little lowbrow for you?"

He snorts. "We're going to my favorite restaurant in all of Vancouver, and I want to park on the street. I have almost two hundred thousand kilometers on this car, and I plan on driving it until she gives up the ghost. Then I'll buy another one. It's a great car."

"You've impressed me."

"Good to know you're so easy to impress. And you've impressed me too." His eyes darken. "You look perfect."

I feel myself blushing a little as he opens the car door for me and holds my hand while I ungracefully slide into the passenger seat.

"So where are we going tonight?" I try again to get him to tell me.

"You really want to know?" I nod. "Nonna's. It's in Chinatown."

"Is it Chinese food?"

"It's Italian. It's with the third generation, and the recipes go back to the original Nonna."

"Sounds great."

He pulls out into traffic and heads south. "How did things go in Toronto this week?"

I shrug. "Some teams have multiple owners, so that makes decision-making tricky. I've petitioned the league to have each team designate a single person to attend the meetings because often people feel ganged up on when they're getting multiple owners' opinions. But overall, the meetings went well enough."

"Did your dad go?"

I sigh. "No. He left a few weeks ago and hasn't returned any calls. I think he went to his place in the south of France. His office just keeps telling me what needs to be done."

"What did you do at the meetings?"

"We finalized the schedule for the next two years, and we're talking about some exposition games in the U.S. and UK They're thinking about games in Australia too. Who knows."

"That would be interesting to share our version of football. It's a little different from the NFL."

"That's part of what we discussed. And there are two teams up for sale in the league. I wish Donnie Cochran was interested in them. Based on their pricing, he has significantly underbid my dad for the team."

"How does your dad feel about that?"

"I'm not sure. Like I said, he's not returning my calls."

Steve stops at a light and looks at me. "Is that normal?"

"I don't know. I haven't been in town a ton since he and Laura had kids, so maybe they're just busy. But while I was in London, he always returned my calls."

Steve nods pensively. "Do you think he might be testing you?"

We're passing the Vancouver Library, a beautiful building and one of my favorite places to go. "Most likely. He plays games like that with people. It's something we've fought over before."

"I've known people like him my whole life. Little surprises me, but I hope he at least saw the newspaper with our picture in it."

"I'm sure if he didn't, some of his friends have pointed it out."

After a few more minutes, Steve pulls into a parking lot, and as we exit, he has to point me toward a tiny little restaurant. I would have missed it completely. Inside, the tables all have the cheesy red-and-white-checkered tablecloths with a candle and a red carnation at the center of each.

"Steve! Gina told me you were coming." A man about our age approaches. He has a tiny limp but a bright smile.

Steve lights up. "Tony! When was the last time I saw you?"

He grins. "It's been a while. "

Steve turns to me. "Tony and I played ball and hockey together in high school. He just finished playing for West Ham United in the UK He was the soccer phenom when we were growing up."

Tony turns to me. "Welcome."

"This is my...Eliza," Steve says.

Tony laughs. "*Girlfriend* doesn't roll off the tongue easily, does it?"

I laugh with him. "It doesn't seem to," I tell him, giving Steve the eye. "But I don't take it personally."

Tony's eyes sparkle as he looks at Steve. "She may be a keeper."

Steve's ears turn pink, and I realize I do need to clarify his reasons for going along with my crazy scheme to outwit my dad. Tanya was right.

"How is Marie?" Steve asks Tony as he leads us to our table.

"She's doing great. She's thrilled to be home after all the years we've been gone. It was hard not having any help from our families while we were in England."

"I'll bet."

Tony steps in close as he offers me a seat. "Are you seeing patients these days?"

"What's up?" Steve's face turns serious as he transforms into doctor mode, and it's really quite sexy. If he takes a stethoscope out of his pocket, I might faint. But instead, he does what I think I like best about him. He asks a question and listens to the answer. So refreshing in my dating life.

"I wrenched my knee—moving home, of all things—and probably need it looked at."

Steve looks down at Tony's leg. "You probably shouldn't be standing on it." He reaches into his wallet. "This has my cell number. Call me on Monday, and we'll make plans to meet up. We'll see what's going on, and if necessary, we can schedule a few tests at Mercy."

"Thanks. I appreciate it."

"Anytime," Steve says, settling in his seat across from me. "So, what are the specials tonight?"

"We have a veal puttanesca that Gina made from my Nonna's recipes, which is to die for." He kisses the tips of his fingers.

"Sounds great."

Here in our corner booth, it's almost as if we have a private room. I look out and see nothing but Steve. He truly is drop-dead gorgeous. I've imprinted our night together in my brain, and try as I might, a part of me wants to jump him right here in the restaurant, which would be disastrous. Might make my father proud though. I stifle a laugh at that weird thought. "This place is great," I say, craning my neck to see beyond our corner.

"I'm glad you like it. Nothing they have is bad, so choose

whatever hits your fancy." He leans in. "And tonight, I'm buying."

The corners of my mouth curl. "Fine. Then I'm ordering the most expensive thing on the menu."

"I can handle it."

I'm sure there isn't much he can't handle.

The server arrives to take our order, and Steve adds a bottle of Chianti.

Tony delivers the wine, and now, his limp seems pronounced. He must be in some pain. He fills our glasses and leaves us again, and we toast to the Tigers.

After a few sips, I muster the courage to start our conversation this evening. It has to be done, and I need to go into it with clear eyes if I have any hope of coming out the other side in one piece. "So, why are you doing this for me? I mean, I know you haven't agreed to the whole thing, but why even fake date me? I really don't have much to offer you."

Steve looks down at his wine for a moment. "I'll be honest, my interest surprises me too. And I don't particularly think these dates are fake. We're getting to know each other. That's real. I don't usually feel much for my dates past a good time, but I enjoy being around you." He looks up at me, and something in his eyes shifts. "I don't have a good frame of reference when it comes to relationships. My parents may still be married, but they don't like each other, and they haven't for a long time. When my dad announced that he wanted to retire, I championed my sister taking over. I have no interest in working with family or leaving the practice of medicine. Dad was reluctant because he felt Olivia wouldn't be respected by our contractors and suppliers. But that isn't the case. She's amazing. I see you in the same position. It's bullshit that your dad thinks you need to have a husband behind you to be successful. I want you to have what my sister has—a thriving career that you enjoy. Your gender doesn't mean crap."

Warmth washes over me. "So, you're a feminist?"

He chuckles. "I suppose I am. I love women—"

"Yes, all the pictures on the internet make that clear."

"You looked me up?" His eyes sparkle with mischief.

"I did. But anyway, I'm grateful to have you in my corner. The owners were a bit much in certain situations at those meetings, but you saw me stand down Sean Rhymes' agent. I don't put up with fools. I know I can do this."

"Then let's do this. Let's make you the owner and general manager of the Vancouver Tigers. We'll beat your dad at his own game."

I'm about to ask exactly what he means by that, but then I decide to quit while I'm ahead. He's agreed, and that's all that matters. The rest is up to me.

Steve holds up his glass, and we toast again.

Now, we have to think about logistics. "We have a few things to work out," I tell him. "It's almost the middle of July. I have until the first of January to get this all settled and show my dad what I've accomplished."

"What do you think he's going to need to see?"

I take a deep breath. "He'll be suspicious if we just get engaged. He has a fixer who works for him, Charles, and he, my stepmother, my half-sister Minni—who's six years old—and my dad will all have to believe the relationship is real. I expect Charles to be all up in our business, but we'll never see him coming. This is going to require that we date, as we already are, and spend a lot of time together. And that will lead to overnights and eventually moving in together—all pretend, of course."

The look on Steve's face tells me he's struggling. I'm not sure with which part. I reach for his hand. "Tell me what's bothering you. If this is going to be too much, just say so, and we can walk away now."

He takes a deep breath and shakes his head. "I assume we're going to have to fool my parents too. Your dad will probably want to meet them?"

I think for a moment. "That's a good point. How will they take this?"

"I'm not sure. I had dinner with them and my sister last Monday night, and although they'd seen the photos from the bachelor auction and were all interested in you, I told them I wasn't made to be married."

Our caprese salads arrive, and the server offers us fresh ground pepper. This gives me a minute to process what he's saying.

"I'm not trying to change that about you," I assure him. "And I don't want to hurt your family." I squeeze his hand. "This is messy. Thank you for considering it."

"We're not going to have to get married, right?" Steve asks.

I shake my head. "My dad said I need to have a social life outside of work and be in a serious-enough relationship that I'm engaged. He wants me to have a support system and other things in my life besides the team, so I don't make the mistakes he did. *But I'm not him.*" I feel my temper flaring all over again and pause for a moment to calm myself. I look up with a smile. "Sorry. I figure after we get engaged and I've taken over the team, we can continue a bit longer. By then The Butterfly should be ready for move-in, and we can have a big breakup and I'll move into my place. Then you can go on about your life, and I'll do everything I can to convince the league, so you'll still have your job as the CMO of the Vancouver Tigers."

Steve finishes his salad and takes a deep pull on his water. "What about intimacy?" He doesn't meet my eyes.

"You mean sex?" I confirm.

He shrugs. "That's a part of intimacy, but being a couple that's sharing and becoming friends is also intimacy."

I take the last bite of the best caprese salad I've ever had and look at him. "I enjoy spending time with you. I also realize we've had sex before, but even as we move forward, I think it's best if we keep that separate from this. As you said, this is about beating my father at his own game. I prefer to manage my personal life on my own terms. If we're spending time together *and* having great sex while we do this, things are going to get confused. So, I still don't think we should."

"You don't think we should what?"

"I don't think we should confuse ourselves and have sex."

Steve is quiet as the waitstaff comes to clear our dirty plates.

"So, we'll be getting that from other people?" he asks after a moment.

"No!" I practically knock over my water glass. "We'll be celibate for the next six months."

He starts to cough and needs a moment to recover. "I haven't been celibate for six months since I lost my virginity at fifteen."

"Fifteen?" I blurt.

"Yes." His eyes widen.

"You've got to be lying." *That isn't possible.*

"When's the last time you've gone over six months?" he challenges.

"Before I met you it had been more than a year."

Steve sits back against the booth. "You were deliciously tight, but—"

I put my hand up. "I don't want to talk about it. Charles will most likely put a private investigator on us if he hasn't already. This will all be for nothing if he catches you with another woman."

Steve looks away. "Fine. Whatever you say. I'll figure it out. But I won't promise I'm not going to take care of myself."

"That's fine," I assure him. "I have a few toys as well."

He rolls his head back and looks at the ceiling. "I can't know that. I'm a giant pervert. I may want to watch and then join in."

"Stop it. We can't go there."

"Tell me about it." Steve rolls his eyes. "What else?"

"That's all I can think of right now."

"I'm going to have blue balls for the next six months."

"I know I'm asking a lot and for not much in return." I

sigh. "I understand if you want to change your mind." I lace my fingers together, feeling a little panicky. "But if you could let me know sooner rather than later, I already feel like getting engaged within five months is too quick."

Steve scrubs his hands over his face. "I'm still surprised your dad is not the other way, trying to protect you from some idiot who wants your money or to use you as a steppingstone for something else."

I shrug. "He knows I don't suffer fools, and of course he'll insist on a prenup. I don't think he's worried about that."

Our main course arrives. I have the baked ziti, and Steve ordered the veal special Tony mentioned. When I take my first bite, my eyes grow wide. "This is incredible."

Tony steps up to top off our wine and water. "These are my grandmother's recipes. Good, aren't they?"

"This is better than good. Holy crap. I want this every night."

"That can be arranged." Tony winks at me, and I see Steve's knuckles go white.

As we eat, we talk a bit more about my meetings in Toronto, and Steve fills me in on what's going on with Hudson. We're done with our meal before I know it, and Steve is walking me out to his car.

"Do you think Charles has already gotten someone to watch us?" Steve asks.

I look around the parking lot. "I suppose it's possible."

He nods and opens my door before entering on the driver's side. "Do you think they'd bug my car or anything?"

"No, but I wouldn't be surprised to see photos of us from tonight."

"Then we have a part to play," Steve says, leaning over to kiss my cheek.

"Thank you."

He nods.

"You're still struggling with the abstinence," I note.

He nods. "Yes, but I'm an adult. I'll figure it out."

"It won't be that bad," I assure him. Or maybe I'm assuring myself.

He gives me a look. "We'll see."

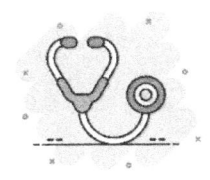

The phone ringing startles me from the spreadsheet I'm staring at. It's still early Monday morning, but I've been at the office since before seven. I answer without even looking at the caller ID. "Elizabeth Rourke."

"Lizzy!"

My heart soars. Only one person calls me that. "Mom! Where are you?"

"I'm still here in Tuscany. I'm leaving for Paris for a shopping trip on my way, but I'll be home in a week or so. I want to spend some time with you," she gushes.

"That's great news. I can't wait. But don't be stressed out if I'm not home much."

"Please tell me you're not working tons of hours for the Tigers."

"It's football season, so I'm working quite a bit, but…" I cross my fingers as I lie to her, but I've got to start somewhere. "I've met someone. He's really great. We're spending lots of time together, and it might be serious."

"What? You're too young to settle down. Don't do anything brash like get married until you've dated him at least a year."

"I won't," I promise. "I can't wait for you to be home. My condo isn't done yet, but we have so much to catch up on." I won't tell her about my deal with Dad. If she caught wind, she'd show up at his door and scream at him. They have opposite feelings on relationships. My mother doesn't like being tied down because she says men try to make all her decisions for her. She's a free spirit.

"I agree," she says. "I have so much to tell you. I may have a guest return with me."

"Oh? Do tell!"

"He's Italian and so handsome. We have so much fun together, and he's a dynamo in the sheets—"

"Stop! I don't want to know about your sex life."

"I don't know why you're so provincial. Everyone has sex. I want to hear all about your sex life with your new man too."

"Not everyone has sex."

She sighs. "I have no idea how I raised a daughter who can't talk about something so enjoyable."

There are so many reasons I don't want to share my sex life with my mother—the biggest being that I don't want to know about hers.

"Anyway, what's the name of the man you're seeing and how did you meet him?"

"His name is Steve. He's the chief medical officer for the Tigers, and he works the other half of the year on staff at Mercy Hospital. He has a gorgeous Victorian house in Chinatown, and he's not intimidated by my love and knowledge of football."

"He sounds wonderful. I can't wait to meet him."

We talk a little more about her trip and the things she's done. Each time she tries to tell me about her new boyfriend, I steer the conversation away.

"Listen, I need to run," I finally tell her. "I'll see you when you get back. Let me know when, and I'll make sure I clear my schedule, as long as it's not a game night. Dad is who knows where, and he left me in charge, so I try to go to all the games."

She sighs. "I don't know how you can enjoy that. I never understood why your dad loved football so much that he had to buy the team."

"I guess I got that from him. But he doesn't understand

why I love art so much, and I got that from you. Speaking of which, one of my new friends is a pretty famous artist—Paisley Martin. Do you know her?"

"Hmmm…" Mom muses. "I've seen some of her work. She's very talented. I hope you can introduce us. My new friend is a sculptor. She might be able to point him in the right direction."

I roll my eyes. I love her so much, but sometimes, she's a lot. "We'll see, Mom. Let me know when you'll be home."

"I will, darling. Have fun with your boy-toy."

We hang up, and I already know she's going to embarrass me in front of Steve. I'll have to give him plenty of warning.

Chapter 14

Steve

I've picked up the last of the takeout containers in the living room and moved the beer bottles to recycling. I have a shepherd's pie my mom made in the oven. I think I'm ready. Which is good because Eliza should be here any minute.

Last night at the Italian restaurant, we agreed that since this is supposed to be a whirlwind romance, we should see each other nearly every night. So, Eliza is going to come to my place this evening. She'll bring an overnight bag and sleep in my guest bedroom.

I haven't had a roommate since I was in school. This is going to be weird. And I never wanted to sleep with one of my roommates, but then again, they were always men. But what's really tripping me up is giving Eliza a key to my house. It makes sense with what we're doing, but the only people who've ever had keys are my parents, my sister, and Jack, in case of an emergency.

What have I agreed to do? I always enjoy hanging out with Eliza, but therein lies the problem. I enjoy it way too much. That's not normal for me, and of course it happens just in time for me to get myself into an impossible situation. But there's no time to ponder that now. Through the open living room windows, I hear a car door shut out front and I know she's arrived.

I take a deep breath. We're likely always putting on a show for someone, so we have to look the part. She knocks on the door, and when I open it, we kiss softly.

Her lips are so pliant. I would love to spend hours enjoying them, but instead, I step back and let her in.

"How did practice go?" she asks as she places her overnight bag inside the door.

I walk to the kitchen to check on dinner. "It wasn't too bad. We still have two players who want to tell everyone else what they're doing wrong but won't put a mirror up and admit they're not doing great either."

I pour a glass of white wine and hand it to Eliza.

"Thank you." She takes a sip, and her shoulders relax. "I don't know what to do about this. Why would Roy, or anyone else, think those two guys are worth what they're doing to the team?"

"Seems to me like the coaching staff has the team split up more than they have in the past," I tell her. "They're in two camps, offense and defense, which is common but not always best. It breaks up the team, almost into cliques."

Eliza nods, lost in her thoughts.

"I hate to add to it, but I also received notice that three players didn't pass their drug tests this week," I tell her after a moment.

"Who?"

I list off the players—two new recruits and the quarterback, Marty Holloway. "I'm having them retested at an independent facility. We believe it's a bad batch of tests."

Eliza sighs and takes a deep pull on her wine. "What a

mess. We're one and five so far this season. Any decent players will be flying the coop at the end of the season, and I really believe we're almost a good team."

The buzzer in the oven tells me our dinner is ready. I excuse myself to pull out our food.

"I love a man who cooks," Eliza teases as she comes to the table.

"This is all my mother. Does it bother you? Do I seem ridiculous? I can tell her to stop."

She smiles. "No way. Your mom's cooking is outstanding. I grew up eating lots of salads and takeout. I hate salad. I like all the things you put on it—particularly bleu cheese dressing that coats carrots, sunflower seeds, and other raw veggies, but I don't like lettuce. It's just bad filler made for rabbits, and I'm not a rabbit."

"Turn around," I demand, just as she's about to sit.

She gives me a confused look. I motion with my finger for her to turn around. She does, and when her back is to me, I stop her. "Wiggle your butt."

She turns and looks back at me, still confused.

"Wiggle your butt around."

She gives a little jiggle, and every ounce of blood drains to my lower half. "You're definitely not a rabbit," I confirm.

She playfully smacks my bicep. "Ouch. You're so strong," she mocks.

"Mom always leaves a bag of salad she's made. But you don't want salad."

"Well, I bet it's not iceberg lettuce."

"If there's iceberg, it's mixed in with other things, and she makes a decent balsamic vinaigrette."

"Sounds perfect. I just don't like salad as a meal."

We sit down, and I hand her the serving spoon and a dinner plate. "Help yourself. The game's getting ready to start."

After we have our plates, we toast to our meal, and she tries a bit of the beef-and-potato concoction. "This is amazing. What can't your mom do?"

"She doesn't give me blue balls like you do."

She sits up straight. "I don't do any such thing."

I scowl. "Look at what you're wearing. That shirt is nearly see-through."

"I'm wearing a bra and a camisole. You can't see any of the good parts, and I figure if I showed up in jeans and a T-shirt, they wouldn't believe we were getting busy."

"I can't believe we're *not* getting busy." I carry her plate and mine into my living room so we can watch the game while we eat.

She sighs as she flops down on the couch.

"Who do you think will win?" she asks after a moment.

"Nice change of subject. I see you for what you are. As for the game tonight, I don't know. They seem pretty evenly matched. I'm sure you have an opinion."

"Honestly?"

"When are you not honest with me?"

"I don't like the owner of the Edmonton team very much. He tried to explain the game to me as if I was some arm candy for my dad, which is a disgusting thought."

I throw my head back and laugh. "I can see him thinking that, but he must have looked like an ass as soon as you spoke. You know your stuff."

She shakes her head. "I didn't say too much at the meetings. I mostly took it all in and watched the politics."

"What do you think?"

"They're a bunch of old white men. And even in the height of youth, most of them couldn't throw a halfway-decent spiral across your living room."

"Can you throw a ball?"

"Across your living room? Absolutely. Twenty-five yards? No way. I could probably do ten yards.

"I haven't tried in years."

We sit back and put our feet up—at least until the first of her outbursts.

"What?" she demands, pointing at the screen. "That was

clipping? Come on, ref. I'm going to send him some new glasses if he's going to miss these obvious calls."

I love this.

"Oh great," she laments a while later. "The ref ran into the player. That's not a good call! The ref didn't even fall down."

My balls are going to go from blue to purple before these six months are up.

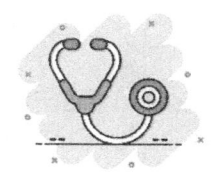

At the end of the evening, we close down the house, and I walk her upstairs to the guest room. We agreed that she'd use my bathroom and do her routine in my room to avoid turning on any lights in the guest room, on the off chance someone is paying attention.

When she walks out of the bathroom in her sleep shorts and tank, with her hair piled on her head, I'm a goner. I roll over, bury my face in the pillows, and groan.

"I'm sorry. I couldn't find where I packed my contact solution and face cleaner. I'll try to be faster in the future."

"It's okay," I say into the pillow, trying to think about my mom and sister and willing my cock to go to sleep.

"Goodnight," she calls as she moves down the hallway.

If it wasn't too obvious, I would take a shower and get a release. But she would know. I sigh. How am I going to do this for six months?

"There he is," Jack says as I slide into the chair next to him at Joe Fortes the following evening.

I signal Nancy behind the bar, and she nods and brings me three fingers of Johnnie Walker Blue over a small block of ice.

"Where are Michael and Nadine?" I ask.

"They should be here anytime," Davis says as he stretches out his long legs. He's drinking soda water.

"Surgery in the morning?" I ask.

He nods. Davis is a pediatric heart surgeon. "We're repairing a heart valve in a seven-year-old."

I shake my head. I rarely see kids in my practice, and I like it that way. It breaks my heart to see sick kids. "They're lucky to have you as their surgeon."

Paisley, his wife, is sitting next to him, and she kisses his cheek. "That's what I tell him." She turns to me. "Where is Eliza?"

"She should be here any time."

"Looking for me?" I hear over my shoulder as Eliza approaches with a martini glass full of pale pink liquid.

I stand. "There you are." I kiss her on the cheek. "What is that?"

"It's a cosmo. I know they're terribly out of style, but I still like them."

"I think that sounds perfect. That's what I'll have." Paisley heads for the bar.

"How did today go?" I ask Eliza in a low voice. This is the first chance we've had to catch up. I was downstairs at the stadium and didn't have two minutes to meet until nearly the end of the day, and she was on a conference call all afternoon.

"There was an offer on one of the franchises, and all the owners had to approve."

"Which team sold?"

"The Maritime Mariners." She leans in close. "It sold for almost twice what Donnie offered my dad."

I shake my head. "Why would your dad consider a low bid?"

"I would think once he hears about this price, he'll make Donnie up his offer."

I nod. "All three of the failed drug tests did fine at the new lab."

"Oh, thank God. Why do you think they failed the first one?"

I shake my head. "I don't know. I'll see how next week's tests go."

Suddenly, everyone is buzzing because Nadine and Michael have arrived.

"This is great. Everyone is here," Paisley says as we scoot over to make room for them.

The three women huddle up while the guys kick back. We talk for a while about the challenges we're having with the hospital.

Davis looks over at the women. "So, you're really doing this?"

I shrug one shoulder. "It's going to be hard."

"You're not interested in anything more?"

If only he knew the mess I'm in. "I think I'm interested, but she's made it clear that's not on the table."

Davis nods, looking at me carefully. "And you're going to do that?"

"It's the only way. I have to ride this out for a while."

"Wow. I don't think I have that much restraint," Michael says.

I look at the melting ice in my glass. "Trust me, it'll probably be the hardest thing I ever do."

"What do you have to do?" Jack asks, looking confused.

I'm not about to rehash the whole thing here in public, with Eliza at the same table. "I don't think I'll have a job with the Tigers next year," I tell them shifting the subject.

"Because you're going to break it off with Eliza? If you are, can I ask her out?" Jack asks.

I glance at Davis, and he's grinning.

"Oh, this should be good," Michael says.

"What are you talking about?" Nadine asks.

"We're teasing Steve," Michael counters.

She looks a little suspicious but turns back to the women.

I lean close to Jack. "You can never date her. Do you understand? Ever."

That gets whistles and noise from my friends.

"You're not going to make it six months." Davis shakes his head.

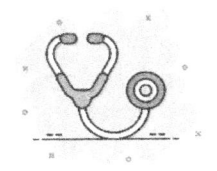

At the end of the evening, I go back with Eliza to her mom's townhouse. She takes her hair out of its ponytail and runs her fingers over her scalp as she toes off her heels.

"Why did approving the new Mariners owner take so long today?" I ask.

"We had to meet with the new owners, go through the business plan and their banking statements. They have to be able to make payroll and get everything accomplished, showing they can work with the other owners. It's a lot of glad-handing. They don't pay much attention to me because I'm just there as my dad's representative."

"Will you have to do the same thing when your dad

gives you the team?"

She stretches, and I try not to watch. "No, thank goodness. We'll just meet with lawyers. I think a few of the owners who are tight with Dad know I want the team. Maybe they're the reason he doesn't want me to have it."

I shake my head. "I don't think you should try to guess. You know he wants what he thinks is best for you. It's a little outdated, but from my view, you're doing great. You're going to get the job done."

"Thank you."

When she beckons, I follow her upstairs, and she points me to the guestroom. "I'll get changed and then feel free to come in and watch sports highlights with me."

"Sounds good."

I change into a pair of shorts and a Tigers T-shirt and join her in her bedroom. She's wearing sleep shorts and a tank top again. She covers herself with a blanket and sits next to me on the loveseat. It's either that or the bed, and if we sit there, I'll have zero control. I'd love to remind her of what we did the last time we were together in a bed.

We watch sports highlights, but it gets boring fast.

"How about a movie?" she offers.

"What are you thinking?"

"There's a Lethal Weapon marathon on."

"Let's do it."

We laugh about Mel Gibson's long hair and how dated the movie is, but we have fun. She fits so well snuggled up in my arms, and eventually, she falls asleep.

I turn off the television and help her get into bed.

"'Night. I wish I could kiss you," she murmurs, half asleep.

Hmmmm... "Why can't you kiss me?"

"Because you wake up all my lady bits, and they'll want way more than a kiss."

She snuggles into her pillow, and she's out.

I'm left with a raging hard-on and the knowledge that,

deep down, she might be interested in me after all.

I pad down the hall to take a shower, and my mind slips back to the night we spent together. I can still recall the look she had when she climaxed and her tight pussy choked my cock. Then I paint the drain with my orgasm and try not to cry that this is my lot in life until sometime after New Year's Day.

Chapter 15

Eliza

"You can put that right there," I tell the mover.

He sets down a stack of boxes in my bedroom, which is really Steve's guest room and the place I've been staying since we reached the phase where we're supposedly spending all our nights together.

It's going to take some time to get everything organized here. I wasn't that organized at my mom's, but I lived alone and didn't care. Here, I'm a guest, so I will try to be more thoughtful.

I'm a little uneasy about this, but with mom and her latest boy toy moving back, it's time for me to get out of her place anyway. I've been ordering appliances and furniture for my condo and putting them into storage as they arrive, since the condo isn't ready yet, but I still had a lot of stuff to move, mostly clothes, shoes, and accessories.

Tanya drops a box. "What the hell is in this?"

I look at the markings on the side. "It says mugs, but I don't have mugs, so I'm not sure."

"I hope the movers didn't pack your mother's kitchen."

I break the tape seal with my keys and open it up. There is a mug here that was on my bedside table, but the rest is about ten boxes of boots and a few more, like my wellies, that don't have a box. I like boots. "Nope. One mug and boots. I need to figure out a way to organize them."

Tanya moves the box to the corner of the room. "Where is Steve? Why isn't he helping his girlfriend move into his house?"

"I assume he's out at the practice facility. We didn't talk about it."

Tanya stops and looks at me like I'm a wild animal that might turn on her. "What part didn't you talk about? Where he would be or that you were moving in?"

"I guess both." I pick up the box that has my hair and makeup supplies and walk toward the bathroom.

"You don't think the confirmed bachelor is going to freak out that you used a key — mind you, one he's never given to any other female outside of an immediate family member — and just moved in your things?"

"He knows it's not permanent, and we talked about it at the beginning. I will be living in this bedroom. His room is down the hall. We even have our own bathrooms."

"But he didn't know you were doing this today?"

"I didn't have time to get into it, but I'll ask for forgiveness if I need to, because I had to. My mom and her new friend return tomorrow. I can't stay with them. I don't want to hear her have sex with this guy."

She wrinkles her nose. "I get that. I don't want to hear you have sex, either."

"Don't worry. Steve and I are not having sex."

Now, she looks even more disgusted. "You need to get your priorities figured out. That man is amazing, and you're going to look back on this and regret that you didn't have sex all over this house when you move out."

I sit down hard in the single spot open on the bed. "This is about getting the team. Steve is great, but I don't have time for that right now, and I don't want to risk getting my heart involved. My priority is the Tigers." I could be reminding myself of this as much as telling her.

Tanya opens her arms. "You deserve more than that. I'm sorry you've been backed into this mess, but try to consider a relationship with Steve as at least a means to scratch an itch. It worked before, right?"

"That was totally different." I look around the room. "That was before he was kind enough to wade into this mess with me and let me live in his house."

"Well, I'm still not convinced. I think we need to find a good martini place and discuss all the merits of his very fine ass and a dick you've never told me about."

I laugh. "I have a box of liquor here. Let's make raspberry lemon drops, and you can tell me what's happening with Jun."

I dig around a minute, and when I find the raspberry syrup and vodka, I motion for her to follow me downstairs. I know there are lemons on the bar cart, and Steve has some glasses.

Tanya moans. "What's there to tell? He wants me barefoot and pregnant. I want to enjoy life a minute before I'm forced to settle down."

"When was the last time you went out with him?" I pour raspberry syrup, lemon juice, and vodka over ice and seal the shaker.

"I guess it depends on what you mean."

I'm looking for Steve's martini glasses, but I stand back up. "Okay, when was the last time you saw him?"

She looks away. "I might have caught his bare backside yesterday morning as he was getting out of my bed."

My eyes grow wide. "What? Are you sleeping with your ex-husband?"

"It might be an exaggeration to call it sleeping."

I give up on my search for martini glasses and pour our drinks into tumblers.

"Are you exclusive?" I ask as I pour.

"I guess that depends on how you define exclusive." She takes a tentative sip of her drink. "Oh, this is good. Dangerously good."

I smile, feeling very proud of my bartending skills. But she's not getting out of this. "You're being very technical here. How do *you* define exclusive?"

Tanya sits back. "I don't want to ask because I think he's seeing other people, and anyway, I don't know that I'm ready for us to be exclusive. That didn't go so well the last time."

Then why are you doing this? I want to shriek, but I don't. I realize she's lonely, and Jun is at least a known quantity. I sigh. "As long as you're protecting yourself, both with condoms and your heart."

She shrugs. "We do the horizontal mambo well. It's our desired ways of living life that don't intersect. He wants to spend all his time attached to a video game, and I want to be outside enjoying what Vancouver has to offer."

I take a deep breath. This sounds like almost as big a mess as I'm in. Jun was a little suffocating when they were married. Going out for drinks when I was in town was hard, not because he wanted to come with us, but because he didn't really want to share her with anyone. "How do you feel about him dating other people while sleeping with you?"

She shrugs. "It's so flipping hard to meet a nice guy in Vancouver."

"I get it. But as you said to me a bit ago, you deserve more."

"Well, I haven't found a fake boyfriend to move in with so…"

I roll my eyes. "Hey, I'm not holding myself up as the shining example here either, but this is just temporary. I'm going to get where I want to be. I want you to do that too."

Tanya shakes her head. "Thanks. I need to get a plan together, not just keep falling into bed with my ex. He's not any different than he used to be, so I don't know what I'm expecting to happen."

I nod and give her a squeeze as I join her on the couch. We spend another hour talking while I work on unpacking. If the movers were being paid by the box, they would have made a mint, because despite that heavy one full of boots, they packed a lot of boxes with very few things inside.

After I wave goodbye to Tanya, I head to the take-out menus and look at local places. I decide on Thai, and the best news is that they deliver. I order myself pad thai with shrimp and sweet basil chicken with steamed rice. I'll have enough for lunch tomorrow and possibly the next day.

While I wait for my dinner, I crank up the music. I work through Katy Perry's, "Smile" and then up comes Taylor Swift. I bop around, hanging clothes and at least trying to clean off my bed so I can sleep tonight at some point. Then "Shake it Off" begins to play, and I have to abandon the unpacking for dancing.

I use my brush as a microphone and sing at full volume, shaking my back side.

As the song ends, I turn and find Steve standing in the doorway. "Don't stop on my account." His smile melts my panties.

I turn the music down. "Sorry. I'm trying to get this all put away. I'll get it taken care of."

He looks at all the stuff, seeming to notice it for the first time. "What's going on?"

"I'm moving in."

His smile freezes.

"Don't worry. It's only temporary." I laugh.

His brow furrows.

My heart races. He's panicking, and I need to head it off before he completely freaks out. "Remember, we said we would move in together after 'dating' for a while." I use finger quotes to emphasize that we've not really been dating.

"Yeah, I remember we talked about it. I just…"

"My mom and her new boyfriend are coming back tomorrow, and The Butterfly isn't ready for me to move in. This is just until I get things figured out with my dad." I pat him on the arm. "I promise, I'm a good roommate. I'm not messy, and you can use all the hot water if you need to."

He looks at me, and I can tell he's struggling with what to say. I've short-circuited his brain.

He looks around the room, stuffed with boxes. "Where are you planning on sleeping?"

"Still in here." I open my arms to the chaos. "It may take some time to clear the room, but I can dig out the bed. This is all clothes, so I'll get it figured out."

"This is all clothes?" He winces.

"Well, and accessories—shoes, purses… I have to admit, I love a good handbag."

"I… I…d…"

I sigh. "I know. This is a lot for you. I'm sorry. Please don't panic. I swear, this is not going to turn into *Fatal Attraction*. Don't worry. Think about whatever rules you need, and we'll put them in place. I really appreciate you doing this for me."

His lips purse, and I hear the doorbell. "I didn't know if you were coming home so I ordered dinner—Thai food," I tell him, my words tripping over each other. "I have more than enough to share if you'd like."

I explain what I ordered, and he nods.

While I get dinner from the door, he pulls out plates and silverware.

I bring the takeout containers to the table, and we sit.

"You mentioned your mom is moving back to town?" he says after a moment.

I nod. "She's been in Italy taking art classes, and she's met some young guy. She's bringing him back."

"What will your dad say?"

I nearly choke on the water I'm drinking. "My dad? Nothing. They have an okay relationship, but they've both moved on."

He takes a bite of his food. "I love sweet basil."

I smile at his compliment, even if it's just about my ordering skills. "I figured since they named the restaurant after it, it might be their best dish."

He nods, and I wait for him to say something about his parents. He's very private, so I won't push.

Okay, maybe just a little. "What about your parents?"

"What about them?" He sighs. "I can't remember when they weren't pissing each other off."

"Do all your friends know about them?"

"They know my parents don't get along behind closed doors. But when you meet them, they're delightful and seem happy together."

"That must have been really hard growing up."

He shrugs. "I guess. I don't have any other experience, though. My friends' parents seem to all still be together, and they're much like my parents when I see them. They don't fight, and they smile a lot. Who knows what's going on beyond that."

"What happens if your sister one day gets divorced? Are they going to disown her or call a priest in to counsel her and her husband?"

"I suppose we're going to find out. My sister just told me she and her husband are splitting up."

"How do you think they're going to feel about what we're doing?"

"I wasn't going to tell them it's fake, because I don't want them to do anything to ruin it, so I suppose when we break up, they'll blame it on each other."

We eat, and I process what he says. "Is that why you're doing this for me? Your parents' experience?" I ask after a moment.

He shakes his head. "I'm doing this because you asked. No one should be in the situation your dad has created for you."

"That's it?"

He shrugs. "I'm not the marrying kind of guy. My parents showed me I'm not made to be married. But I can be a nice guy, so when you asked, I agreed."

"Okay," I squeak. I don't know how I feel about that.

"That doesn't mean I wouldn't mind getting naked with you," he adds with a devilish grin. "Maybe if you just have to walk down the hall, you'll be less likely to escape in the middle of the night."

I'm glad this is all out on the table, and I need to make sure he understands that I hear him. "What we did was fun, but our relationship has changed since then. You are a nice guy, and I'm so grateful that you're helping me. But if you're truly not available, I don't want to get my heart tangled up with you. And that's not what this is about anyway. This is about me getting the team and keeping my life from being controlled by my dad. Anyway, all that to say, it's still probably best we don't sleep together again."

He looks down at the table. "I guess we understand each other then."

I nod. "Thank you for sharing dinner with me."

"It was great." He's silent a moment. "What are they telling you about your condo at The Butterfly?"

"Good question. They say December, but they've been running behind, so I'm guessing it will be February."

He nods. "What kind of unit did you choose?"

I explain the floor plan I went with, which will give me a view of the harbor, and the various finishes I picked. "I worked with an interior designer to get the tiles I wanted, not that I didn't like what they had, I just wanted something more ornate. And since the elevator opens inside my apartment, I wanted to be able to put out a small table for deliveries and what not. Have they ever had a problem with key fobs that went to the wrong floor?"

"What do you mean?"

"They've told me I'll wave a key fob, and the elevator will go to my floor. There are almost a hundred units in the building, most on the lower floors, but I was wondering if the fobs they give us could accidentally take someone to the wrong floor. I wouldn't want someone walking into my place. Or if I leave my keys and bag on the table by the elevator, I don't want to worry someone might come and take it."

He shakes his head. "It's never happened that I'm aware of. I can set up some time for you with my sister. She could explain their system and its safety measures."

"Oh, okay." I collect our empty plates, and Steve follows me into the kitchen. "What else has your dad—well, your family—built?"

"He's known for interesting architecture. He did the stadium a few years ago."

My head whips up. "He did?"

"Yep. He has some signage there."

The lightning hits me. "Of course, Boss Construction. I didn't put it together."

Steve nods. "He also did the convention center years ago. That was one of his early projects."

"That's amazing."

Steve loads the dishes in the dishwasher, and I put the takeout containers in the recycle.

"The stadium has some issues," I say. "I hope The Butterfly doesn't."

"A builder can tell the architect that there are issues, but if they don't want to fix them, the builder can't do it without their approval and a change to the plans."

"Is that why the offices at the stadium have such a lousy view and there aren't enough women's restrooms?"

He laughs. "Yep. Don't blame the builder. Blame the architect, and in the case of the stadium, blame the city and your dad."

"He says the builder got it all backward."

Steve shrugs. "I wasn't there." He stands and wanders

over to the window.

He seems a little distant now, but I'm not sure if it's because he told me about how he grew up or the fact that I shut him down again about having sex. Or maybe it's because I picked a stupid argument. But the silence forming between us makes my mind go crazy.

His phone goes off, and I jump.

He looks at the message and types a reply. "I've got to go to the hospital."

The timing is a little suspicious, but that's fine. "Oh. Okay. I'll see you around then."

He nods. "Sure."

"I'll have my room all taken care of in the next day or two," I call as he walks away. "I'll try to keep my mess to a minimum."

He doesn't turn around, just waves over his shoulder. I hope this is going to work out okay.

Chapter 16

Eliza

I was awake until two o'clock, unpacking until I'd cleared the room enough that I could go to bed. Steve didn't come home.

I hope he didn't feel like he couldn't be there. Am I overblowing how awkward things felt last night? Argh. I'm dragging this morning, so maybe I'm just not thinking clearly. I put on a cute outfit, which always helps, and stop for tea on my way into the stadium for work.

My phone pings just before lunchtime. I'm hopeful that it's Steve, but it isn't.

Mom: We've landed and are through customs. Come home early and see me.

My heart soars.

Me: I'll make it a short day and head over about 3.

Mom: That's too long! I'll be waiting. It's been so long since you've hugged me.

Me: I need a Mom hug. Can't wait.

Mom: Plan on dinner. You can tell me all the ridiculous things your father has done while I was gone. I'm determined to push through as long as I can.

I practically skip over to Tanya's desk. "My mom is back, and I'm so excited to see her."

"I'm happy for you. How is she doing?"

"She seems good." I laugh. "She wants hugs."

That makes Tanya laugh as well.

"Did you see Jun last night?" I ask after a moment.

"He texted to come over, but I ignored it." She shrugs.

"Oh yeah? Why?" Maybe she did hear what I said the other night.

"I need to know what I want before we get together again." She crosses her arms and gives me a look. "Did you ask Steve about why he's doing you the favor?"

I nod. "We talked a little about his family history, and he said again that he doesn't like the position my dad has put me in, but he also said it was just because I asked. He wants to be a nice guy."

Tanya's mouth pops wide. "No way. He must want something else."

"He made sure I understood that he didn't ever want to get married, but he still thinks getting naked would be fun."

"So did you fall into bed and bang his brains out all night?"

"Nope. I told him the truth about how I feel. Now that I know he's a good guy, my heart is bound to get tangled up. That's a recipe for disaster if it's not what he wants, *and* my focus right now needs to be on getting the team. I'll just try to be a good roommate."

"No!" Tanya says loud enough that people are looking at us.

I nod. "Oh yes." She rolls her eyes. "Listen, I gotta run. I've agreed to meet up with Mom about three and stay for dinner, so I need to get some things done before I go. Catch you later?"

She sends me off with a nod and a wave.

"Hello?" I call as I walk into Mom's place.

Mom runs out in her bathrobe. She holds me tight, and I feel so loved and safe. Until this moment, I didn't realize how much I'd missed her.

"I'm so glad you're home," I tell her.

She steps back to look at me. "Your room is empty. Where are you living?"

"I have a friend I'm staying with."

She perks up. "You do? Is this the man you mentioned?"

Despite the rocky ground I'm on with Steve at the moment, I have to believe we're still going to do this as planned. So, I guess I have to go with it. I smile. "I told you, his name is Steve McCormick."

"Why is that name familiar?"

"He's the team doctor."

She smiles widely. "Of course. He's cute."

A guy who has to be younger than me appears behind Mom wearing a pair of ripped jeans that hang low and no shirt. "Oh sweetie, I want you to meet Antonio."

I try to calm myself and pull my eyes away from his

washboard abs. Painting a tight smile on my face, I extend my hand. "Nice to meet you."

He lifts my hands and kisses my knuckles. "Mi sono innamorato di te." He winks at my mom, and she giggles like a schoolgirl.

I look at her, puzzled.

"He says he's falling in love with you."

I pull my hand away. I don't need this. "Tell me about your trip," I suggest, changing the subject.

We move into the living room, and Mom spends the next two hours telling me all about her classes, and she overshares her romance with Antonio. I love her, but I don't want to know that my mother is getting more sex than I am. And apparently, it's a lot more sex.

"What's going on with your father?" she asks.

I sit back. She and Laura are close, so she probably knows better than I do, but she has been out of the country. "Good question. I have no idea. I think he ran off to the south of France without telling anyone. He's not returning my calls, and I'm getting all my orders at work from his secretary."

Surprise crosses her face. "Your father? The same man whose first love is his work?"

I snort. "I don't want to speak ill of Laura, but she has hexed him. He's determined to be a better father with Minni and Logan."

She tilts her head. "How do you feel about that?"

"I think it's great. But I always knew he loved me."

She nods. "He did. I never liked that he thought money would buy your love, but he tried."

"I fell in love with football because of spending summers with him going to games."

She scoffs. "I know that's why you want that smelly team. You could do anything. You're beautiful, smart, and you don't have to worry about money. Why would you want to work in professional football?"

I roll my eyes. "I love the game. Plus, it doesn't hurt that they are prime specimens."

She smiles. "Now, I understand. So, why are you dating the doctor and not a player?"

"He's much more fun," I say with a smile, hoping I seem convincing.

"As long as you don't think he's after your money."

I choose not to ask the same question about the boy toy she's brought home. "His father owns Boss Construction," I explain. "They built this building, the stadium, and they're building The Butterfly."

"Of course. That's why his name sounded so familiar. All I care about is that you're happy."

I nod. "I am, though it's still early. I think he's a bit freaked out that I moved in, but once my place is ready, I can move in there."

After a little while, Mom orders in food, but it's mostly just lettuce, so there's not much I'm interested in eating. By seven thirty she's yawning, and I'm heading out. I can tell she's exhausted.

"Next time you come, you bring that handsome man you're living with."

"I promise." I hope that's a promise I can keep.

When I get back to Steve's house, I can tell he's been home and left again. It's still early, so I break down and hope I don't sound too needy when I send him a message.

Me: Hey. Are you coming home soon? Mom ordered salad for dinner, so I was thinking about ordering Greek if you're interested.

Steve: I would love that, but I have to go back to the hospital. My patient from last night is struggling with the pain meds, and I want to see why.

Me: Okay. I'll order extra and you can reheat when you get home.

Steve: That's great.

I order the Greek platter for two, and when it arrives, it's enough to feed at least a half dozen. We're going to have plenty of leftovers.

I eat while watching a series on Netflix, and then I work on organizing my room. I give up waiting for Steve around eleven thirty and go to bed, only to stare at the ceiling.

He has to be avoiding me, and I hate this.

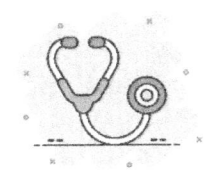

On Friday morning, Tanya knocks on my door and walks into my office. "Did you jump his bones yet?"

I push back from my desk. "I think the better question is, did you give in to Jun and jump *his* bones?"

"I agreed to meet him for dinner last night," she says. "We did sushi at our favorite place in our old neighborhood."

"How did that go?"

"He tried to order for me, and it went downhill from there."

"Oh no. You're kidding. I'm sorry."

She shakes her head. "How's your mom?"

"She's great. Her boyfriend is younger than we are."

"Go, Mom!" Tanya raises her fist in celebration.

I put my head in my hands. "I don't know. It kind of creeps me out. I'm really glad I'm not living with them. It would gross me out to be there. As it was, they were nearly naked. But I'm blaming it on jetlag and Mom being tired and a little giddy."

"What did Steve think?"

"He wasn't there. I haven't seen him since we had dinner the night I moved in."

"Why?"

I put my head in my hands. "I think he's avoiding me. You were so right. He freaked that I moved in, and then I told him I still couldn't sleep with him, which didn't make things any better. Since then, he's only been home when I haven't been there."

"He's still going to help you?"

"I hope so. As far as I know. I don't know what I'll do if he's changes his mind."

"What is he telling you about why he's gone?"

"He said he had to go to the hospital."

"Have you followed him?"

"No way."

I don't know how I'm going to manage this for the next five months. But when I look up at my computer, my email is blowing up with an article in the *Vancouver Sun* about a doping scandal. That seems to be how they're referring to our mishap with the drug tests almost two weeks ago, and that isn't helpful at all.

"What the hell?"

Chapter 17

Steve

"How long are you going to avoid her?" Davis asks over the top of his glass before taking a drink.

I look over at him, all smug on his couch. "I don't know what you're talking about."

"Last night you hung out with Michael, the night before Griffin, and the night before that you showed up at Jack's and slept on his couch. Now you're here. What's going on?"

I sit back. "I don't know. She moved in."

"Wasn't that part of your plan?"

I nod. "But I thought we'd be more than roommates."

"Did you talk about that?"

"We did, and she wants this to be all business. But we've had sex before. I thought she'd change her mind."

"You think pretty highly of yourself."

I open my mouth to tell him off. But then I close it and take a deep breath. "It's more than that." How am I going to explain this? "I think about her all the time. Her perfume lingers after she leaves. I can't get her out of my mind, and it's driving me crazy."

"Have you really talked to her since she arrived?"

"A few times over text. But we're not talking about anything other than work."

Davis shakes his head. "Just because your parents don't have a relationship to brag about doesn't mean you're going to do the same."

"Tell that to Olivia."

Davis looks at me, confused. "She's married with two beautiful children."

"They're separated, and he's dating someone else."

He sighs. "Marriage isn't always easy. Some days are harder than others, but if you can establish early on how you're going to talk to one another, it's a great thing. And..." Davis leans in. "Make-up sex is always the best."

I roll my eyes. "I just don't know where her dad gets off. I love Tom Rourke, but he's requiring that his daughter find a life partner in order to pursue her chosen career. And he wants her to do it in six months. Does he think it's so easy? He's been married four times."

"I'm surprised he's not worried about her settling for some guy who's out for her money."

"Oh, don't worry. I have a lot of hurdles to clear for them to accept me."

We talk for a while longer and then Davis shows me to his guest room.

Paisley's little sister walks down the hall.

"What's up, Arabella?" he asks.

"I have to go potty." She rubs the sleep from her eyes and looks at Steve. "Why are you here?"

"He's going to sleep in the guest room."

"Okay," she says as she walks into the bathroom.

"I'll see you in the morning," Davis tells me.

I nod and close the door behind me. The room is nice

enough. It's mostly dark blues and white. I stay in my clothes and lie down on the bed, staring up at the ceiling.

What do I really want from Eliza?

I'm such a coward to be here, away from her another night. I pull out my phone and look through the text messages she's sent that I haven't responded to.

The first night I left, I had an emergency surgery. One of the knee replacements I did earlier this year was having problems, and we looked at what was going on as soon as an operating room opened up. I slept at the hospital before driving to Surrey the next morning.

Eliza: Goodnight. Feel free to wake me when you get home.

Eliza: Good morning. It doesn't look like you made it home. Are you avoiding me?

Then last night she sent:

Eliza: I finally finished off the Greek food tonight. No more Greek for a while. I was thinking Blue Water Café? Tanya is up for joining me tomorrow night. Interested in coming along?

A few hours ago, she sent:

Eliza: Goodnight. I miss you around here. I've begun looking for a new place to live. I'm sorry. I should have talked to you about moving in before I did it. We mentioned it at the beginning, and I thought you were okay with it. But I realize this happened quickly because my mom came back. I hate that you're not coming home because I'm here. I'll be out as soon as I can find a place.

I shut my eyes. *Fuck.* I'm screwing this up. I don't want

her to move out. The problem is my dick wants her to move into my bed, and that's where I'm stuck.

Me: I'm sorry I'm being a dick. I don't want you to move out. I've been stuck in my head. Did I miss dinner at Blue Water? How about a quiet dinner tomorrow night at Cioppino's?

Eliza: Please come home tonight.

I stare at her words. I'm not sure what to do. What happens if I go home? Could I convince her that we might be something real? Do I want that? The idea of something long term completely panics me.

I finally sit up and text Davis that I'm heading home.

Davis: I'm glad. You're welcome anytime. And Paisley wants to arrange a dinner for the four of us.

Me: Thank you for everything. You're a great friend.

Davis: Anytime. See you next week at Joe Fortes.

I walk to the elevator and ride it down to the parking garage for guest parking.

It's after two in the morning, and the streets are moderately busy, but I hit mostly green lights. I would love it here if it was always like this.

When I walk into my house, I find Eliza in flannel pajama bottoms with hedgehogs on them and a long sleeve T-shirt. It's all baggy on her, but I don't care. She looks amazing.

She runs into my arms and holds me tight. "I'm so sorry," I tell her.

"I'm the one who's sorry. I should have talked to you before moving in. I get things in my head and just leap without thinking."

"You were right the other night. I heard what you said, and it sent me thinking about my parents. They're a lot, but we need them to make this work. Can we go have dinner with them soon?"

She nods. "I'd love that. My mom wants me to bring you over too."

"Let's plan that, then. I want you to see where I grew up, and I want to introduce you to my sister, Olivia."

"That would be great."

"Plus, I'm sure she'd love the cover of you being there when she tells our parents that she and her husband have broken up."

Eliza laughs, and the peace that blankets me is warm and so very welcome.

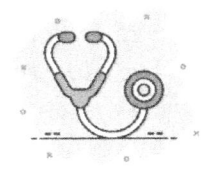

After talking until the very early hours, Eliza stayed in my room with me last night. We didn't have sex, and how I slept with a hard-on all night is beyond me. But I loved seeing her hair splayed out on my pillow and having her perfume invade my senses.

I spoke with my family earlier today, and we're meeting for dinner tonight at my parents. I gave Olivia the heads up that Eliza was okay with being her shield if she wanted to tell Mom and Dad about her and Paul.

Now, as we stand on the threshold of my parents' home, Eliza has a bottle of fancy Irish whiskey and a beautiful bouquet for my mom.

"Be prepared. They'll be wonderful tonight," I mumble out of the side of my mouth.

Eliza gives my hand a squeeze just as Mom opens the door.

"Welcome to our home," Mom says with delight.

"Mom, I'd like you to meet Elizabeth Rourke."

Eliza hands her the bouquet. "Thank you for having me. I'm a huge fan of Gerber daisies. I hope you like them as much as I do."

"These are beautiful—so many colors." She motions us in. "Please come in. It's wonderful to have you at our home, Elizabeth."

"Please, call me Eliza."

She nods. "John? Steve is here with Eliza."

My dad walks out in jeans and a button-down shirt.

"Dad, this is Eliza, my girlfriend."

My dad puts on his thick Irish brogue. "Welcome to our humble home."

I didn't see Olivia, but I hear her when she snorts at that. There is nothing humble about this house. Dad's office is filled with awards he's received, and he keeps trying to expand them out into the hallway, but Mom is pretty firm that they stay hidden away.

"Behind my dad is my big sister, Olivia."

Eliza smiles. "Wonderful to meet you. I brought something for Emma and Dylan."

Suddenly, the kids are circling around us, and Eliza reaches into her bag and brings out a sketchbook and colored pencils for Dylan and for Emma, a palette of fingernail polish. Emma lights up and looks at her mom.

"They peel off when you want them gone and don't require nail polish remover."

"Can I, Mom? Please?"

Olivia looks at Emma and ruffles her hair. "Yes, but you know the rules at school."

The kids disappear, and Eliza hands Dad a bottle of Redbreast Irish whiskey. "This is my father's favorite," she explains.

Dad's eyes grow big. "I love Redbreast. I think I've had this with your father."

"It's very likely. This is his drink of choice."

"You know what makes it better than any bourbon, Canadian, or Scotch whiskey?"

She shakes her head, but there's a twinkle in her eye, and I have a feeling her father has told her this before.

"It starts out in American whiskey barrels, but after a year, they move it to their port barrels, and it has a nicer finish."

"I didn't know that," Eliza says.

Dad smiles. "Would you like to try some?"

"Sure, as long as I'm not the only one drinking."

Dad pours whiskey for all the adults, and we sit in the living room and talk.

"How long have you two been together?" Mom asks.

"A few months," I tell her, exaggerating. "Eliza was living at her mom's while she was out of town, but when she came back last week, I talked Eliza into moving in with me."

Mom's eyes brighten. *Ooh.* This fake relationship is going to not end well.

"It's only short term," Eliza quickly adds. "I have Penthouse B at The Butterfly as soon as it's ready."

Olivia grins. "You do? That's great. What do you think so far?"

"I was really drawn to the smooth lines of the building, but like many others, I'm frustrated that it's taking so long."

Olivia nods. "Tell me about it. Those rounded exterior concrete slabs were ordered from a supplier up north, and they were not up to spec when they arrived. That's a challenge sometimes with something new like what the architect designed."

"What made you pick these plans for this spot?" Eliza asks.

"I loved that it was across the street from an elementary school on one side and had full views of the Lions Gate Bridge, Stanley Park, and Coal Harbor," Dad answers.

She nods. "My view is split between the school and West Vancouver. If I stand in a certain place, I think I should be able to see the Lions Gate. I would have loved one of the other penthouses, but they were all sold when I returned from London."

"I think you'll see more than you realize," Dad says with a grin.

Olivia and Eliza continue to talk for a few minutes and make plans to meet for lunch in the coming weeks.

When Mom calls us in for dinner, she's made a beautiful bone-in prime rib with all my favorite fixings.

"Did you make your blueberry cobbler?" I ask.

She glows. "I did. I had some frozen berries from this summer's crop."

"You're going to love this meal," I tell Eliza.

We sit down, and Mom eventually asks Olivia the question. "Sweetheart, we haven't seen Paul in a while. What is he doing these days?"

"He's been spending time with his twenty-two-year-old girlfriend."

Dad stops eating and looks at her and then Mom. "What do you mean?" he asks.

Olivia glances at the kids, who have raced through their meals and are busy with the dog. "Paul decided he didn't love me any longer and moved out almost five months ago. He wasn't interested in counseling or trying because he was in love with Svetlana."

"She's really nice," Emma pipes in from the floor. Guess she wasn't as busy with the dog as it seemed.

Olivia's eyes close as she digests the information Emma has just delivered.

"What does your priest say?" Mom asks.

Olivia smooths the napkin on her lap. "I'm not going to ask a man, who really has no idea of what a marriage is, for any advice."

"He could counsel you on how to stay together," Mom

implores.

Olivia looks at Eliza. "I look forward to having lunch with you, and I promise we won't talk about the next thing I'm going to do."

Eliza nods, her brow furrowed.

"Mom, priests—and I know it's been more than one—have told you and Dad to stay together, and you're both miserable. Paul saw it and knew he didn't want to have anything to do with the hell you're in. No. I'm doing what's right for us and our family. I can't work with someone who doesn't want to try. I hope I can move on to a healthy relationship and show my children that they deserve that, rather than having to be miserable with someone."

"Don't talk to your mother like that," Dad growls.

"You want me to lie to her?" Olivia challenges.

Dad pounds his fist on the table, and everyone freezes. "Don't talk to me that way."

Mom's hand reaches for Olivia's. "I'm sorry you feel that your Dad and I are so unhappy. Marriage isn't always a bed of roses. Sometimes it's a rocky beach with crashing waves, but that doesn't mean at the first sign of things being hard that you cut and run."

"I agree," Olivia says. "And that's not what's happening here. But we're doing what's right for us, and it's divorce."

"But you won't be able to take communion any longer," Dad points out.

Olivia shrugs. "I'm okay with that."

Olivia looks at me, ready to change subjects.

"Mom, have you and your friends figured out what your girls trip is going to be this year?" I ask her.

Just like that, she shifts gears. Amazing. "We have. We're going to Italy."

"That's where my mom just returned from," I offer. "She was there about eight months. She had the best time."

This subject carries them through much of the rest of the evening, my mom peppering Eliza with questions. By the end of the night, she's connected our moms together.

As we're slipping our coats on, Olivia gives Eliza a hug. "Don't let them jade you about marriage. Paul and I just weren't meant to be. I see that now. I thought he'd change his mind about kids when we had our own, but he didn't."

"Don't you worry," Eliza tells her. "I have my own baggage to overcome. My mom never remarried. She enjoys her freedom and doesn't understand why anyone would want to be tied down. My father is working on his fourth marriage, and this one looks like it's going to stick. She's nearly our age, of course, but he's one of those who's so deliriously happy he thinks everyone should be the same."

"I can tell you and Steve are that happy, so don't let my ex and his wayward dick sway you either."

Eliza reaches for her. "You're amazing, and the right guy is going to see that in you."

"I'm busy running the largest construction company in all of BC. I'm not so sure about that."

"Are you even getting out there?"

"Right now, the kids and I are working on our routine."

She kisses us both on the cheeks and gets her kids into her car. They wave as she heads down the hill and into Vancouver to where she lives.

We say goodnight to my parents, and as we drive down the hill ourselves, I sneak a glance at Eliza. "Tonight was a peaceful night, and even that was a forest fire."

She looks at me with a small smile. "You can tell they love you both very much."

"I agree. It wasn't always that way. Dad was so angry at me for sticking with medicine and making it so the company would go to Olivia, who wanted it, by the way."

"Did he have requirements before she could get the company?"

"She was already dating Paul, but he wanted her married, so I think that sped things along. I was pretty sure Paul was only interested in her money, so that was difficult. I really had to go to bat for her. The construction business is very male dominated, and Dad worried that if she didn't have her husband working by her side, the business he'd worked so hard to build would crumble."

"It hasn't," Eliza points out.

"No. In fact, because it's a woman-owned business, it's opened up a lot more work. She's on the way to doubling the size."

"That's great."

"Yes, but it was hard on Paul's ego. He struggled over Olivia being his boss at the office, so he quit. Then he got caught up in Olivia making more money than he did."

"Did they have joint accounts or separate accounts?"

"Joint, so it was both of their income."

"Ahh, he has little-penis syndrome," Eliza says.

I nearly choke as I pull up to the garage. "What?"

"He needs his salary to make up for his little dick."

I chuckle. "You need to tell that to Olivia."

"If it comes up, I will. I have her phone number, but I'm not about to text her right now."

I laugh as we walk into my house. I pull her to me and hold her tight. "Thank you for joining me tonight. I hope it didn't scare you too much."

"It takes a lot more than that."

Chapter 18

Eliza

I run my hands through my hair and balance my chin on my hands at my desk. Something is not making sense in this spreadsheet. Why is the electric bill at the training facility so high this month compared to other months?

Someone clears their throat, and I look up to see Tanya and Darius standing at my door. "We gave up waiting for you by the elevator," Tanya announces.

"Oh crap! Sorry. The morning got away from me, and my mom called."

"Oh?" Tanya says.

I pull my handbag over my shoulder. "She wanted to tell me about Antonio and bug me about dragging Steve over for dinner."

She shakes her head. "I'm so jealous of your relationship with your mother. My mother would get married and not tell anyone."

"Well, maybe that's because she's still married and living with your dad."

"You know what I mean. You two talk to one another."

We get in the elevator, and Darius is studying his phone. He hasn't said a word.

"What's going on, Darius?" I ask.

"The agent to a quarterback I have my eye on has approached us about a move."

"Mid-season? I mean, Marty is doing well, and I assume since you have an eye on him, he's not junior material."

"Well, that's the thing. Marty's agent has asked how firm we're going to be about not letting him out of his contract at the end of the season."

"Are you telling me that with all this crap going on, we're going to lose a few players?"

"The doping scandal has everyone worried."

"It's not even a scandal," I protest. "Marty was in the group that had the false positive, but it was just a bad batch of tests. Everyone knows that." I don't know who I'm trying to convince. Probably myself.

Darius gives me a hesitating nod.

My head is beginning to hurt. I shut my eyes. "Why didn't Steve tell me Marty wants out? We're together every night. I—"

"He doesn't know," Darius says. "Only Coach and I know."

I scoff at that. "I bet half the team knows. This would be hot gossip among the players." I think for a minute. "Would Coach tell my dad if a player was trying to get out of his contract?"

"Normally, I would say yes, and your dad would head it off. But for some reason, Coach isn't telling you. Do you know why?"

I shake my head. "I don't know if he doesn't respect me… I'm pretty sure he doesn't like me, but maybe there's something else going on."

We walk the block over to the restaurant, and the hostess seats us quickly.

"What are you going to do?" Tanya asks once we're settled in.

"I need to find my dad." I shake my head. "Ugh. Let's talk about something else."

Darius nods and nudges my shoulder. "It sounds like you and Dr. McCormick are getting very close."

I manage a smile. I feel bad for not telling one of my closest friends what's really going on. Steve's told his closest friends, and I've only told Tanya... I may be rationalizing, but Darius is trustworthy. So I spend the next couple minutes telling him all about my dad's requirements and how Steve is helping me out.

"I'm not surprised Dr. McCormick is doing this for you," he says. "He's really a great guy. And I bet sex with him is *ah-maz-ing*."

I debate how to respond, and Tanya steps in. "She's told him no sex."

Darius gasps and holds his hand to his heart. "That is sacrilege. Such a fine specimen, and you're not taking advantage of him?"

"We have an understanding, and I don't want to talk about it," I inform him, looking around to make sure no one is listening.

This calls for another shift in conversation, so we talk about the team and their rough start so far until we order. But after the server leaves, Tanya turns back to me. "Are you going to tell your mom about what's really going on with Steve?"

I shake my head. "No way. She'll be furious and go right to my dad. I hate lying to her, but I can't take the chance that she's going to screw it all up. She and Laura are close, which doesn't help."

Darius' hand goes to his heart. "Is there a Tom Rourke wives club?"

I think about my dad's two other ex-wives. "There just

may be. But I don't think he and Laura are going to break up. They're happy together."

"You never know what goes on behind closed doors," Darius warns.

"I agree, but she's in cahoots with my dad about me having a life outside of work. They're both so delirious they think everyone needs what they have."

"I think I'm going to vomit," Tanya announces, which gets her a funny look from the table next to us.

The server has just returned, and she also stands back.

"Oh," I say. "It's just hyperbole. You know, realizing your parents are still having sex."

The server looks at me strangely as she puts our plates down in front of us and dashes away.

"I guess she isn't surprised that her parents are still having sex," Darius stage-whispers.

I suppress a snort.

"Tell us everything that's going on with Steve," Tanya says.

I tell them about meeting his family and friends and how much I enjoy the girlfriends and wives. "Now that we're over the hurdle of me moving in, we really are developing a wonderful friendship. We get along well, and he's funny."

"And don't forget he's hot," Tanya reminds me.

Darius nods. "Very hot."

"That's true," I tell them. "But it's just not particularly relevant in this situation."

As we walk back to the stadium, Darius and Tanya get into a discussion about something going on in the office, but I lose the thread of conversation. My brain is fully absorbed with trying to figure out where my dad could be. There's one person I'm sure would know, but would he tell me? I think I have to find out. I need to talk to Charles, my father's fixer. I believe they talk at least once a day, regardless of where my dad is.

When we get back to work, Darius waves goodbye and heads out to practice.

"Don't forget to call or text me if there's something I need to know," I tell him.

He nods. "Promise."

Tanya waves and heads to her office as I detour by Charles' office here at the stadium. He has offices at all Dad's businesses, but this is closest to where he lives, so he's here the most often.

When I arrive, I'm relieved to see he's in. He's looking at his computer when I knock on the door jamb. He looks up but doesn't smile or really acknowledge me.

"Hey, Charles. I need to speak with my dad. Do you know where he might be?"

He gives a subtle shrug.

"I want to tell him Nicolette has returned and warn him."

Charles clears his throat. "When I talked to him this morning, he was at home."

The hair on the back of my neck stands up. "I thought he'd left the country."

"Not to my knowledge."

He would know Dad's calendar, so that bothers me. And then I start to get a little angry. What does Dad think he's doing? If he's so worried about me managing the team, why did he disappear and leave me to do just that? He gave me no notice or instructions—other than about my personal life, of course—and he's not returning my calls. What is that about?

But I don't say any of that to Charles. I force a polite nod and turn to go. "Okay, thank you."

"How are things going with Dr. McCormick?" he calls after me.

"We're doing fine, and as I'm sure you're aware, we're spending a lot of time together."

He smiles. Now, he knows I know he's monitoring me. I know my father well. I hate him for all this, but at least there aren't any secrets.

As I walk back to my office, I debate going out to Dad's

now or waiting until after work when the traffic is bad.

I decide to head right downstairs to my car and go now.

The drive through town is still crazy. As I cross through Stanley Park and over the Lions Gate Bridge, the day is gorgeous—must be why so many people have flocked to our vibrant green landscape and beautiful waters. I look out and see a giant cruise ship. I feel so lucky to live here. I've traveled the world, and Vancouver, in my opinion, is the most beautiful place of them all.

My brain cycles through Mom's return, her boy toy Antonio, Steve, the team, Coach Roy, Marty Holloway wanting out of his contract, the owners meetings, Donnie Cochran and his stupid lowball offer, and then somehow, I end up on my high school boyfriend. I wonder where he is today.

When I pull into Dad's circular driveway, I'm kicking myself for not coming out here sooner. With Minni in school, it makes sense that they wouldn't just leave the country. But I'd still like him to return my calls. Hopefully, I can keep my cool to explain that.

I knock on the door, and after a moment, Laura opens it. "What brings you here in the middle of the day?"

I paint a smile on my face. "I've left a few messages for Dad, but he's not responded. I thought I'd come talk to him face to face."

Laura pales, and she looks away as if she's suddenly nervous.

"What's going on, Laura? Why is he avoiding me?"

"It's not what you think," she says, finally meeting my eyes.

"What do I think? I don't know what to think. Until today, I'd been telling myself you went to the south of France and didn't tell me."

Laura's eyes fill with tears. "He didn't want you to know."

"What? That he was hiding here the entire time? Letting me run the team he's not sure I get to take over?"

She shakes her head. "No... He should be the one to tell you. But he's sleeping right now."

"Dad's taking a nap? He runs dozens of companies. Since when does he nap?"

Laura still looks nervous, but she heaves a deep breath and lets me in. "Let's check, just in case."

I follow her down the stairs to the main bedroom. The room is dark, with the blackout curtains closed. *What is going on?* It's the middle of the day. The light from the doorway shines on the bed, and I see Dad lying propped up by pillows. He's definitely sleeping. There's a slightly sour smell in the air, but even more disturbing are the many, many pill bottles next to his bed. My heart races.

Laura nods and directs me back upstairs.

"What's going on?" I ask again when we reach the kitchen.

"He didn't want you to know."

"Know what?"

She sighs. "He's a strong man who has always taken care of you. He didn't want you to see him so weak."

"What's going on?"

"He was diagnosed with stage-four colon cancer this spring."

All of the air rushes out of me, and I see stars. *How can this be?* Questions flash through my mind, and I'm floundering. I feel so lost. Tears spring to my eyes, and I reach out to Laura, probably the only person who loves him as much as I do. "What can I do?"

"He's been in radiation and chemo, but this round has been tough."

My mind races. I know nothing about colon cancer. I don't know what the prognosis is. I need to talk to Steve.

Tears fall freely. I'm not ready to lose my father. Laura and I hold each other. "Why didn't you tell me?" I finally ask.

"Because he expressly told me not to. I figured you'd eventually reach out to Charles, and he and I agreed he'd send you here so you would find out."

"Do they think Dad can kick this?" I ask.

"Your dad is the strongest-willed man I know. If he wants something, nothing out there is going to stop him. And he wants to be here for you, and for Minni and Logan. He expects to walk you down the aisle when you get married."

"Is this why he's given me all these requirements about my life if I want the team?"

"It may be a factor, but no. He really feels like he missed out with you by working all the time, and he figures you have enough money that you shouldn't have to work that hard."

I talk to her about Donnie's offer and how I'm sure he's taking advantage of Dad.

She shakes her head. "I'm not a fan of Donnie Cochran, but he's always been a friend to your dad, since I've known him."

Suddenly, I sit up straight. "Is this why my mother decided to come home? Does she know about Dad?"

"I don't know if that's why she's come home, but he told her. He knew you'd need her support if anything happened."

The tears pop up again, and I wipe my eyes with the heel of my hands. I'm sure I look like a panda bear with big black rings around my eyes.

Laura makes a pot of tea, and we sit down and watch the barges on the water as they line up to get their goods unloaded and reloaded.

I text Steve.

Me: I'm at my dad's. Will you be at your house tonight?

Steve: Yes. Is everything all right?

Me: I'll tell you what's going on later. Promise.

There's a noise over Minni's old baby monitor.

"Your dad's awake. I'll go check on him and then call

you down."

I nod and dash to the bathroom to clean up my face as Laura disappears.

"Hey…" After a minute I hear her over the speaker. "How are you feeling? Can I get you some chicken broth or something to settle your stomach?"

"Not right now," Dad grumbles. "What time is it?"

"It's a little after four. Elizabeth has stopped by."

"What did you tell her?"

"The broad strokes. She's been worried about you."

"She doesn't need this stress."

There is some noise. I can't make out everything Laura says. "—she's an adult and can handle this."

"Tell her I'm not seeing anyone."

My eyes well up again. I can't believe he'd send me away.

"I won't tell her that. You're going to man up and see your daughter. She's upset that you haven't told her, and everyone around her knows."

"Fine. You can send her down."

"I will, and I'll bring you back some warm broth."

I hear more noise and begin the trek downstairs, passing Laura on the way. She gives me a sad smile. When I walk into the room, Dad is sitting up, and the noise I heard was the blackout curtains being opened.

"Hey, Dad."

"Buttercup, I'm sorry you have to see me like this."

"I was getting worried about you. I left a few messages, and things are going wonky at the stadium with you out of touch. Do you want to hear about it?"

"Actually, that sounds better than everyone else who wants to know how I'm feeling."

"I would like to know that too, but we can talk about the team first."

I start at the beginning, telling him about how Rhymes injured Hudson and I released him from his contract.

Dad's eyes widen. "Are you sure that was smart?"

I nod. "The hit was beyond dirty. It's bad enough when it's an opposing team, but when it's your own teammate—and he tore a ligament in Hudson's knee—it was the appropriate move."

"I trust you," he says.

I feel a warmness in my chest.

"What is this crap I'm hearing about a doping scandal?" he asks after a moment.

I shake my head. "There's no scandal, although I'd like to know who leaked it to the *Vancouver Sun*. We got a faulty batch of drug tests, so we sent three of our team members to an independent facility for retests. Everyone was clean, but the *Sun* failed to share that part right away."

"Did you get that sorted out?"

I nod. "I did, but the story ran last Friday, and the small article correcting it didn't come out until Monday."

He shakes his head. Unfortunately, that's not the end of it.

"With all the chaos, I'm getting a lot of calls from various agents looking at trades and getting out of contracts."

Dad shakes his head. "We're not even halfway through the season. This could turn around at any time."

"We have a few players who are trying their best to undermine their teammates' confidence with constant critiques—and by the way, their own play is far from perfect. I'd like to get rid of them. I think it would do a lot for morale."

"Why isn't Roy whipping them into shape?"

I shrug. "He's trying to work with what he was given."

"You know the termination triggers in his contract. If more than twenty-five percent of the team wants to be traded, and he doesn't have a winning season, he won't have a job."

Dad has a coughing fit, and I can tell he's already tired and we've only been talking a short time. I guess I'll save the rest of my speech about getting rid of players until later.

"Charles tells me you're seeing Steve McCormick," he

says when he's recovered. "He's a good guy, but make sure he's not trying to get into your pants to keep his job."

I smile at Dad. "He's already telling people he doesn't expect to keep his job. He's disappointed, but he knows that isn't our choice."

"He's a bit of a player, so just keep your wits about you." Dad's blinks are becoming longer. I need to let him rest.

I stand, lean over, and kiss him on the cheek. "Daddy, I love you. I wish you would have told me sooner."

"I plan on beating this thing."

"Good, because I plan on you walking me down the aisle and spoiling your grandkids."

He shuts his eyes, and I head out.

Laura meets me at the top of the stairs. "You were so good for him today. That's what he needs. He needs to be thinking about things besides his health."

"I'll be back in a few days. I'm going to find out more about his prognosis. Who is his oncologist?"

"He's with Stein at Mercy Hospital."

I nod and thank her as I go. For the first time today, I'm relieved. Because I know someone at Mercy Hospital.

Chapter 19

Eliza

Questions play on repeat in my head as I leave Dad and Laura's and drive to the only place I want to be, and that's with Steve.

What will I do if something happens to Dad?
How will I manage Laura and Mom?
I have so many plans with the team, and I want to show Dad they can work.

I drive directly to Steve's place. When I pull up in front of his house, the only lights on are the ones on timers.

My eyes sting with bitter tears.

I let myself into the house and pace around the living room.

Me: Where are you? Are you coming home?

My phone rings, and it's Steve.
"I'm out with the guys. Is everything okay?" he asks.

I struggle with what to say, but I really need him. "No. I..."

He murmurs something to the people he's with and then returns to the phone. "I'm walking out now."

"You don't have to do that," I protest.

"Where are you? At my house?"

I nod, forgetting he can't see me.

"Eliza? Where are you? I'm on my way."

"I'm at your house."

"I'm coming. I'll be there in ten minutes."

"Thank you," I murmur.

He leaves the line open, and I don't feel quite so alone. "I'm getting in my car."

I hear the engine start up and suddenly the line is clearer as I move to the speaker in his car.

"Do you want to tell me what happened?" he asks, and I know exactly why he's a great doctor. There is true concern in his voice.

"It's about my dad."

"Look up from your phone and get out of the crosswalk," he mutters.

That makes me smile.

"Do you want to tell me what he said?" Steve asks again.

"I will when you get here."

"Okay."

"I'm sorry I took you away from your friends."

"Don't worry about it. I see them all the time. Things come up, and they know it."

I wrap my arms around me, all too eager to sit down with Steve.

"Ugh," he says. "I swear I'm coming. I can't believe I'm hitting every fucking red light."

"Please, just get here in one piece."

He chuckles. "It's great to see you care."

"Of course, I do," I sputter.

The garage door opens, and we disconnect. In moments,

he walks across the backyard into the house. "Are you okay?"

I race to him, wrap my arms around him, and let the tears fall.

"What's happened?" There's an edge to his voice.

"My dad is sick."

Steve becomes rigid. "What kind of sick?"

"He has colon cancer, and it's stage four. I don't even know what that means."

Steve's shoulders fall. "It means the cancer has spread to other organs and possibly the lymph nodes."

My stomach hurts. I don't know what I'm going to do without my dad. He wasn't perfect by any means, but I always loved him, and I knew he loved me in his distorted way.

Steve cups my face with his hand. "Do you know where it might have spread?"

I shake my head.

"I'll make some calls, and after the game on Saturday, I'll go with you to talk to him."

"You'd do that?"

His head tilts to the side. "Hey, try not to stress about this. We're in this together. We'll get it figured out and make sure he has the best doctors and care."

My mind begins to reel again, thinking of all the things I wanted to show Dad, and then it hits me. Selling the team to Donnie is all about him being sick.

I double over and hold my sides.

"Come here." Steve pulls me close, and I can feel his beating heart.

I look up at him as my heart swells. "Thank you." Then my lips touch his, and there's no stopping us. We crash together, and the kiss curls my toes, making me feel dizzy and weightless.

My head tilts to the side, and I lean against him as his hands roam my body—over my waist, down my thighs, up my torso to graze my breasts. He purposely avoids my erogenous zones, making me whimper each time he comes close to touching me where I want him.

"Tell me to stop if you don't want this."

"I want you to make me forget," I breathe.

"I'm here for you." He turns me around, and his hands wander everywhere at once, lighting my skin on fire.

"Oh fuck, you're driving me crazy!" I gasp as I rub my ass against his cock.

"Good!" he whispers in my ear. "Because I am going to make you fucking scream before I'm done!"

He wraps his arm around me and clasps my breast, bringing the other hand around to work the zipper of my dress. His lips follow the zipper, kissing my back as he slowly exposes it.

As he goes lower, he releases my breast and goes to his knees to kiss the small of my back, his free hand now goes under the hem of my dress and up the inside of my thigh to knead my ass.

There's a mirror on the wall beside us, and he watches me place my hands on the wall for support as my head rolls forward and my eyes close. He uses both hands to lift my dress. "Mmm, fucking beautiful," he whispers, just before he kisses my ass, randomly, all over.

I gasp and my hips roll, wiggling my ass as he kisses it. He licks me occasionally, and when he knows I'm really turned on, he nips with his teeth.

Holding up my dress with one hand, he glides the other up and down my thighs. I spread my stance in invitation, and he touches me, feather light, on the soft flesh of my inner thigh.

I squat just a bit, aiming for more contact for my pussy, and Steve finally relents and strokes my crotch firmly through the triangle of fabric that is now damp and warm.

"Oh!" I say softly.

He backs off and strokes my center lightly, not quite giving me what he must know I want. He returns to kiss and lick my ass cheeks again. I'm panting hard now, trying to push against his fingers.

I arch my back, pushing my ass in his face, so he nips it with his teeth, and as I gasp, he grabs my hips with both hands and turns me around to face him.

I lean back against the wall, panting, my face flushed and my eyes blazing. "Fuck!" I gasp. "You are so bad!"

"And you love it!" he tells me with his devilish grin. He is still kneeling, looking up at my eyes, then down over my body. "Now, lose the fucking dress, Eliza!"

His lips curl into a salacious smile, and I shrug off the dress. It falls in a heap around my ankles, and he gathers it up so I can step out of it.

Tossing the dress aside, I look at him with a brow raised. But I say nothing as he grabs my hips and kisses the tops of my thighs, tracing my sexy black panties with his tongue. He kisses my mound through my panties, and I can't wait for a repeat of him filling me up.

He sits back on his heels and looks me up and down, appreciatively. I'm quaking with arousal. I lean back, my shoulder blades against the wall and my hands pressed flat against the wall behind my ass. My normally pale skin is flushed and my chest heaves, my nipples trying to push through the fancy black lace of my bra.

"You're so fucking beautiful." Steve says in a low tone while one hand rubs his cock through his pants. "But some of that has to go!" he tells me, gesturing with his free hand. My eyes return to his, and he knows I understand.

My fingers shaking, I hook my thumbs into my thong at my hips, as if I'm asking permission.

He looks up into my eyes. "Go ahead, Eliza…"

A slight whimper catches in my throat, and his smile grows. He knows I'm loving these naughty games.

He watches me push my panties down my hips, the damp crotch sticking momentarily to my lips. Steve smirks. When the lacy thong falls to my ankles, he holds it for me as I work my high heels loose. Then he casually tosses it over his shoulder in the general direction of my dress.

He gazes at me with hunger in his eyes, taking in the little sculpted triangle of hair, which points down to my hairless pussy. He growls at the sight before looking back up at my face.

I stand frozen under his gaze, fighting to control the urge to pounce on him. This moment has been a long time coming, and I want to let him do it his way, have me however he wants. I owe him that. Plus, I love the way he looks at me, like I'm the first drink of water he's seen since crossing a hot, sandy desert.

Steve traces up my body with his eyes. When he comes to my bra, he focuses on the nipples, which are making little points behind the black floral design. I shudder from the stimulation and want more.

"And now the bra, Eliza," he whispers.

My hands go to the clasp between the cups, and in a flash, the bra is gone. This time, it is my turn to casually discard the item. The anticipation grows, increasing my arousal, as I know what he can do with his dick and fingers.

"So fucking beautiful," Steve murmurs again.

I pinch both nipples, pulling and twisting. "Do you like that?" I purr.

"I'm the one in charge of your climax. Just remember that," he growls.

"Yes, sir."

Bringing his hands to my legs, he begins kissing my thighs and stomach, avoiding my center. Then he kisses the slight crease where my thigh meets my body as his hands gently travel up the backs of my legs.

I bring my heel higher up the wall, moving my knee outward to spread myself open to him. I sigh as I run my fingers through his dirty blond hair.

When his hands clasp my ass and pull me forward, I widen my stance, shoulders still against the wall.

Steve knows what I want, what we both want, and dips his head to wetly kiss my inflamed pussy. As his tongue licks through my center, barely grazing my clit, I whimper and clench my fingers in his hair. "Please," I whisper.

He stands quickly and grabs my ass, hoisting me up.

I let out a squeak and wrap my arms around his neck and my legs around his waist. Steve turns toward the kitchen as I frantically kiss his neck. He doesn't have time to go upstairs and instead walks me over to the sturdy oak kitchen table.

This is where we eat our meals. Now, he is going to eat me here. He kicks a chair aside, places my ass on the table's edge, and pulls aside the vase of flowers before pushing me backwards. I whine as he latches on to a swollen nipple and swipes his tongue over it as he sucks.

His hard dick rubs against my swollen center through his pants, giving me stimulation and frustration at the same time. I keep my legs wrapped around his waist and grind myself, begging and moaning, "Oh, please, Steve."

He switches to the other nipple, giving it the same aggressive treatment as the first. Then he reaches for my thighs, pulling his mouth off my nipple and going straight to my center.

"Ohhh," I groan as he starts with long licks. He reaches over and pulls the chair back into place, settling in for yet another great meal at this table.

I know I'm not the first girl Steve has gone down on, but right now, I'm thankful to every woman before me, as his skill is unmatched. He reads my body and my physical responses like a fine instrument.

He laps at the entrance to my channel, then sucks me into his mouth and licks me clean of my sweet nectar. I moan, then gasp when he pulls his head back and my clit pops free.

He groans with pleasure as I writhe on the table. I put my hands on the back of his head and pull his face into me, placing my legs over his shoulders.

"Oh, Steve, oh fuck yes!" I moan, rolling my hips as he devours me.

He keeps his tongue moving up through my center, and occasionally, he licks higher to play against my clit.

My response is immediate. "Ehhh!" I squeal, and my fingers ball into fists, pulling his hair. Steve brings two fingers up, slipping them into my pussy as he finally swipes my clit steadily with his tongue.

I see stars and white light as I explode, thrashing on the table as I climax. He works his fingers in and out of my grasping center and laps repeatedly at my clit while reaching out to twist a swollen nipple with his other hand.

I scream at the ceiling, and my ass comes off the table, my legs still on his shoulders. He keeps his fingers working in time with his tongue lashing at my clit as he sucks it between his lips.

My screaming soon moves to a gasping, strangled attempt to breathe. I can't do this again. I release the hair at the back of Steve's head and slap my hands down on the old oak table. I squirm, trying to get free of his hungry mouth. "Nnnno...no...more! Ohh fuuuuck...Steve...no...more," I squeal.

Steve eases the pressure on my G-spot, releasing my clit from his lips but still licking. "Damn, you taste so good."

I squirm again, my pussy tightening on his fingers until he withdraws, leaving me feeling empty. But still, I beg to be released from my torture.

Steve stares at my exposed center as I catch my breath, and I know he's ready.

He has me down to just my heels but has neglected to take off anything himself. "If you're going to take me, you're going to need to get naked."

He licks his lips as he undoes his belt. He hands me a condom. "We need to get tested and make sure we always have some sort of birth control."

"I'm on birth control, and I never miss a day."

He drops his clothes and stands before me naked, his cock jutting out and bobbing.

As I watch him roll on the condom, I lick my lips. I need him inside me like I need to breathe.

He pushes the purple head into my entrance and stretches me wide. "Holy fuck, Steve!" I whisper.

He chuckles at me. "I could say the same about you, Eliza."

Chapter 20

Steve

I hold her in my arms and feel at peace. This isn't something I'm used to. Her breath becomes rhythmic, and I want so much to do whatever I can to make this all go away for her. My mind whirls. First, I'll put a call into Tammy Winters. We were residents together, and she's a gastroenterologist. I know the generalities about colon cancer, but she should be able to give me some insights on the disease. We need to know where the cancer has spread. I won't get Eliza's hopes up until I know more.

Her panic when she realized why her dad might be selling the team was heartbreaking. We've got to be a believable couple. This may be the only chance she has to reach her dream.

I want this for her.

I fall asleep, focused on that thought, and in the morning, when I roll over in bed, Eliza isn't here. I head to the kitchen to make coffee, and I can hear the shower going in her room. We had a late night, and we both need caffeine.

I pour water in the kettle to make her tea, and I arrive at her bathroom door just as she's getting out. "I thought you could use this."

She pulls her towel tighter around her and seems suddenly shy. "Good morning."

"How are you feeling this morning?"

The corners of her mouth turn up. "A little sore, but in a good way."

I reach for her towel, but she can't look at me. I hook my finger in the fabric, and it opens up. "Look, I know why you're hesitant. But I promise to treat you with care. Let me help you through this."

She nods. "Thank you."

I lean down and kiss her, and I'm ready to go again.

She breaks away. "If we do that, we'll never get to the office."

I lean my forehead against hers. "You're right. I need to get some things done. It's a quiet practice day, and the team is ready for the Express."

"Good. Hopefully, we don't have more—"

My finger stops her mouth. Regardless of where she's going, I don't want to put it out into the ether and bring the bad luck that accompanies it. We don't want any more injuries, bad drug tests, or problems, and speaking of any of it would be tempting fate. I've worked too many years in professional and semi-professional sports to know that karma will always bite you in the ass. "Get dressed, or you'll need another shower this morning."

She smiles, and my heart races.

I go back to my room to shower, and as I'm heading out for the day, Eliza appears. She's dressed all prim and proper in a pencil skirt and white button-down blouse, but I know what's underneath.

"Don't," she threatens.

I hold up my hands. "What?"

"I see the look in your eyes."

"All I can think about is what's underneath that armor you're wearing."

"Save it for later," she tells me.

"Don't worry. I will."

She leaves for the stadium, and I head to my office at the practice facility. The physical therapists are here with the trainers as the team filters in. Since it's the day before a game, they'll have a short practice to run over specific plays they've designed for our competitors. I message Tammy.

Me: Hey stranger. I have a question about stage-four colon cancer. Do you have time to talk today?

Tammy immediately pings me back.

Tammy: I'm off today, and I'm around now if that works for you.

Me: Calling now.

"Hi!" she says boisterously when she answers.

"Hi yourself. What's going on with you?"

"Just trying to stay out of trouble. I've got my daughter home today from school, and we're going over to Science World a little later."

Science World is a great museum. I've even had a few fun dates there.

"I'll be quick. My girlfriend's father has stage-four colon cancer. All I know is that success in beating it depends on where it has spread. Can you fill me in on what else I need to know?"

"Right. If it's spread to the lymph nodes, lungs, or brain, the success rate goes down dramatically. But liver is usually okay, as is GI tract."

"Okay, that's what I remember from school. Her father's being treated at Mercy. Who are the best surgeons in the lower mainland?"

"My favorite is a surgeon out of Port Moody at Eagle Crest Hospital. I refer a lot of patients there. Her name is Gina Luu."

"Okay. And for an oncologist, who would you recommend?"

"There are several, thankfully. I like Jim Wang or Terry Stein. Both are at Mercy. What else do you know about the patient?"

I sigh. "Not a lot. I should be able to meet with him tomorrow after the game. His daughter just found out when she happened to stop by. It sounds like he's in the middle of a radiation and chemo treatment."

"Ahh, those can be rough. But if his body can take the aggressive therapy, it can be really beneficial."

"Okay, thanks. I'll find out more tomorrow. If I have other questions, can I call you?"

"Of course. I owe you. You fixed Mandy's leg when she fell off her bike. You'd never know she had a compound fracture, and the leg is doing great."

"I'm glad."

I hang up and stick my notes in my shirt pocket. Hopefully, things are on the way up for Tom.

I find a spot to watch from the sidelines as practice gets underway, but it's a painful experience. As it has been much of the season, the workout is a cluster of errors, tempers, and overall dysfunction.

"The Winnipeg Express are the worst in the league," Assistant Coach Majors confides. "Tomorrow should be a cakewalk, but I'm not so sure."

I sigh. I look up at the owner's box and try to spot Eliza. She must be ready to choke the life out of someone. But I'm not sure she's actually up there.

When I look back at the field, Coach is walking toward me. "When is Hudson off the injured reserve list?" he demands.

"He's out for at least another month."

He curses under his breath, and I wait patiently for him

to calm down so we can have an actual discussion. But then he just turns and leaves me standing here. Something isn't right. But it doesn't make sense that he'd do something to sabotage the team. Their winning and losing is tied to his compensation, as well as his having a job next season.

After practice, the team filters out, and once the last player is gone, I realize I'm the last guy in the building. We're not even halfway through the season, so it's not a good sign that everyone is already so checked out.

Once I'm in my car driving back to my place, I call Eliza. It goes right to voicemail. "Hey, beautiful. I'm just leaving the Surrey Training Center. I'm heading home. Hope to see you soon. I thought we might order in dinner and watch a movie."

I don't hear from her on the way home, so I decide to just wing it and put in an order for Chinese takeout.

I've just received the bounty of boxes, and I'm sitting at the kitchen table staring at a lot of food spread out in front of me, when Eliza finally walks in.

She immediately takes a seat opposite me. "What did you order?" she asks with a smile.

"Chinese. I got your favorite—kung pao chicken."

She claps her hands. "Yay! I'm starving."

We dig into the food, talking and laughing as we eat. I tell her what I learned from Tammy.

She nods. "My dad is seeing Terry Stein. So at least we know he has a good doctor."

"I agree. I know there's a lot on your plate, but I was surprised you weren't at practice today."

"I was going to get there, but instead, I think I spoke to almost every single agent today."

I put my chopsticks down. "Why?"

"There's quite a swirl of rumors in the air. Apparently, my dad is disbanding the team. They started calling first thing to let me know. They figured it wasn't true, but they had to make sure, you know." She rolls her eyes.

"Disbanding? Where did that come from? I thought he

was going to sell."

"Well, my dad is in the south of France and is leaving Laura for the nanny," she says conspiratorially. "And he's going to stay there and sell all his companies because he has no one to run them."

I snort. "Except for the people, including you, who are running them today."

She shakes her head. "It's such bullshit. Some agents said their players were being warned that we couldn't make payroll."

I stare at her, waiting for her to say she's teasing, but she doesn't. "What did you say to that?"

"Nothing they didn't already know, but the rumor is out there, so that's problem enough."

"What are you going to do?"

"I'll bring it up when we meet with my dad after the game tomorrow, and I'm leaning toward sending out a memo to the team to address the issue."

"You know whatever you send will be in the paper."

She nods. "I know." After a moment, she drops her head into her hands.

"What's wrong?" I ask. I mean, there are an array of things to choose from, but I want to be supportive.

She looks up at me. "Have you noticed that none of this began to happen until I was running the team?"

"That's not true. Your dad was running the team when they picked up the three free agents—Rhymes, Cotton, and Pelletier."

She sighs.

"Come on. You're exhausted. Let's watch a movie and go to bed early."

"I know why you want to go to bed early."

"Of course, you do. Have you seen your body? Your mind is incredible too. But the way we come together…"

She smiles at my feeble attempt to lighten the mood. I'm angry over these stupid, unsubstantiated rumors. I'm angry about everything that's making her life harder than it needs to be. This is so wrong on so many levels.

Eventually, we curl up on the couch, and her head rests on my chest as we scroll through Netflix. We settle on a romantic comedy, and as the movie plays, I can feel her body relax against mine. The soft glow of the TV illuminates the room, casting a warm light on us as we enjoy each other's company.

As the credits roll, I turn to her, cupping her face in my hands. Our eyes meet, and I know without a doubt that I want her more than anything. I lean in, capturing her lips with mine. Our kiss is deep and passionate, and I can feel the heat between us building. "Let's go upstairs."

Game day starts early this morning, so we're up and out the door.

During warmups, I watch from the sidelines as running back Nathan Cotton's anger boils over. He can't seem to catch anything the quarterback throws to him, or else he trips over his feet. Losing his temper isn't going to help anything, but that doesn't stop him from yelling profanity at everyone within earshot.

I watch another throw, and the football bounces on the ground. Cotton picks it up and throws it into the stands in a fit of rage. Everyone on the Express's bench is watching.

I want to say something, to offer some advice or encouragement, but I'm not sure what would help. I can see the frustration etched on his face. It's clear that he's struggling, but he's not owning it.

And unfortunately, a few hours later it's clear the

warmup has set the tone for our day. It was a rough game, one we should have won, but didn't. And managing that disappointment is only the first task on Eliza's to-do list. Next, we're headed out to see her father.

After the postgame activity has wrapped up, Eliza and I pile into my Toyota 4Runner and head over to West Vancouver. I spent time here growing up, but I can tell the community has changed. She directs me to Cliff Drive, which is one of the more exclusive addresses in West Van, and we pull up into what looks like a nice home with a gated circle driveway.

I remember my dad talking about this house when it was being built. It was an engineering marvel, as it was attached to the cliff side and should be earthquake proof up to something like an eight-point-five quake.

As we get out of the car, Eliza reaches for my hand, and I give it a light squeeze.

We've got this.

A woman roughly our age opens the door as we walk up, and a whir of a little girl runs out and jumps into Eliza's arms. "Lizzie!"

A dog joins us, as does a little boy, and soon it's chaos. My confirmed-bachelor heart is terrified and ready to race back to the car, but the woman who opened the door shoos the dog out, sends the little girl back inside, and she picks up the little boy, balancing him on her hip. "Sorry about that," she says with a smile. "Minni is always excited when her big sister comes to visit."

Eliza slips her hand in mine. "Laura, I'd like you to meet Steve McCormick. We haven't been dating that long, so don't terrify him with too much."

I chuckle nervously.

"He does seem a little skittish." Laura's eyes twinkle. "Come on in. What can I get you to drink? Your dad is resting right now, but I promised I'd get him up in a little over thirty minutes so he could talk to you."

We follow her into the kitchen, and there's a platter of

kids' munchies out. It looks surprisingly good.

"What would you like?" she asks me. "Eliza and I usually drink tea, but if you would prefer coffee or something harder, that works too."

"Tea is fine."

Laura sets the little boy down, and he runs over to show me his fire truck. I look at it carefully. "It has two ladders," I point out. "That means it's ready for some big fires."

He nods and then runs off.

"Beware," Laura warns. "He's going to get every single one of his cars for you to comment on now."

I smile. And here I thought I'd scared him away... "That's fine."

We sit down, and Eliza explains that besides being her boyfriend, I'm the team doctor.

"Very nice," Laura says.

"Eliza told me the news about Tom," I tell her after a moment. "I know she's nervous about such daunting news, as I'm sure you were too."

Tears glisten in Laura's eyes, and Eliza throws her arms around her. "We're going to get through this together."

Once they separate, I see my opportunity. "As a medical professional, I want to help break things down and give Eliza some details," I explain. "Can you tell me what you know?"

She looks at me a moment and then nods. "I first thought something was up when Tom became tired more often. I mean, the man is twice my age and usually runs circles around me. Then suddenly he wanted to sleep all the time."

"That's a good sign to pay attention to. I assume he had blood in his stool?"

She nods. "He had cramps, and his stool was not something you'd want to see."

"So he got a colonoscopy, and they found polyps?"

She nods again. "They biopsied them and immediately sent him to a surgeon to remove them."

"Who was your doctor?"

"We got in quickly out in Port Moody."

"Ah, was it Gina Luu?" I ask.

Laura's eyes grow wide. "You know her?"

"I reached out to a friend who's a gastroenterologist at Mercy Hospital, and that's who she said she'd refer someone to."

"That's good to hear," she says.

"And then who did the surgery?" I ask.

"Terry Stein at Mercy."

"I know Terry. He's the best." I think for a moment. "Do you know where the cancer has spread?"

She sighs. "It's in his liver, and when they did the partial removal of his colon, they also took a bunch of lymph nodes. They think they got it all, but he's still going through radiation and chemo."

"How is he feeling?"

"Very tired."

"I'm sure your doctor has told you this, but everything sounds pretty positive."

She nods. "They said if he can get through this, the survival rate is better than fifty percent."

"That's great news."

"It's what we're hoping, but he's struggling with the radiation and chemo this time." Eliza reaches over and takes her hand. "I'm trying to stay positive."

We talk a few more minutes about Tom's struggles, and when it's time for Laura to wake him, she disappears downstairs. She's gone for close to half an hour before she comes back up and invites us to see Tom.

I'm rather nervous to talk to Tom as Eliza's "boyfriend" and not the team doctor.

"Well, it seems my daughter has shown an interest in you," Tom announces as we enter the room.

I smile, though his voice is scratchy, and he's not his usual exuberant self.

Eliza blushes. "Dad!"

"I think the interest is mutual." I smile at Eliza, and her return smile makes my heart beat faster.

"You're usually quite the player," Tom admonishes.

"I've not been known for long-term relationships—that's true," I concede. "But I have nothing but respect for your daughter, and we're enjoying ourselves." I shift my attention toward him. "But we're here to talk about what's going on with you."

He shakes his head. "I have plenty of doctors, and I didn't break my leg."

I open my mouth and then close it. He's not making this easy.

"You may have plenty of people telling you things," Eliza reminds him, "but you've been silent when it comes to telling me what's going on. I'm grateful for Steve, who's talked to people to make sure you're getting the best care."

His eyes narrow. "My health is none of your concern."

"Sure it is," she counters. "I'm your daughter, and I've worked my whole life to partner with you on the team and accomplish all the things we've talked about. You being part of that is important."

"I don't want to talk about that right now," he huffs. "You know my feelings on the subject."

With that, I stand and excuse myself. I know Eliza can manage her dad, and he seems hesitant to talk with me there. She smiles at me as I close the door and go back to find Laura upstairs.

I locate her in the kitchen, her eyes red-rimmed and puffy.

"Are you okay?"

She nods. "I try so hard to be a pillar of strength for him. But he's a stubborn old coot."

"He's giving Eliza the business now. I stepped out so they could break it all down. Will he be too brutal? Should I go back?"

"He's direct, but he won't be too hard on Eliza. She's

used to it."

"I don't think he likes me dating her."

A smile plays over her lips. "I think he called you a womanizer."

"You heard that?"

She nods. "I have a baby monitor in his room, in case he needs me."

I smile. "How are you faring with all of this?"

"Mostly okay, but I have my moments. It took us so long to meet, and we've only been together about ten years. I'm not ready to let him go."

"I think it's great that you two found each other. Colon cancer is certainly something you can manage. From what my friend told me, stage four can be treated much like diabetes or other chronic diseases."

"That's what they tell us too, but this last round of chemo has been really hard on Tom."

I nod and drink another cup of tea with her, listening to her and allowing her to vent a bit.

Eliza eventually comes upstairs. She seems upset, but I won't ask her about it now. I'll wait until we're in the car.

She spends a few minutes with her younger sister, and then we say our goodbyes.

As we drive back into town, I try to gauge whether she wants to talk. "How did it go with your dad?"

"He's as ornery as ever. He was upset about the game."

That reminds me of something I wanted to ask her earlier. "Have you done a background check on Coach?"

"I personally haven't," she says. "Why? What are you thinking?"

"I'm wondering if he's had any infusions of cash recently, and if so, from where."

She chews on her lip, and my attention immediately locks on. I have to force myself to keep my eyes on the road. "I think that could be something to look at," she finally says. "Anyway, I couldn't really disagree with my dad. The loss was disappointing, to say the least."

"It was a game we should have won," I agree. "It's too bad, but the worst part is having Pelletier suspended."

Mathieu Pelletier is a tight end and definitely one of the problems for our team. He's struggled to get along with everyone, and during the game, he got too aggressive with the referee and got himself kicked off the field. He then had an additional fit, and the league suspended him for two games.

"I think that's what has my dad the most upset. He wanted to know why Darius had approved Pelletier to play for the team in the first place."

"I didn't think he did." I'm very confused. How can management not be on the same page?

"He didn't," Eliza confirms. "Pelletier was in Darius' never-hire group, as were Cotton and Rhymes. So that means there's a disconnect somewhere."

"But Coach loses his job if the team falls apart, and he seems really hot under the collar about it all."

"I agree. It doesn't make sense, but somewhere, the wires got crossed, and it's not good for the team. I need to get us back on track," she laments.

When we arrive back in town, we stop for a quick bite at the Cactus Club.

"Hey," Nadine and Michael walk up just as we're walking in.

"We watched the game today," Nadine tells Eliza. "I'm sorry."

Eliza gives her a pained smile. "Thanks. It's driving me crazy that they lost, but sometimes, when something should be an easy win, the team doesn't get their heads in the game."

"How did your dad take it?" Michael asks.

Eliza shrugs. "He wasn't happy, but at least he saw it from the comfort of his living room and not standing next to me in the owners' box."

Chapter 21

Eliza

A week passes, and it's another game, another loss. Losses on the road are hard, but this one — to our biggest rival, the Yellowknife Polar Bears — particularly stings. We should be getting used to it, though. We're one and nine, having only one victory so far this season. The *Vancouver Sun* is recommending that team leadership at all levels be changed.

I thank our host in the owners' box and head down to the locker room to wait for the all clear so I can enter. That's usually after a short team meeting and everyone's showers. A few of the players will meet with the press, but given our losing streak, I'm not sure many will want to talk to anyone.

Once I get downstairs, I lean against the wall and look through my text messages.

Darius: When we're ready to pull the plug and hire a new coach, I've identified a candidate.

I chuckle.

Me: Hang on to that. I'm meeting with my dad tomorrow. I'll keep you posted.

Tanya: Even Jun, who hates football, was cheering for the Tigers to pull it off. We're so disappointed. When the team is all yours, I know you'll fix this. Then you can do whatever you want.

Ahh. I love her. She's so wonderful. Jun, on the other hand, sucks. He keeps playing with her and won't get out of her life. I'm not sure what to do about that.

Me: Thanks

Mom: Don't let the loss get you down.

I need to plan dinner with her and Steve...and I guess Antonio if he's still in town.
Me: Thanks, Mom. I needed to hear that.

Mom: Come by when you get home and bring that handsome boyfriend of yours.

Me: We land after midnight tonight. Maybe tomorrow.

Mom: I'll give you some time to catch up on sleep. Let's meet at Botanist for brunch on Sunday. How does 11 sound? I can grab a reservation for four.

Me: I can be there, but Steve plays golf with his friends on Sundays.

Mom: I don't want to wait longer than that to see you. Maybe Steve will change his mind.

"Can you believe this wait?" a woman who has appeared next to me says.

I look up at her. She's a typical WAG—beautiful, fit, and bubbly.

I shrug. "They lost today, so I'm sure they're not having a pleasant conversation. There's quite a bit to discuss."

"I bet. My friend is on the staff, though, not a player, so hopefully, it won't be too bad for him."

I nod and return to my phone, now looking through my email. I see several messages from agents, and my heart sinks. This is going to be a tough year to hang on to the people we need to get my goal of the Grey Cup.

The woman looks at her watch and then the door. "I only see him when he comes to Yellowknife, and occasionally when I get down to Vancouver. I know they have a flight to catch, but I've missed him so much."

I look at my watch. Takeoff is in three hours, and it's a little less than a three-hour flight home. I want dinner, and I hope I can talk Steve into grabbing some food with me away from the team.

"—I mean, as the team doctor, I'm not sure exactly why he needs to be there while the coach yells at them."

My brows lift. "You're waiting for the team doctor? Steve McCormick?"

She nods. "He's so hot, and the things that man can do with his tongue…"

"Does he know you're here?"

"I texted last week and told him I'd be here after the game."

I nod and force myself to smile. *That doesn't mean he responded*, I remind myself. Though it would certainly fit his reputation if he had. I'm strategizing on how I'm going to play this when the door opens, and Steve puts the doorstop in place to allow everyone in. He surveys the crowd, and when we lock eyes, I see panic in his gaze.

Uh-oh. My heart sinks. *What have I gotten myself into?*

The woman races over to him, jumps into his arms, and attaches her lips to his.

I walk right past them and into the locker room toward Coach Roy. As I look around, the place is a mess. We're guests, and I can't believe we don't have better manners than this. Actually, I can. But I still don't want to pay a cleaning fee because of their destruction.

"I'm sorry. The guys are cleaning up," Coach Roy says as I come into sight.

"Great. They certainly need to." I look around again, and Steve is talking to the woman, who is no longer attached to his body. The next time I look back, she's gone, and Steve is talking to a player.

I'm angry. Whatever that was, and whether he meant it to be anything or not, it's put this whole thing we're doing at risk. For all his talk of wanting to help, he's not being very smart about some things. I force myself to take a deep breath, and I survey the scene in the locker room as the players clean up and clear out for a few more minutes. Then I talk with Coach Roy to get his thoughts on what happened — he has nothing particularly insightful to offer — and finally there's nothing left here for me to do.

Steve is watching me from across the room, and he motions for me to meet him in the corner. It's too public to explode at him the way I'd like to, but that's probably not the right call anyway.

"Here is my cell phone," he says, holding it out as I approach. "I didn't get any of Tara's messages. She's blocked. There is no side piece here in Yellowknife. I promise."

I nod. "I understand that you don't owe me anything, but you've said you want to do this, so I'm trusting you to help me. You know how important it is that everything appear above board, even when you're on the road."

"I do understand that, and it is. I swear. You can see I've blocked her in my phone. You'll see that with several women. I am committed to getting you to your goal." He finds my eyes and lowers his voice. "I made a reservation at Bullock's Bistro. It's a nice place, and no one else will be there from the team. Will you come?"

I sigh. I want what he says to be true—for so many reasons—and I guess I have no choice but to continue moving forward. "That's fine."

He nods, relief flooding his features. We make our last rounds of the locker room, ensuring that everything is in order before we head off in a rideshare to the restaurant. It's not very far, and we're quiet on the ride. I don't want an audience, as I know if Charles were going to interview someone from this trip to get the inside scoop, it would be the rideshare driver. So Steve and I make polite conversation about a sprained ankle on one of the tackles and a sore finger on one of the running backs.

When we arrive at Bullock's Bistro, we're shown to a quiet table. After we have our drinks, we order, and once the server is out of earshot, Steve takes a deep breath. "E—"

I hold up my hand to stop him. "I am well aware that you and I are not on the same page when it comes to our relationship. There's no playbook for this, and we're moving forward differently than I had envisioned. The green monster of jealousy reared its ugly head when that woman told me you had plans." I take a few breaths before I continue, so I don't cry. "I admit, you being there for me as I deal with my dad's illness and with all this crap about the team has been both a huge help to me and made this very difficult. I don't want feelings involved, but…"

I take another breath and steady myself. "Charles will be living in our back pocket for the foreseeable future. So, if you want out of our deal, just let me know. I'm sure I can find another way to…" The tears fall. I really have no idea what else I can do, but I don't want to feel miserable and worry like this.

Steve pulls me in and holds me tight. "Listen, I'm so sorry this happened. I've seen Tara once. Since then, she's wanted to come down to Vancouver a time or two, and I've always conveniently told her I wasn't available. I blocked her number ages ago, which is why I didn't get her text message about meeting up after the game. The commitment I've made to you is very important to me, and honestly, you are the only person I'm interested in regardless of that." He pauses a moment, as if that admission surprises him too. "You are the only woman who occupies my mind, and I am not sleeping with anyone else. I promise, I'm going to continue doing whatever I can to help you, until you tell me to stop."

Our meals arrive, and the server is quick at reading that we want to be alone.

"Thank you," I tell Steve. "I know this is a mess. I'm a mess. I am trying so hard to distance myself, but I'm not doing a very good job."

He smiles. "I'm in the same boat. I think of you all day, and when I'm not with you, I miss you." He leans in and gives me a soft kiss.

When we finally start our dinners, we move back to talking about the debacle of the game.

"What happened at halftime?" I ask.

"Coach is frustrated. He had each of the assistant coaches meet with their teams—the offensive team met in the main room, the defense was in the shower room, and special teams met in one of the treatment rooms."

"What's the value of that? Have you ever seen that before?"

Steve shakes his head. "He's desperate."

"We need to figure out what's going on. I don't like it."

"I think you need to be very honest with your dad."

I nod. "Laura says every day he's getting better. So maybe if we go tomorrow or Sunday…"

"That works. Davis and Paisley are having a group over for dinner tomorrow night. Would you like to go?"

"I'd love that. But we have to meet up with my mom soon or else she's going to show up at your house."

After we finish our meals, we zip to the airport and reach

the plane just as the team is boarding. Before we take off, I send a text message to Charles.

Me: Would you have time to meet with me tomorrow morning? I know it's Saturday, but I don't want to wait.

Charles: I can meet you at Dr. McCormick's at 9 a.m.

Nine o'clock is going to be early, but I need his help to get to the bottom of what's going on and why.

Me: I'll be ready with coffee.

Charles: See you in the morning.

Chapter 22

Steve

When I wake up, Eliza is already out of bed, and I can tell she didn't sleep well. "Are you okay?" I ask.

"I'll get there," she says, searching for her robe. "Charles isn't my favorite person, but we need his help with this."

"He's not going to stand on the table and accuse us of having a fake relationship."

Eliza sighs. "I know."

"How about I run out to Tim Hortons and pick up coffee and donuts?"

"I'm not sure he'll eat them, but I will."

"What's your favorite kind? I should know that as your boyfriend."

The tension leaves her shoulders. I know yesterday with Tara was hard. I hate that I didn't manage the situation better, or even see it coming. But it did get some of our feelings out on the table, so maybe that's a good thing? I don't know what to think. Usually, when a woman confesses she has feelings for me, I'm gone before she's done talking. But I don't feel that way with Eliza. I don't want to hurt her, and I really want to see this deal through. I was telling the truth when I said she was the only woman on my mind. I just don't know quite what that means for me.

"My favorite donuts are the sour cream."

I nod. "I'll make sure there are a few of those in the dozen." I reach for my wallet and keys. "I know how you take your tea. Do you know how Charles would like his coffee?"

She shakes her head. "I can text him and ask?"

"I'll get my coffee, and I'll pick him up black coffee. I should have any fixings he might want."

"That's a better idea. It seems less planned that way. I don't think he'll eat donuts, but he's surprised me before."

I race off to our neighborhood Tim Hortons, and after circling the block twice for a parking space, I luck out when I find someone pulling out. When I walk into the store, the line is long. I don't know when it isn't, but they're efficient, and in less time than I expect, I'm stocked with a dozen donuts and a tea and two coffees — black for Charles, Earl Grey for Eliza, and a double espresso for me.

As I drive back to my place, I spot the fruit stand and swerve over to an open parking spot. I race in to pick up a fruit tray and some fresh-squeezed juice. Regardless of whether Charles eats any of this, I want to do it right.

When I pull up, I see Charles' car already parked out front. He's a good twenty minutes early. Figures.

I walk in with my goodies and extend my hand to him. "Nice to actually meet you. I've seen you around the stadium and at games."

Charles nods. If I had to guess, he's in his late forties. His head is shaved, and his blue eyes are piercing. This morning he's wearing an expensive tailored suit. He's not wearing a wedding band, but he is wearing a Patek Philippe watch that easily cost a half-million dollars.

I place my bounty on the table. "I don't know how you take your coffee, so I have a cup of black, and we can add anything you might like."

"Black is fine," Charles says.

"I also picked up donuts, fruit, and orange juice."

"The coffee is fine." He turns back to look at Eliza, seated on the loveseat in the living room.

"I was just telling Charles about my concerns."

I nod and hand her the tea.

She clears her throat. "If these hires were insisted on by my dad, that's fine. We'll live with his decision. But if they were authorized by someone else, I need to understand who, as they seem to be in conflict with Darius Johnson's advice, which Dad usually follows. As you know, Donnie Cochran has made an offer on the team, and the more the value goes down, so will his offer."

Charles eyes her, his face expressionless. "It was my understanding that you are looking to take the team over."

"I am, but as I'm sure you know, my father isn't sold on that idea."

He nods. "It's unlikely that your father would want to sabotage the team."

"I agree," Eliza says.

I swallow a bite of a maple donut. "Did you mention that Darius has documentation about the problems these players had with their previous teams?"

Eliza shakes her head. "No. Thank you for reminding me. You can reach out to Darius, Charles, if you'd like those details. All three were on a do-not-hire list he'd created because of issues with their previous teams."

Charles is quiet a moment. "I'll wait on that," he says. "Please don't tell *anyone* I'm looking into this. I want to see if there's a money trail. I will also broach the subject with your father."

"Okay." Eliza nods. "And I'm going over tomorrow to see him."

"I'm going with you," I volunteer.

"Oh, right."

Charles looks away, seeming in deep thought.

"What can I do to help?" Eliza asks. "This team is important to me. I've worked very hard to be in a position where my father feels ready to give it to me."

"I'm aware." Charles looks at Eliza and then me. "I'll pull the banking information and let you know what I find out."

"Thank you, Charles."

Charles stands and takes his coffee with him as he goes. As predicted, he never touched the fruit or the donuts.

Eliza shows him to the door, and when she returns, I pull her in for a deep embrace. "He's going to check this out. That's good news."

"I know." She nods and looks away for a moment. "I think he wanted to say something about my dad's requirement for me, but he didn't know if I was playing you or you're a willing participant in my scam."

"I thought the same thing. But if we keep this up, we'll be fine."

"I hate this," she mumbles into my shoulder.

I give her an extra squeeze. "I need to head over to the hospital and check on a patient. We'll need to leave for the Martins' about six. I think we're better off taking a car service over. That way we won't be drinking and driving."

She nods. "I'm good with that. I have an appointment for a manicure, pedicure, and bikini wax."

"I look forward to closely inspecting that bikini wax."

She rolls her eyes, but she also smiles, so I think we're back in a good place.

I head out shortly after that, and while Eliza does her thing all day, I check in on my patient and then run into Michael at the hospital.

"What's up?" I call as I see him coming down the corridor.

"I had a delivery of twins early this morning. Now, I'm going to take a nap before I meet up with Nadine to go to Davis' place tonight."

"That sounds like a good idea. I'm a little tired myself."

"Really?" Michael teases. "Are you bringing your friend this evening? Is she why you're tired?"

"You mean Eliza?"

He nods with a cheeky grin.

"Yes. She's coming with me. Try to be kind and not give her too hard a time."

"We'd never be anything but kind to her. However, you? I can't help it if I happen to tell the stories of some of your past friends."

I roll my eyes. "She's stuck with me for the time being, and it would be miserable if she hated me."

"No promises," he singsongs as he walks away.

I realize I should prepare Eliza for what to expect tonight. These guys are a good group, but sometimes, when we're together in a private setting, we revert to being fifteen years old and find humor in the worst places, not to mention how much we tease one another.

After stopping by my office at the hospital, I head back home to work out. I end up going on an hour-long run and then lifting some weights in my home gym. I'm in the middle of that when I hear a catcall from the doorway.

"Wow," Eliza says. "I could sell very expensive tickets to what I'm seeing right now."

I give her a side grin. "I need to shower before we go. Care to join me?"

She shakes her head, allowing her hair to flow over her shoulders. "I just got my hair blown out, so I have to pass."

"Hmmm...that's a shame," I lament as I follow her upstairs. We have almost an hour before we need to leave.

She walks to her room, and at first, I'm confused, but then I realize she's looking through her clothes. "I don't know what to wear tonight," she explains when she catches me watching her.

"It won't be dressy. Paisley is usually in jeans, and Nadine too, though the girl who comes with Jack will most likely be in a micro mini dress. And I think Henry will be there with Allison, and she could be in a dress or a pair of jeans."

"So, you're telling me I should wear jeans."

"I'm not telling you anything. You wear what you feel comfortable wearing. If you want to go naked, I'll bring a blackout curtain, so the guys don't get jealous."

She narrows her eyes. "Okay. Yoga pants and a fleece pullover then."

I shrug. "If you'd like."

"I'm just teasing. I wouldn't embarrass you that way."

"I wouldn't be embarrassed. You look hot in your yoga pants."

Eliza smirks. "I'll get it figured out."

"I'm going to take a shower. The option to join me stands if you change your mind."

"I'll try to remember that."

I shower quickly, and when I walk out, Eliza is standing in my bedroom, dressed in jeans that hug every curve and a blue sweater. She's staring down at her boots. She doesn't look happy.

"What's wrong?" I ask.

She reaches down and zips her boot up. "I've met your friends before, but it was out and about. Being in someone's home is more intimate, which makes me nervous."

"No need to be," I assure her. "I'm sure Davis and Paisley will have put away their whips and chains."

Eliza's eyes grow big, and I can't help but belly laugh. "I'm just kidding. You already know they're easygoing and very likeable. I can't vouch for their manners tonight, but I'll do my best to keep them in line."

"Just know I had pictures of Henry, Phillip, Griffin, and Davis on my wall when I was a teen. It's a little surreal."

I shake my head. "Why does everyone say that?"

"I bet you had the picture of the Terrazzo triplets on your wall."

I look at her, my mouth falling open. "They weren't on my wall. They were on the back of my door."

Eliza laughs. "I thought so. What would you do if they were my friends and we were going out with them?"

"I'd try to think of a way to have them join us for a night."

"Ha." She shakes her head. "In your dreams."

I stop and look at her. "Actually, not really. I don't want to share you with anyone."

She blushes. "Oh."

I reach for her. "Hey. Don't stress about this. We're having fun, and everything is going well. Let's enjoy ourselves. This is no pressure, right?"

"Right."

I squeeze her hand. "I'll meet you downstairs."

We're bringing a bottle of expensive scotch that I got when I was on my last visit to Scotland. But I busy myself with pouring it into a cheap bottle—after pouring the cheap scotch right down the drain—as a joke. If I'm lucky, no one will share with me. Eliza picked up a nice bouquet on her way home from her day of beauty, so we're ready to present ourselves as guests. I check for messages from the hospital, and there are none, so I'm good to go.

My phone pings, signaling that our driver is out front. I walk to the base of the stairs. "Eliza? The car is here."

"Almost ready."

I hear her run across the floor. What is she doing?

It takes a good five more minutes for her to walk down the stairs, but when she does, she looks absolutely delicious. She's changed to a green wrap sweater that shows off her eyes, as well as a wonderful amount of cleavage.

"Maybe we should cancel and just stay home," I suggest.

"You're funny. I'm ready." She takes a deep breath.

"We're not heading out to war," I tease.

"I know, but these are your closest friends."

I shrug. "They already like you. And we're not that kind of crowd. We have enough people who judge us. We get together because we trust one another, and we can be ourselves. That doesn't mean they won't give me a hard time tonight and tell you all sorts of secrets that I would prefer you never know, but it should be fairly painless for you." I hand her the flowers, and she looks at me funny when I pick up the cheap bottle of scotch. "It's a joke."

I lock the front door behind us, and we walk out together.

"What stories can I expect they'll embarrass you with? Booze? Sex? Drugs? Rock n roll?"

"They've witnessed plenty of my embarrassing moments. I hate to spoil the fun. But I can tell you they're looking forward to filling you in and getting to know you better."

"I'm excited to meet them too. You said you told them about our arrangement, right?"

"Yes. When we were first considering this, I talked to my friends about what your dad was asking. But everyone here values privacy, so you don't have to worry."

She smiles. "I think I'm going to like them."

We slide into the backseat of the car, and in no time, we arrive at a large high rise that overlooks Stanley Park and Coal Harbor. "I've heard about this building," Eliza says. "Each apartment is multiple floors, right?"

"Yes, that was an issue for the builder, which wasn't my father, thankfully. He was disappointed that he didn't get the building, but with eighteen stories and less than a dozen owners, Vancouver's City Council was not happy."

"I know they want affordable housing, but when real estate is limited, it's hard for anything to be affordable. Even the suburbs are overpriced for what you get."

We take the elevator up to the penthouse, and the door opens to a gathering of people. The party is already underway.

"Sorry we're late," I announce.

"It was all his fault," Eliza adds.

They all turn and greet us.

Davis steps in and takes the scotch. "Really?"

"It's my recent favorite." I give him an honest smile.

"Steve has told me so much about your art," Eliza says to Paisley. "And I loved what I saw at Julia Martin's fundraiser, especially the silver-dipped driftwood. It's remarkable."

"We don't have any of her pieces here," Davis pouts. "She sells it before it even walks in our door."

"That's not true." Paisley pats him on the chest. "The painting above the fireplace is mine."

"Okay, that's true. But everyone here has one of your driftwood pieces but us."

Paisley rolls her eyes.

We walk farther into the crowd, and I make sure to reintroduce everyone to Eliza.

"Will you stop?" Nadine teases. "You may date a lot of women, but we like Eliza, and we definitely remember who she is."

"Let the teasing begin…" I warn Eliza, and she squeezes my hand.

Davis holds up the bottle I brought. "Anyone else want some of this rot gut beside Steve?"

There are no takers, and I'm loving this. "Suit yourselves."

Davis opens the bottle, takes a sniff, and pours us each a glass with two fingers over ice. "You're a scam artist," he says as he hands it to me.

I shrug. "I thought that way you'd have some of Scotland's finest small-batch left after tonight."

Davis shakes his head, all smiles.

The girls steal Eliza away, and I sit down to talk with my friends.

"So how is the roommate thing going with you two?" Davis asks.

"Pretty good. The plan is proceeding. She met Mary and John, plus Olivia and her kids."

"How did that go?" Jack asks.

"They loved her. Olivia appreciated the cover Eliza provided while she told my parents that she and Paul are divorcing. I think it kept them from totally going off the deep end."

Everyone shakes their head at that.

"I haven't heard from Olivia since, though. I wouldn't be surprised if my parents were burning up her phone lines."

"How is Eliza's family feeling about things?"

I shrug. "Her dad has someone following us to make sure we're authentic."

"Wow, that's some serious damage control."

I look over at Eliza. Allison is telling her a story, but she looks at me and smiles. It makes my heart sing.

After a moment, a woman comes in and taps Paisley on the shoulder. They speak for a moment, and then Paisley nods as she disappears.

"Okay, everyone," Paisley announces. "Dinner is ready."

As the crowd moves into the dining room, I walk toward Eliza. "Everything good?"

"Definitely. I've learned I'm a step up from the cheerleaders you typically bring to these parties."

"I could have told you that."

She smiles. "Also, you gave a week-long trip to San Francisco to a woman who went with you to some silent auction?"

I grimace. "I might have done that. She indicated that she was feeling more serious about things than I wanted, so I gave her the trip and encouraged her to take a friend."

Eliza crosses her arms. "You dumped her in front of your friends."

"Whenever I spend time with a woman, I'm very clear. I don't do relationships. When they start to think differently, I bail. Usually anyway," I add.

I lace my fingers with hers as we walk in to eat, although I'm not sure why. Everyone here knows we're in a fake relationship, so there's no need to, but it feels right. I'm doing something like a relationship with her, I realize, whether I meant to or not. And I'm okay with that—for now. It's the two of us against the world.

We take our places for dinner and enjoy a chicken and pasta dish that is outstanding. The drinks flow freely, but my friends hold off with their true shenanigans until after the dinner dishes are cleared.

"Eliza," Michael starts. "You're the favorite of all the women Steve has brought to meet us."

"I guess that's a good thing." She looks at me and smiles.

"Well, I thought you might want to know what you're getting into, so you can go into this with your eyes open."

"Michael…" Nadine warns.

"It was different with us, because Nadine and I went to middle school and high school together."

"Yes." Nadine looks at him. "And you were a dick then. You shouldn't be a dick now."

The crowd laughs.

"All I want to say is that Steve cheats at golf because there's no way anyone can really be as good as he seems to be and not be on the tour."

"You've found me out." I laugh hard. "There are a lot of things you could have said, but you're going to lie and tell her I cheat at golf?"

Michael shakes his head. "I'm not lying. I don't know how you do it, but there is no way you're that good."

Eliza's hand goes to my thigh. "Trust me. He's that good."

"Ohhhh," the chorus from my friends is loud.

I lean over and kiss the side of her head. "What can I say? I'm gifted in many ways."

"Oh gawd," Allison complains. "Paisley? Can you get

the microscope out so we can measure their dicks?"

"Hey, I've got a big dick," Henry exclaims.

"Of course, you do," Nadine says patronizingly.

The table is in hysterics. I lean over and whisper, "I told you we behave like fifteen-year-olds."

"It's great," Eliza says.

The conversation doesn't improve as the night progresses, but we all have fun, and we make plans to host them at my place after the season and the holidays are over.

On the drive home, I pull Eliza onto my lap. "You were the sexiest one there tonight."

"I'm glad you think so." She moves her hips over my hardness. "I didn't want to break anyone's spirit by telling them you certainly don't need a microscope to measure. More like a measuring tape."

I throw my head back and laugh.

Chapter 23

Eliza

Steve is playing golf with his friends today, so I'm meeting my mother for brunch at the Botanist on my own. He offered to adjust his plans, but I'm a little overwhelmed by all the meeting and greeting we've been doing. I can hold my mother off a bit longer.

Or at least I hope so. She's waiting for me quite eagerly when I arrive.

I lean down and kiss her on the cheek as I approach the table. "Hey, Mom."

"You have a beautiful glow about you," she says with a sparkle in her eyes.

I look around for Antonio, but he's nowhere to be found. I decide not to ask about that just yet. Instead, I sit down and spread the napkin over my lap. "What looks good today?"

"I think I'm going to have the egg white spinach and feta cheese omelet."

I look at the menu. "I'm going to go with the crab avocado eggs benedict." With that decided, I study my mom. "Are you feeling okay?"

She smiles. "I am. I saw your dad this week."

"I saw him the other day."

Her expression changes. "Why didn't you tell me?"

She could be talking about a dozen things, but I know she's not. "Tell you he was sick?" I venture, hoping that's it.

The server interrupts our conversation at the very best time, and I take a moment to gather my wits as my mom orders. She asks for essentially everything on the side. She'll pick at it, but she never really eats much.

When the waiter departs, she folds her hands in front of her. "Why are you with Steve?"

"He's handsome, funny, smart, and loves football as much as I do."

"Are you just with him because of this thing your dad is requiring?"

I look at her, not sure how to play this. I can't keep it from her, it seems, but I'm sticking with our script as much as I can. "Steve doesn't know."

Her eyes narrow. "He doesn't know? Your dad cornered him the last time he was there. And if you're so crazy about each other, why isn't he here with you?"

"I told you when you chose today that he had plans. Why isn't Antonio with you?"

She sighs. "I asked him to stay home so you and I could be alone."

"This is the first time we've been together since before you left that it's only the two of us. Let's enjoy ourselves. We'll get everyone together soon."

"You learned this deflection from me." She shakes her head. "You shouldn't have to manipulate a man into getting engaged to you. Marriage is serious."

"I know it is. And honestly, I resent that Dad feels I have to have a man in my life to be complete."

"I entirely agree. I swear, I don't know where he comes up with these things. But you know there's no arguing with him. Maybe this is a sign that the team isn't the right choice for you."

I shake my head. "That's about what you want for me, not what I want," I point out. "In a way, you sound just like Dad."

She looks away for a few moments. "I'd hate for you to make a rushed decision just for a silly team. I just want you to be happy, and I want you to be free to live your life, however you choose."

"Mom, I know what I'm doing with Steve. We're all good."

She crosses her arms. "I want to meet him."

"We'll make that happen. He had plans for golf this morning. He would have changed them, but I insisted he go. There's nothing nefarious about him not being here — promise."

"How do you feel about him?"

"Honestly, I like him much more than I should. He is kind and generous. His family is as screwed up as ours is, and we get along well. It's like we complement one another."

"Then why is it more than you should?"

"Because I know we're only having fun."

"Your dad thinks you've got some deal with him."

I feign disgust. "I was seeing him before Dad gave me his ultimatum. I like him, but he's not a guy who gets serious with anyone."

"You have my bad picker."

I shrug. "I don't know about that, and anyway, I think your picker's fine." I suppress a shudder as I think about Antonio. "Dad changed after you were married."

"Money does that to some." She studies me a moment. "I just worry about you. I don't want you to jump into something with Steve just to get the team."

"You're going to have to trust me, Mom. Like I said, I know what I'm doing."

I'm worried she's not going to let it go, but then our breakfast arrives, and as she picks at her food, Mom tells me about her friends and what they've been up to while she was gone.

"Eliza?" Allison stops as she passes our table, and I see Paisley right behind her.

"Hi!" I exclaim. I stand and hug them both. "Mom, this is Allison Pate and Paisley Martin."

They exchange pleasantries.

"Are you arriving, or are you just finishing?" I ask.

Allison sighs. "We're just finishing. I'm planning my wedding, and it's not as easy to get married to a Martin as Paisley made it out to be."

Paisley giggles. "That's because we ran off to an island to get married, and I was not marrying the prodigal son."

"Who are you marrying?" Mom asks.

"Henry Martin. He's currently the chief operating officer of Martin Communications."

I lean in. "Mom, don't be fooled. Allison is a fabulous actress who's put her career on hold for Henry."

Mom smiles widely. "Of course. I've worked with Julia Martin many times at fundraisers in town, and I knew you looked familiar. And Allison, I'll spare you my lecture about giving up your job for a man."

Allison nods. "My mother already gave it to me. Don't worry."

"What are you two working on so early this morning?" I ask.

"Location," Allison says. "I can't find a place I like that hasn't been used by dozens of other people."

I nod. "You know, Steve's sister is building the MacLean Museum. The gardens were completed first, so they'd be established when the building opens in the spring. I'm not promising, but I wonder if we could get you access to the gardens. There's a spot that they've designed specifically for weddings, and I know they haven't started booking yet. You could be the first. It would be a big win for them to host your wedding."

Allison smiles. "Really? I love that idea. When could we go see it?"

"I'll find out and try to get something set up for you."

"I will owe you big," she says with a squeal.

"It's not a problem," I assure her. "I'll call Olivia this afternoon. She can tell me who to talk to, and I'll get that set up."

"I hope you'll join us when we see it."

"I'd love that," I gush.

After another moment, they say their goodbyes.

"How do you know them?" Mom asks once they're out of earshot.

"Their partners are close friends with Steve."

"I'm so glad you're branching out. You know I adore Tanya, but it's good to have a wide circle of friends."

"Speaking of Tanya, I'm meeting her for a stroll down the seawall at Stanley Park."

"Isn't it too hot for that?"

I shrug. "Two weeks a year it's hot. We'll be fine. At least it means fewer people on the path."

Mom pulls out her credit card when the bill arrives.

"You know I make a decent living. Can't you let me pay?"

She waves me away. "I don't mind. It's all your dad's money, no matter how you split it up."

"Did you come back because he was sick?"

She freezes a moment, and then looks down. "I did. Laura called me to tell me. She's a genuine gift to your dad and me."

"I like her best of all the subsequent wives."

"Angela was a bitch," Mom says.

Angela Garman was a bitch. Her father had something to do with the creation of Bluetooth technology, and she was a spoiled brat. She wasn't even nice to Dad. I nod. "I agree. Laura is good for him. She makes him slow down and not be so focused on his work."

"That's all we want for you," Mom reminds me. "We just have different thoughts on how to get there."

My head is spinning. "I know, and I have to sort that out for myself."

She nods, and before she can wax poetic about anything else, I kiss her goodbye, promise again that she can meet Steve soon, and take off for Stanley Park.

I arrive early enough to change into a pair of shorts and a tank top, slather myself with sunscreen, and put on my sneakers before going to meet Tanya by the First Nations Totem Poles.

When I emerge from the restrooms, Tanya is waiting for me, water bottle in hand. She sees me and holds up her other hand, which also holds a water bottle. I have to laugh. "You know me too well."

"I figured you hadn't unpacked your water bottles yet."

I nod. "You're too good to me."

"I know, but that's the job of the BFF."

As we walk along the seawall, the heat is terrible, and it's very crowded anyway, but I don't care. It still feels great to be outside. We talk about last night's dinner with Steve's friends and today's brunch with my mom.

"So, you think your mom is in on what's going on?" Tanya asks.

"Well, she knows about Dad's requirement now. She doesn't like it, but she also doesn't understand why I want the team, so she's not much help. I tried not to fully tip my hand about how I'm handling things with Steve, but she's definitely watching me closely. One moment she agrees with me that you can't find your soulmate on a specific timeline, and then she agrees with my dad about me needing to find more balance in my life."

"That sucks."

I smile. I could say anything, and Tanya is a good

enough friend that she'll agree. That is one of the many things I love about her.

"Agreed. But it is what it is. Tell me how things are going with Jun."

"He had a date last night. She wanted to sleep with him, but he couldn't get it up."

I stop and look at her. "And you know this why?"

"He called me after."

"That must have been interesting. 'Hey, just checking in. I had a date and a serious case of ED.'"

"It wasn't like that, but honestly, I thought it was fantastic. He was all upset because he had this beautiful, busty redhead all hot for him, and he couldn't perform."

"Serves him right."

"Truly."

We walk to the point, where we stop to watch a sea plane land in the harbor. I never tire of seeing these planes touch down on the water.

"So, what is your current plan with Steve?" Tanya asks as we start walking again.

I blow out a puff of air. "I have to stay the course. I'm focused on getting the team. I refuse to allow my father to sell it to Donnie Cochran."

"What are you doing about the bad hires?"

"We got rid of one of them. I'm still waiting to hear from his attorney, but Darius makes sure our contracts have a strong termination clause."

"Thank God for that."

We're approaching the Lions Gate Bridge and a fork in the road. We can continue on or walk through the park, which is the opposite of the seawall trail. It becomes a dirt trail underneath the red cedar and Douglas fir trees that line the paths. Their roots prevent things from getting too muddy with all our rain in the winter. I think we're both ready to be out of the sun, so we opt for the shady choice.

"But you still don't know how it happened in the first

place, right?" Tanya presses. "Are you thinking about doing any investigation?"

I consider how I answer. Charles asked me not to say anything, and I hate having secrets from Tanya, but I need to honor that. The best way to keep a secret is not to tell anyone. "I haven't decided yet. I still need to ask my dad about it and make sure he's not the one behind this."

"Oh my God! You're right. He could be testing you."

My heart races at the thought. "I'm going to be very pissed if he is. But I haven't been able to feel him out yet."

"When are you going to see him?"

"I thought about going today, but I think after we're done, I'm going to go home and take a nap. I've had a lot going on between the team, my mom's return, my dad's illness, and Steve."

"I think Steve is the biggest reason you're so tired."

I shrug. "At least he's over his freakout."

When we finish our walk, I give her a hug goodbye at the totem poles. "See you in the morning."

"Sounds good. Make sure that hottie of yours recognizes what a great catch you are."

Smiling, I wave goodbye. "He knows."

I take out my phone and find a text message from Steve. He was pulled off the golf course to go to the hospital. His patient is not doing well.

And there goes any chance of a pleasant night together at home.

Chapter 24

Eliza

Bright sunlight streams through the windows of my luxurious Château Frontenac Hotel room on this fine Saturday morning in mid-August. It's been another week, and another game—though it was a win this time and a win on the road. Maybe the season will be better now that we're two and eleven. Steve and I are traveling together this weekend, and we have a breathtaking view of the walled city of Quebec. We overlook the St. Lawrence River, and across the water, the trees cover the hillside down the small mountains. It's stunning.

I'm still floating after the Tigers' fantastic Friday night win against the Quebec City Coeurs. It felt so good to see we could actually do it, and I'm going to be celebrating for the rest of the weekend.

"Are you ready?" Steve asks.

I turn and look at him. He's wearing jeans and a rolled neck sweater and looking absolutely delicious. "What's our plan?"

"As many times as I've been here, I've never explored. I thought we'd take in the Battery and wander the streets."

I smile. "Sounds great." Donning the warmest coat I brought, I worry it will not be enough. It may be August, but the wind is fierce, and the evenings are chilly. But nothing can get me down today. "Outside of Vancouver, this is my favorite city," I tell Steve as we head out.

We lace our fingers together and wander in and out of cute little shops. In one of them, I find the perfect gift for my mother—a piece of hand-blown glass art that will work perfectly in her living room. I don't usually shop for Christmas this early, but I couldn't help myself. Then we stop at a boulangerie for pastries.

"I can see why you like it here," he says. "It's like a little slice of Europe in our own backyard."

"That's exactly how I think of it." I grin at him. "What is your favorite city?"

"I went to medical school in Los Angeles, and it was pretty great. I knew before I started that I wanted to be in sports medicine."

"What made you want to come back to Canada? There's much more money to be made in the U.S. with their for-profit medical system."

He shrugs. "I guess I love Vancouver. It's beautiful and green. There's so much to do and see. And despite how I feel about my parents' marriage, I love being close to them."

I link my arm with his. "I feel the same way." I stop and look at a giant frog statue. It's at the entrance to a toy store. "I might find something for my younger brother and sister in here."

"I was hoping this was a different kind of toy store," Steve whispers. There's a mischievous glint in his eye.

I shake my head. "I know there's one of those around here too."

We go inside and browse for a bit, and I walk out with

the perfect things for my younger siblings, and Steve has found something for his niece and nephew.

We've just returned to the sidewalk when suddenly, Steve pulls me into a store. "I bet they have something I'd like to see you in."

I look around the lingerie shop, and I know he's right. The salesclerk approaches. "What can I help you with?"

In broken French, Steve tells her to find something very naughty.

She smiles and takes me to the back room, where she demands I strip down. She measures me and returns a few moments later with a soft pink, lacy ensemble—without bra cups or a crotch in the panties.

"I think your boyfriend will really like this," she says in French.

I laugh. "I think you're right."

When I walk out with my selections in hand, Steve's face falls. "You didn't model for me."

I grin from ear to ear. He's like a puppy who's been refused table scraps. "I don't think she wants to hear us having sex in the dressing room."

Steve's eyes grow large.

"It wouldn't be the first time," the saleswoman says.

On the way to the register, Steve adds a few things to my items, and then he pays for it all.

As we leave, the salesclerk calls after us. "Have fun."

I try to peek in the bag. "What did you add?"

"You'll see."

I shake my head.

We continue exploring the historic city, discovering hidden gems in its quaint alleyways and historic buildings. We have lunch in an incredible bistro that serves us a tasting menu of salmon cooked six ways—tartare, pan-fried, roasted, broiled, grilled, and pan seared—each with different rich sauces. We share a lovely bottle of Canadian white wine, and in the end, I'm stuffed. "I could have had an entire meal of any one of those salmon bites."

Steve wipes his mouth with his napkin. "Agreed. Which was your favorite?"

"I don't know. The tartare set the bar pretty high, but each time I was expecting the next thing not to be as good, it exceeded my expectations."

"I think what really surprises me is that I'm not overloaded, just pleasantly full."

I sit back in my chair. "That's definitely a good thing."

When the check comes, Steve pays our bill, despite my protests. He's paid for everything this weekend, including the gifts I bought for my brother and sister.

"Let's go back to the hotel room," he says when we've finished. "I'd like to see you model your outfit."

I blush. "Let's go."

When we get to our suite, Steve closes the door, pushes me up against the wall, and kisses the silly grin I've been wearing all afternoon off my face. He holds my hands over my head and spreads my knees wide. His kiss sears me and prepares me for how he's going to fuck me.

"I want you now," I beg. "Please."

He steps back and pulls me toward the bathroom. "Nope. I want to see you model your new purchase. And how well you do will determine how many orgasms you get today."

I pick up the bag, but he takes it from me. "No, there are some surprises for us later." He places the small box with the lingerie in my hands, and as I turn to walk away, he swats me on the ass.

"I won't be long," I assure him.

"Good. Because that will help your orgasms too."

I strip out of my blouse and pants and wriggle into the bustier. I lace it up, and despite the lack of cups, it hugs my breasts and keeps them sitting high. I'm not sure why I bother with the panties, since they're crotchless, but I wear them anyway.

"Are you ready?" I call as I walk out.

Steve is standing with a pair of nipple clamps dangling from his finger. "Any objections?"

I shake my head. I can hardly wait.

"You look fucking gorgeous. Turn around."

I quickly spin, my pulse pounding in my ears.

"Again, slower."

I turn more slowly, and when my back is to him, he asks me to stop. "God, you have a beautiful ass. Climb up on that table on all fours and show it to me."

When I do so, his hand slides up and down my seam. "You're so wet. Does this turn you on?"

"Yes," I moan as he grazes my clit.

"How do you feel about red handprints on that ass?"

I shiver.

"That's what I thought."

He comes around in front of me, and I can see his cock pushing hard against his zipper.

"Can I help you with that?" I ask.

Steve and I pull his pants and boxers down and off his body together. His dick bobs. He sits down on the edge of the bed and curls his finger at me.

I approach, pushing his knees apart and running my fingernails up his thighs to his hips. Then I run my tongue up the inside of his thigh. He shudders, and I smile.

I lick up the bead of pre-cum that seeps from his head and moan. "You taste better than lunch today." I run my tongue up his fat shaft and back down again.

His prick pulses, and he growls. "Oh fuck!"

I smile my naughtiest smile and giggle at him, giving him a little more of what he wants by focusing my tongue around the tip of his dick.

I sense that Steve is on the verge of just taking over and fucking my mouth when I stop. "Do you want to come in my mouth, my pussy…" I sit back and play with my nipples. "Or maybe on my tits?"

"Put it back in your mouth," he commands.

I suck hard at the tip and roll my head, swirling my tongue around him, each time taking him deeper into my mouth.

"Fuck, Eliza, that's so good!" Steve moans when he reaches the back of my throat. "Fuck, you're good at that!"

His hips begin to roll up and down with me. He reaches for my nipple and pinches it tight.

I close my legs. "I knew you'd like this."

Still pivoting in and out of my mouth, he attaches the clamps. They feel magnificent, but my clit is desperate for friction. I moan again, sending vibrations through his shaft, and reach to strum my clit.

But Steve pulls on the chain connecting the clamps. "Don't touch yourself."

I suppress my whine of frustration. I know when he unleashes this orgasm, I'm going to explode.

He pulls out of my mouth with a big pop and leans back on the bed. "Climb on."

He doesn't have to ask me twice. He hands me a condom, and I roll it on before lining him up with my pussy and lowering myself.

We moan together as we join, looking deep into each other's eyes.

"Oh fuck, you're so tight," Steve tells me hoarsely.

It takes a few times rolling my hips to settle down on him completely.

Steve removes the clamps from my nipples, and they sting, but he's quick to lick and suck them. He holds me by the hips, and I rock gently on his dick as we look deep into each other's eyes. The sound of our breathing, the squelch of my pussy, and the creaking of the bed are the only sounds in the room.

I can feel a myriad emotions pass between us as we silently communicate. Steve slides his hands up my back and pulls me in for a passionate kiss. As our lips and tongues wrangle, I slowly increase the rocking of my hips, not bouncing up and down but rolling forward and back. I grind my clit on the base of his cock and my G-spot against his shaft.

I soon feel a climax building, deep within me. I have to break the kiss in order to breathe, and I rest my forehead on his. Our eyes meet and lock again. I lower my head to his shoulder and groan deep into his chest. My internal muscles pulse as the first wave of my orgasm crests.

I tighten and spasm as I climax, and Steve flexes his own muscles, making his cock twitch inside me. "Oh fuuuuuck..."

He holds me tight as my breathing slowly returns to normal.

"That was incredible," he whispers.

It was exactly that, and as we lie in bed, our limbs intertwined, I realize this weekend has brought us even closer. I've never felt this way before, and I think I'm getting myself into a huge mess, even as I get closer to my goal.

Chapter 25

Steve

The Tigers are officially halfway through the season, and we have a Friday night game this week, and it's away again, this time in Toronto. The weather is hot and humid, and their fans are enthusiastic. They should be. Toronto is in line to go to the Grey Cup this season.

The odds makers are putting the Toronto Pirates in the killing-the-Tigers range, and looking around the locker room, I'm not surprised. No one is excited to be here. This is not how professional football should be played. I sigh, scrubbing my hands over my face. This is not a season I'm going to look back on particularly fondly if it's my last one with the Tigers.

I hear yelling from the other room and poke my head out to make sure it doesn't become physical.

"You fucking slept with my girlfriend," Nathan Cotton says, pointing his finger aggressively at the Tigers' tight end.

"Well, if she isn't getting it at home..." Mathieu Pelletier shrugs.

Fantastic. Thing one and thing two are fighting. Just what Eliza needs — another problem. I wade in just as fists are thrown, and the coaching staff, players, and I soon pull the two apart. The swear words are flowing, and people are taking sides.

"You, get out," Coach Roy yells at Pelletier. "I'm tired of the problems you're causing. You threw the first punch, and you're done."

"I don't have to take this shit." Pelletier slams his helmet on the concrete floor and kicks it.

Dean Frankel, the team kicker, is standing three feet away, and the helmet nails him in the shoulder. That helmet probably weighs twenty pounds, and the look on Dean's face says it all. That hurt. I race over to check him out.

The room around me is in chaos, with most of the team still holding Cotton away from Pelletier.

Then two large police officers materialize and take Pelletier down to the floor to handcuff him.

"He assaulted another player. I want him arrested," Coach declares.

The litany of expletives explodes from Pelletier as he's led out of the room in handcuffs.

I'm glad the incident is over, but this is not the way to start a game. Today's going to be a disaster, no matter how they play.

I examine Dean in one of the treatment rooms as the coaches talk to the team to fire them up, but it's not helping. I can feel their eyes watching us as I look at his shoulder. When I rotate it, pain contorts his face.

I look over at Todd, one of my assistants, and I can tell he agrees with me. It's a broken clavicle. We can't be a hundred-percent certain without an X-ray, but given Dean's limited range of motion and pain, if it isn't broken, it would surprise me. And there's nothing that can be done. If the break is severe, we'll have to do surgery, but in the meantime, it's going to hurt a lot.

"Just shoot me up with morphine and let me play, Doc," Dean begs.

The coach's eyes plead with me too.

I sigh, shaking my head. "I need permission from Eliza Rourke before I agree to let you back on the field." I put ice on the injury.

Coach's mouth turns from a straight line to a frown as I text Eliza.

Me: Mishap in the locker room. Come ASAP.

Eliza: I'm on my way.

As the team files out for the pregame warmup on the field, Coach catches my eye and tips his head toward the office.

"I'll be right back," I assure Dean.

When I walk in, Coach motions for me to shut the door. "We didn't bring another kicker," he says.

I nod. "I understand, but without an X-ray, I don't know the extent of the break. I just know it's broken."

"He needs to play. You'll need to morphine him up and get him on the field."

That's against the rules. I know a lot of clubs play that way, but there are fines if the league finds out. "Not without Eliza's permission. I'm also concerned that if he plays, it will have legal ramifications for him and his assault case against Mathieu Pelletier."

Coach rolls his eyes. "Dammit! Work with me, or I'll find someone else who will."

I slowly shake my head. "I understand you're mad, but the only people who can hire and fire me are Tom and Eliza Rourke."

"And since you're fucking Eliza Rourke, you think you're in a good place to threaten me?"

I step back. "Watch what you say."

Eliza chooses that moment to walk in. "What happened?"

Coach gives her a rundown of the altercation between the players. He's a little light on details of the accident part of the situation, so I step in.

"Pelletier booted his helmet, and Dean Frankel was standing less than three feet away. He took the brunt of the force in his right shoulder."

Eliza's face morphs to horror as she looks back and forth between Coach and me.

"My assistant and I have examined him. It's broken," I tell her. "Without an X-ray, I don't know the extent of the break and whether it requires surgery. He has offered to medicate with morphine and play today."

"Absolutely not," Eliza says. "After the scandal in the NFL a few years ago, we forbid pain masking. If he can't play with Advil, he can't play."

Coach glares at me and then at Eliza. "We don't have a kicker."

I snap my fingers. "Jerome Standing is one of our trainers, and he was a kicker at university. We can put him on a one-game contract."

Eliza looks at me, her eyes sparkling. "That's exactly what we'll do."

Coach has steam pouring out of his ears. "Your father is going to hear about this."

"I hope he does, because if you put Dean in, he'll fire you. I will tell the league, and we'll be fined because you ignored league rules. And the penalty for that is twenty-five thousand dollars. I have no problem deducting that from your paycheck if you try to put him in."

Coach stands up and walks out the back door, away from the field.

Eliza turns to me. "Did he just leave?"

"I think he did."

She shakes her head. "I can't believe what a cluster this

is. Get Jerome into a uniform and let Coach Majors know he's head coach today."

"Will do. I'll work with Dean to get him X-rayed and drugged up before the pain really starts to hit him hard."

Eliza nods. "Thank you for calling me down."

"It wasn't pretty."

By now, the team has warmed up, and they're filtering back into the locker room. Eliza smiles as she walks out, and I pull Coach Majors aside. "Coach Roy has stepped out. I'm not sure if or when he's going to return, so it's all you."

Coach's eyes grow wide. "Okay. I can do this."

"Jerome Standing, the trainer, was a kicker at university. He's going to stand in for Dean today."

Coach Majors nods. "Thanks."

We get Dean to the hospital and into X-ray. Thankfully, his clavicle doesn't look like it needs surgery, but it's a pretty severe break. It's going to be a long and painful recovery, and yet another needless injury this team has caused itself.

By the time I return to the stadium, it's forty-two to zero, and it's official: the Toronto Raptors are killing us. I head up to the visiting team's box to see what the mood is like there.

The attendant opens the door for me, and it's instantly loud and rowdy. No one seems to be paying attention to the game. I spot Eliza, and she's off to the side, talking animatedly to a guy about our age who is buffed out. He's pulled her away from the crowd and has angled his body at her. He's looking at her like she's an ice cream cone on a hot day and he wants to lick her all up.

The hair on the back of my neck stands up straight. *Who is this guy, and what is he trying to do?*

I step up to Eliza and put my hand at the small of her back. "Hey."

She smiles up at me, and the guy looks me up and down.

"Does Dean need surgery?" Eliza asks.

"Depends on how it heals, but for now, it's okay. It's immobilized, and he's flying high as a kite." I look around the room. "Did the press pick up on what happened?"

"No. I gave Roy some cover by saying he went with Dean to the hospital. But I'm pretty upset." She turns toward this guy. "Oh, Vince, please meet my boyfriend, Steve McCormick."

I can tell he's a bit disappointed as he extends his hand. "Vince Harding. Nice to meet you. You work for the team?"

"I'm the chief medical officer." I force a smile, getting my jealousy in check. "How do you know Eliza?"

"I'm an assistant coach for the San Diego Pelicans. We used to work together."

"What brings you up to Toronto?"

"Eliza invited me. We're still in preseason."

I nod, schooling my features. *Can that be true?* "Yes. I'm aware. Well, we're glad you're here."

"Toronto just scored again," Eliza announces.

Vince shakes his head. "It's really weird. The game is the same but different."

I nod. "The obvious differences are the longer field and twelve men on the field, but it's more than that. We could get a point here."

The Tigers kick the ball but can't keep it the end zone. They tackle the Raptor on the one-yard line.

"They can get a single point?" Vince asks.

Eliza smiles. "They can if the Raptors can't move the ball out of the end zone."

"Most of the differences are subtle," I point out, returning my attention to Vince.

"There isn't a big difference in the caliber of the players between the two leagues," Eliza says. "The difference lies in the salaries, size, and scope of the game—and the hype. The Grey Cup is almost always a classic. It's generally a high-scoring, close game and very exciting. The Super Bowl over the years has more often than not been one sided. People watch it for the commercials." She shrugs.

I stand closer to Eliza. "Professional football north or

south of the border is great entertainment with incredible athletes, so let's not compare. Both leagues provide a great product for fans, and Canadians love the NFL too."

Eliza smiles at Vince. "We're very passionate about our game, and I hope to work with companies to garner sponsorships that will up our profile."

"If anyone can do it, you can." Vince says, touching her arm.

I fight the urge to deck the guy. But I know my fists aren't what's needed here. I can do better than what happened in the locker room.

We turn toward the flat screen that's showing the game below. We're starting the fourth quarter, and the stands are nearly empty. I pull Eliza in close. "I'm sorry."

She sighs. "What did you expect after what happened before the game started?"

"I know, but the loss still sucks."

A few minutes later, TSN, the channel covering the game, breaks away to join a baseball game.

Vince looks at Eliza. "Do you want to get out of here?"

"Our flight home leaves at midnight," she says. "It's a redeye so the guys can take Saturday and Sunday off."

"We could hang out until then," he practically whines.

Eliza looks at me, and I know she's looking for my permission, but I'm not giving it. She's the one who's said Charles is always watching, and at away games in particular.

"I need to get down to the locker room." I lean in and kiss her, and it grows into a deep, wet kiss quickly. Yes, I'm marking my territory like a big ol' cat, but I don't care. What an ass to invite her out with me standing right here.

When Eliza steps back, I have to reach for her arm, so she doesn't topple over.

Yep. I did that to her, asshole. Hands off. I extend my hand to Vince. "It was great to meet you."

I wink at Eliza and leave the box. The game isn't over yet, but I couldn't stay after that goodbye. I'll just wait in the locker room until the team arrives.

When the team trickles in, they're a dejected group. Coach Roy is sitting in the visiting coach's office.

I give him the update on Dean, and he nods. "Thank you for being level-headed. Jerome was the best player out there this evening."

I chuckle. "He's probably thrilled he got put in, even if it was last minute."

"Pelletier's agent was here a minute ago," he says. "I held firm on the contract. That means two of the three bad apples are gone."

"How did we end up with these guys, anyway?" I ask.

Coach shakes his head. "I have no clue. I would have preferred a new college grad to what we ended up with."

"I thought you were there when we picked them up?"

"I was at the draft, sure. But these guys were all free agents. I just got an email that they'd been hired while we were in the free-agency period."

I cross my arms. "Well, maybe we can live with Cotton."

Coach just shakes his head.

The locker room is nearly silent as the guys start to undress and prepare to shower, all except Cotton, the third problem child, who's swearing like he caught someone peeing in his corn flakes. He's blaming everything and everyone except himself for the loss.

Coach Roy steps out and looks around the room. "Sit your asses down."

All the players take their seats on benches around the room. "Today was a total shit show. Frankly, I was so pissed that I walked out and left you all behind. I'm sorry about that. That was the wrong thing to do. But we're halfway through our season, and we can still bring this back. It's going to take work, though, and you need to want to be here."

My phone beeps as Coach continues with his speech.

Eliza: Is everyone decent? Can I come into the locker

room?

Me: Yes. Coach Roy is apologizing for leaving them in a lurch and giving updates on their teammates.

A moment later, Eliza steps in and stands just inside the doorway.

" — I'm sorry I let you down," Coach continues. "It won't happen again. We're going to put this game behind us and be ready for practice on Monday. And I want everyone in the weight room Monday morning long before practice. By the time you walk out at eleven o'clock, I want you to each have run ten kilometers, done one hundred crunches, and one hundred burpees. Be ready to work hard. You want out of your contract? That's not happening until the end of the season. We're going to be the team we were designed to be. Now, you have two and a half hours to get yourselves dressed and on the bus to the airport. Don't be late, or we will leave you behind."

Eliza smiles at Coach Roy when he's finished. I step out of their way, so they can meet in the office.

I work on getting my trainers and our things together, and I instruct one of our junior trainers to get Dean and Jerome's things and to pick up Pelletier's things and keep them separate. I glance back toward Eliza and Coach Roy, but I can't really see what's going on. There aren't any raised voices I can hear, at least.

When I look up again a few minutes later, Eliza is standing off to the side, waiting for me. She's blushing, but that's probably because several of the guys are walking around naked before they get to the shower.

I wave her into a treatment room and suggest she shut the door. There's a large window in the door, but at least the more modest guys won't be worried about walking around nude in front of Tom Rourke's daughter.

"Are you going to meet us at the plane?" I hold my breath, waiting for her answer.

She smiles. "No, I'll just go with you. Couldn't you tell I wasn't interested in Vince?"

I shrug. "He was interested in you."

"Of course, he was. Because he can't have me anymore. He dumped me to date a cheerleader, but he wanted to string me along until she dumped him. I didn't play those games, and I moved to London."

"So, you didn't invite him today? How did he know you were here?"

"Good question. The invitation to come to a game is an open one I've offered to many people. So he just showed up. All my social media says I'm in a relationship, but that didn't seem to deter him."

I stalk closer to her. Something inside me wants more.

"I will admit, my favorite part was when he thought you were a trainer on the team, and you told him you were the team doctor." Eliza chuckles.

"That was your favorite part?" I shake my head. "I would have thought that kiss was your favorite."

"The fact that you were so possessive was a bit of a turn on, but we weren't out to everyone. We are now."

"Coach mentioned it earlier. I think everyone knows. Who cares?"

She shakes her head. "We'll talk later. But know that I wouldn't have gone with him without you."

My heart rate slows for the first time since that kiss. "Good to know." I try to play it cool, but my dick is thinking about all the things it wants to do to her.

Soon. Very soon.

We manage to get the team on the bus, and Nathan Pelletier is the only player not on the flight home.

Chapter 26

Eliza

Steve and I spent all day in bed yesterday, partially to recover from the red-eye home and partially because Steve made it his mission to hear me moan his name multiple times in a row.

The warmth emanating from his body is overheating me now. I pull away, and he tugs me in closer. "I'm cold." His fingers begin to explore my hips. "You're so soft."

I moan in response. Every nerve is in overdrive. I've lost count of the number of orgasms, and I know I'm going to be sore for a while. Rolling over, I face him. He's all smile, and there's the twinkle in his eyes that I love so much. It means he's up to naughty no good, and that's always fun.

"I think you know you're making me wet right now." I bring my hand up his leg. "And I bet you're pretty hard, aren't you?" I pull myself on top of him, my legs framing his hips. I kiss down his chiseled chest while grinding my wet crotch on his hard rod.

"Don't stop doing that," he groans.

I run my nails behind me and between his legs. Steve curses under his breath. When I reach his balls, I go straight to kissing and licking, still not touching his throbbing cock. Steve shakes his head, smiling at my teasing. I wink at him in response.

Finally, I run my tongue up his shaft. I go to the side and repeat the action, getting reacquainted with his cock.

He growls. "Oh fuck me! C'mon, quit teasing!" Steve rolls me on my back and positions himself between my legs. Stroking himself, he watches me as he slides our last condom on. "I've never wanted to do this with anyone else like I want to with you. You're my energizer bunny."

He holds my ankles for balance and thrusts into me repeatedly, hard and fast. The squishy sounds are punctuated by the slap of our bodies colliding.

I begin to strum my clit. Every nerve in my body is on a collision course with an amazing climax.

"Now, Eliza. Come for me now," he commands.

The cork pops, and I see stars. Steve is right behind me, groaning my name. He collapses after a moment, and we're both breathing heavily in our orgasmic haze.

"How does it get better and better?" he asks between breaths.

I smile at him as my cell phone pings. I groan. The real world is reaching out, and it's time to come out of hiding, unfortunately.

I find my phone on the nightstand.

Dad: Dinner at our house, 4 p.m. with Steve

I look over at Steve. "My father is demanding that we arrive at the house today at four for dinner."

"He wants me to join you, or you want me to join you?" he asks.

I turn the phone around so he can see the text. "Both of us."

"Okay then." He nods.

"I wonder what could be so urgent. Do you think Charles has said something? In the last two weeks, he's cleared Dad and me, but that's the only update he's had so far."

Steve shrugs. "Who knows."

"I should touch base with Charles to find out if he's talked to Dad. I don't want to go into this blind."

"That's smart."

Me: We'll be there. Should we bring anything?

Dad: No

That's not particularly helpful, so I text Laura next.

Me: Is Dad in a good mood or bad mood today?

Laura: He's feeling better. He was unhappy Friday night about the game.

Me: Understandable. That was a mess. We'll be there about four. Dad's really milking this early dinner hour.

Laura: six happy faces on their side crying emojis.
Laura: He wants you to hang out with him. I think he's getting bored with just us.

Me: What can I bring?

Laura: I will deny this completely, but if you were to bring him a good bottle of Irish whiskey, he'd be thrilled and think he'd gotten something over on me.

Me: We'll come with a bottle of Redbreast. See you

later today.

"Do you mind going to my dad's?" I ask Steve.

"No, actually. Not at all."

We slowly make it out of bed. I give Charles a call while Steve's in the shower, and after I shower, I end up in a yellow, floral-print sundress. Steve wears golf shorts and a collared knit shirt.

"We look like we're going to the country club," I note.

He nods. "We can do that if you'd like."

"Not really my scene. I suck at golf."

"I can think of a lot of things I'd like you to suck, and a golf ball isn't one of them."

"You're hilarious," I deadpan.

That makes us both laugh. We climb into the Toyota 4Runner and start working our way through downtown and over Lions Gate Bridge.

"What did Charles say?"

"He said he hadn't spoken to Dad yet because he doesn't have anything new. It's taking longer to find useful information than he thought. But he said I should talk to Dad about what's going on."

"Okay, do you want me there for that?"

I shrug. "We'll play it by ear."

When we finally arrive, Minni runs out and greets us. "You're back," she says, seeming surprised to see Steve.

"Is that okay?" he asks her.

"It depends."

Steve looks at her, waiting.

"Do you give piggyback rides?"

"You're too big for anyone to carry on their back," I tell her.

But she looks at Steve, waiting for him to respond. Sometimes, I can see my father in her—he challenges and then waits silently.

"I might give you a piggyback, for the right price."

Her hands go to her hips. "What?"

He shrugs. "Depends on if you think—"

"Amelia Danielle Rourke, you are too big for a piggyback ride. No," Laura calls from the front door.

"I almost had him," Minni whines.

I hug Laura and put a bottle of cranberry juice in her hand. "I assume you have vodka?"

She smiles broadly. "I do, and I also have limes."

"Then we're set."

We talk for a few minutes before my dad shuffles in. "There she is," he says.

"Daddy." I give him a tight hug, and despite the heat, he's wearing wool pants and a wool cardigan over a collared shirt. "How are you feeling?"

"I'm sick and tired of people asking me how I'm feeling," he grumbles.

I nod and slip him a bottle of bourbon in a paper bag. He feels the weight of it and smiles. He's not mad anymore.

"Both of you come meet me on the patio," he says. "I want to talk to you."

"I'll be right there." I put three tumblers in Steve's hands and send him off.

As soon as they're out of earshot, and I confirm that Minni is busy painting and watching one of her shows, I turn to Laura. There are dark circles under her eyes, and her hair is a bit frizzy, not Laura like at all.

"How are you doing?"

She gives me a tight smile. "I'm great."

"Okay, that's what you tell people who barely know you, the ones who don't see your exhaustion."

Laura's façade crumbles. "I'm so worried about him."

"What are they telling you?"

"He's doing great on the meds, and his blood count shows his immune system is responding."

"That's fantastic. Why are you worried?"

"Because it's almost too easy."

I let that sink in a minute. This has been tough, and she doesn't have anyone to share the burden with. "I understand exactly what you mean."

"We've not been together long enough that I'm ready for him to die. I knew when we married, he would die before me, but I figured we'd have a few decades before that. He has more energy than most thirty-year-olds."

I nod. "But he's doing well," I insist.

"He is, but he looks so frail, and he's slowed down."

"How is his mind?"

"Sharp, and I shouldn't keep you," she says, suddenly coming back to herself. "He was flipping angry watching the game on Friday night. The network didn't even come back after the third quarter."

"That's no surprise. The team was not on their game. There was a mishap in the locker room, and it threw everyone off."

"Well, go talk to him. I appreciate you checking on me. Maybe you and your mom can meet me for lunch one day this week."

Internally, I cringe at the idea of being out of the office for two hours, not to mention managing Mom and Laura simultaneously, but I know she needs it. I'm sure Mom isn't managing this well either.

When I nod, she hands me a drink, and I head out to the patio to find Dad.

The door is open, and I can hear my dad drilling Steve.

"What are you getting out of being involved with Elizabeth?" Dad presses.

I can smell cigar smoke, but I can't tell where they are.

"I like her, probably a lot more than I should, and that's all I need to get out of it. That's the point of a relationship, right?"

"You do realize there's no way I can hire you back next year if you're still dating her."

Steve is quiet a moment. "I checked, and there isn't a no-fraternization policy. But if you don't want to renew my contract, I have other options. I don't do this for the money. I do this because I love the game, and I love working with athletes. But the Olympics will be here in a few years, and I'm always approached by those teams. You do what you need to do."

"When do you get your trust fund?" Dad quizzes.

My ears perk up. We've never really discussed this. Not that it's any of Dad's business. Jeez...

"I got it at twenty-five, and it's sitting in an account at the Royal Bank of Canada," Steve says matter-of-factly. "Upon my father's death, I'll have more money than I know what to do with. But I'm sure you already knew that."

My father is quiet a moment. "You know I told her she needed to be engaged to get the team," he finally says, his voice different somehow.

I wish I could see Steve's face, but I can't.

"I *wasn't* aware of that," Steve counters smoothly. "Why would you do that? She's worked her whole life in football to be close to you, and I know she has big plans for the team. Why would you do that to her?"

I lean in closer to hear his reason. Maybe it will finally make sense.

"Because the team is a black hole, and all I do is throw money into it. She's too smart to waste her brain power on that team."

"Shouldn't she make that decision?"

Dad huffs. "I don't know what you're up to, but it's no good. I don't want you dating my daughter."

"I care deeply about Eliza," Steve says calmly. "I don't understand why you can't see that she deserves that from everyone in her life. I've always been cautious about women because they either wanted my money or the influence my name offers. Eliza has been in the same boat. We're not sure what we are right now, but we're enjoying ourselves, and I have nothing but respect for her. I would think that's what's important to you."

My heart beats wildly. That's a giant admission. I want to show Steve how much I appreciate all that he's said, but maybe after I shake some sense into my dad.

Before my dad says something I won't be able to forget, I walk outside. "What are you two talking about?"

Steve crosses to me with a smile. "You."

I blush at his honesty. He's my chief defender, and standing up to my dad like he did wins major points with me. But he does it from a place of calm and control. I need to do the same. Who knows how much of what he said he means.

"Did you tell Dad about what happened on Friday?" I ask.

He shakes his head. "I left that for you."

I take a deep pull on my drink. "Start from the beginning. I wasn't in the locker room at first, so tell him how it all began."

Steve looks at my dad. "We'd been at the stadium for a short time. The team was getting dressed for warmups when Nathan Cotton—and I was told this; I didn't witness this part. Cotton confronted Pelletier for sleeping with his girlfriend. He got a typical response, and that led to a fight, but Pelletier threw the first punch."

Dad takes a puff of his cigar.

Then Steve tells him about Pelletier kicking the helmet.

"Wait, didn't Rhymes do that before?" Dad asks.

Steve nods. "I'm guessing that's where he got the idea. Only he did it better than Rhymes."

Dad sighs. "How bad is the injury?"

"It's a clean break. We immobilized the shoulder, and as long as it heals okay, we won't have to do surgery."

"Why didn't he go back in the game?" Dad presses.

"Because of the twenty-five-thousand dollar fine for drugging to mask pain," I inform him. "And until the X-ray, we weren't certain how severe the injury was."

Dad looks at me like I'm stupid.

"We didn't have anyone on the bench, but Jerome Standing on my team — he's one of the physical therapists — was a kicker in university at McGill. So he went in on a one-day contract."

Dad looks at Steve. "That was smart thinking."

I nod. "It worked out, but the problem wasn't that. It was Cotton."

"I leave recruiting and retention to Roy."

Now, it's finally time. I take a deep breath. "That's what I thought you'd say." I put my empty glass down on the small teak side table. "I've engaged Charles to look into how Rhymes, Cotton, and Pelletier came to the Tigers. Darius had them all on his list of players we shouldn't hire, and Coach Roy has told me he was surprised to find out they were on the team. Charles is looking for a money trail, to start with. But he tells me you've been cleared."

Dad's brows furrow. "You engaged Charles?"

I sit up, ready to defend my decision. "Was I not supposed to?"

"I'm just surprised. Charles isn't one of your favorite people."

I sigh. "I know he has your best interests at heart. Knowing that you send him after me to get information you could just ask me for upsets me, but that doesn't mean he's not good at his job. If there's anyone in the world you can trust, Dad, it's the people who are here with you right now."

He blows out a bellow of air. "And I trust your mother."

"Fine, but someone gave the go-ahead to sign these three guys, and as a result, they're screwing up our season."

Next, I tell Dad about the offers two other CFL teams got. "Those numbers mean that if you decide to sell to Donnie Cochran, you're undercutting yourself."

"I thought you wanted the team," Dad counters. "After running it for a month, you've changed your mind?"

It's been two months, but I don't think I'll point that out to him. He may not want to be honest with himself about how long he's been out of commission. "No, I didn't change my mind. I have plans if you'll let me take over, but it's your team until you tell me otherwise, so you need to do what you want to do."

"Dinner's ready," Laura says through the curtain.

With that, Dad nods and looks toward the house. This conversation has concluded for now.

Dinner is fun, but I can tell Dad's getting tired. We eat, and then Steve and I make our excuses to leave.

"Thank you for inviting us," I tell Daddy.

"You're managing all these issues well. Thank you."

I smile and nod, but my heart sings. I want to do my own touchdown dance.

As Steve and I drive back into town, I watch what's left of the sun drop below the horizon. "Thank you for coming, and for defending me today."

Steve glances over with his brow furrowed.

"I was listening for a minute before I came outside."

He nods. "I didn't let on that I knew about his requirement, but everything else I said was true."

My heart fills with warmth, even as fear makes it beat a little faster. How am I ever going to navigate my way out the other side of this? "Thank you."

Chapter 27

Eliza

Coach Roy's total breakdown a couple weeks ago seems to have sent the team into overdrive, and we've won the last two games. I'm calling that forward momentum, and I'll take it. This weekend is Labor Day, and it's time for the Labor Day Classic. Each team will play their main rival over the long weekend. It's a big deal, and there's lots of advertising for all the eyes paying attention. Sponsorship this weekend is what I'd like to see weekly for our league.

I look up from my computer to find Marlene in Dad's office is calling.

"Hello, Marlene. How are you today?" I answer.

"Just fine," she says. "Your father asked me to call and have you come meet him at the house at two o'clock this afternoon. And he'd like you to come alone."

I look at my watch. "Alone?" My stomach drops. He doesn't want me to bring Steve. Does that mean he's going to start the negotiations to give me the team?

"Yes. Your father was very clear that he wanted to meet with only you."

"Okay, I'll leave now," I tell her. "Thank you."

As I gather my things, I send a message to Steve.

Me: I've been called to meet with my dad, and he wants me to come alone. I'm leaving now. I don't know when I'll be back.

Steve: Call me when you get in the car. I've crossed my fingers and toes for you.

I stick my head into Tanya's office. "I'm heading out. My dad wants to meet with me."

Tanya's eyes grow big. "What does he want?"

I shrug. "I don't know, but I'm hoping with every ounce of my being that we're going to meet with lawyers to begin the transition of the team over to me."

Tanya claps her hands. "My fingers are crossed."

I race out of the office and hop in the car. After pulling out of the parking garage, I call Steve.

"What do you think he wants?" Steve asks.

"He's talked to both of us. I hope that means he feels confident that he can start the transition of the team."

"Do you think he'd do that before we got engaged?"

I sigh. "I don't know. My guess is that his requirements are based on his health scare. Maybe since he's doing better, he's ready to relax a little."

"How are you feeling about that?"

"I'm not ready to say goodbye to either of my parents if that's what you're asking."

"I totally understand. I chose sports medicine precisely because I don't lose patients very often. Let's talk about more positive stuff. What will be the first thing you do when you take over the team?"

I know my response immediately. "I would do more at the league level. I've been wanting to work with more big sponsors. You know, Tim Hortons sponsors all the Canadian NHL teams. I want that for the Tigers. I've become friendly with Allison, and I thought I might talk to Henry about Martin Communications. They have the named sponsorship at the NHL arena. The least they could do is run banner ads in the stadium."

He chuckles. "You've convinced me."

"I have a long list of sponsors I'd like to approach, but it would require a committee of owners and marketing teams to make it work for the whole league. Plus, we'd need to get more television time, not only with the Sport Network but even with ESPN in the States."

"I know your dad is going to be so proud of you."

"Thank you. I appreciate you saying that. I really hope that's why he's called me to his home."

"Call me when you're on your way back. I'll be home."

"Steve, I'm so grateful for all your help with this. I…"

"I know. I'm happy to be here to support you."

We disconnect the call, and my palms are sweating. I'm so nervous.

My heart races as I pull up to my father's home. Whatever he says today is going to change my life.

I take a deep breath and step out of my car, smoothing my dress. I ring the bell and wait patiently. Minni must be at school. She's usually out the door the minute my car is in park. When the door opens, I'm surprised to see my father himself. He smiles and steps back to allow me in.

"Where's Laura?"

"I sent her out, and the kids are gone too. That way we can talk freely."

My stomach drops. I don't think I'm getting good news.

Dad's face is grim, and I worry something is wrong. "Elizabeth," he says, his voice slow and serious. "We need to talk."

My heart sinks. I still myself and look into my father's eyes. "What is it, Dad?" I ask, keeping my voice steady.

He directs me to sit with him in the living room. "I don't know what to think about Steve."

A slight twinge of anger wraps itself around the fear in my gut. "I'm doing as you asked. I have a growing relationship with Steve McCormick. I care for him, and we're falling in love. I also have developed friendships beyond Tanya, and I'm getting out more. I do occasionally work late, but that's normal."

He looks at me, and the slight whistle to his breathing fills the room. "I've been thinking about your future with the Vancouver Tigers," he says. "And I've come to a decision."

I hold my breath, waiting for him to continue. Why can't he see that his expectations have nothing to do with my desires and ambitions?

"I'm happy that you and Steve are forming a relationship, and that you're doing as I asked and finding things to do outside of the team."

I nod, silently begging him to hurry and spit out what he wants to tell me.

"Laura and I have been talking. Sharing your life and having a family is more important than a job. We're in an excellent position. The money you have will never require you to work. You can be a wife and mother."

I feel tears building. We haven't made any progress at all. "Dad, I'm not sure I want those things, and if I do, it isn't any time soon. I love my work, and I want that to be part of my life. I shouldn't have to choose one or the other."

He nods. "I know that, but you're a lot like me. You become singularly focused. I'm offering you this because I love you. We think it's time for you to think seriously about your future together."

"Dad, Steve knows nothing of your requirement to get engaged," I lie smoothly. "We're taking this slowly."

My father's face hardens. "I'm changing our deal. I want

to see you married and working toward having a family with Steve McCormick."

The air leaves my lungs. He has officially lost his mind. I desperately want the team, but I know this isn't something Steve wants. It's too much to ask him, and I can't even believe I would consider it. I struggle for something to say.

"Laura and I have always known you'd be the one to take over the Tigers one day," my father continues. "But we believe it's important that you have more than just someone in your life. I propose that in order for you to inherit the Vancouver Tigers, you have to be married and at least working on having children. Only then will you understand all that life is about and be able to manage the team permanently."

My mind is reeling as I try to take in my father's words. He's changed our deal entirely. How dare he use my dreams as a bargaining chip to control my personal life?

"Dad," I protest, my voice rising. "I can't just start a family because you want me to. What about my own dreams, my own ambitions?"

Dad's expression softens slightly, and he reaches out to take my hand. "Elizabeth, I know this isn't what you wanted to hear. But you must trust me. The Tigers are more than a business to me. They're my legacy. And I want that legacy to continue with you. But not only is the team a financial black hole, it can be all-consuming, taking over every aspect of your life. If you and Steve are falling in love, as you say you are, you need to be practical about your future. This shouldn't faze him. Running the team is an enormous responsibility, and I want you to be prepared for it. Trust me, Elizabeth. It's for your own good."

I feel a lump rising in my throat as I look at my father's face. I know he loves me, but I can't help feeling like he's using my love life as a tool to further his own goals. As I look into his eyes, I know I have no choice. He's forced me into a corner, but I'm not going to stay here.

I take a deep breath, trying not to feel my dream slipping

away. "It's your team, and you can do with it what you want. What you're asking from me is too much. I won't sucker Steve into marrying me to get what I want. That's manipulative to him and demeaning to me."

I can see the color rise in Dad's face. He's used to everyone capitulating to him, especially when he thinks he's right, like I know he does now. But he's pushed me too far.

"I'm fully capable of managing the team and being successful without a man to prop me up. I appreciate that you care about me and don't want me to repeat your mistakes, but I'm not you. You don't know what my future holds." I clasp my hands in front of me and pinch the skin between my index finger and thumb to prevent the tears falling. Everything I've worked for, he's dismissed. It's like he doesn't see me at all. "I can't accept your terms."

"Then I'll sell the team to Donnie," he threatens.

I shrug, willing myself to appear nonchalant. "I'm disappointed, but I won't be forced into this. I don't want to end up like you, jumping from one marriage to another. My personal life is mine to manage. No thank you."

Dad doesn't respond to that, and I take it as my cue to leave. I can't keep it together much longer anyway, and there's nothing more to say. My heart is heavy as I make my way back to the car and then back across the bridge to Steve's home. The weight of my father's words bears down on me, trapping me between getting the team and the career I want and asking something unreasonable of me—and of the man I've grown very fond of.

As I pull into the driveway and turn off the engine, I feel no better about the choice I've had to make, though I know it's the right one. I'll just have to talk to Steve and figure out a way to move forward. I have no idea where this leaves us now. I worry it means we're through.

Taking a deep breath, I go inside, and Steve is waiting for me, a smile on his face as he greets me at the door.

"Hey, you," he says, his arms wrapping around me. "I

thought you were going to call me on your way home. Did you tell Tanya the good news before telling me? What did your father say?"

My heart aches. This is all so humiliating. My own father doesn't see me as a competent person. "I think I'm going to need a drink." That's all I can say without bursting into tears.

"Of course," he says. "What would you like?"

"I'd like two fingers of the strongest thing you have "

"That would be the Elijah Craig bourbon. Are you sure you want two fingers?"

I nod. "I'll take it neat."

"It's pretty strong. How about we add ice and a bit of water? This could give you quite the hangover."

I sigh. "That's fine."

Steve looks at me apprehensively as he hands me my drink. "How was the traffic driving back?"

"It wasn't too bad, and it gave me the time I needed to think."

"Please tell me your dad hasn't decided he's going to sell the team to Donnie Cochran."

I look up at the ceiling. "Well, I don't know. But that's not really what we talked about today."

"Well, that's good news. Isn't it?"

"He's changed his requirements for me," I say quietly.

Steve stops mid-sip, and his brow furrows. "What do you mean?"

"It seems he doesn't trust me to manage my own life. Before he will give me the team, now, he says I need to be married and working on children."

Steve's face contorts. "Ohhhh." To his credit, after just a moment, he meets my eyes and reaches for my hand. "I'm so sorry, Eliza. That's not fair to you at all. It's not right."

"It's asking too much. And to give him grandchildren? That's... It feels medieval or something. This isn't who I thought my father was. I don't know if his illness has... I can't..." I take a deep breath and pull myself together. I look up at Steve. "Obviously, this is not even remotely what you agreed to, and it's certainly not something I would ask of you—or of me. From the beginning, my goal has been to satisfy my father without letting him manipulate my life. Maybe that's not possible. He's convinced that this is the best way for me to learn how to run the team."

"And that's ridiculous, because you're running the team already," Steve nearly shouts. "And what will keep him from changing his mind again once you jump through his next hoop?"

"I don't know, but I'm not going to. I'm watching my life's dream slip away." My voice trembles.

Steve runs his fingers through his hair, and suddenly, he's focused. "We'll figure this out," he says, his voice gentle. "We can talk to your father, explain that we're not ready for marriage yet. Maybe we can come up with some kind of compromise."

I nod, grateful for Steve's support, but I know it won't be that simple. My father is stubborn, and he has one hundred percent convinced himself that he's right. This was a mistake from the beginning.

Chapter 28

Steve

"Eliza, I'm so sorry," I tell her. She's staring off into space, seeming despondent. "I can't believe this is happening."

"I know," she replies, shaking her head. "It's too much, and I told him that."

I nod, unsure what else to say. I feel completely unmoored, so I can't imagine what she's feeling.

After a moment, she picks up her glass and downs the rest of the whiskey I poured her. "I think I'm going to lie down," she tells me. "I need to get my head around this."

I feel completely useless, and a little in awe of what it seems she's just done. I'd like to understand better what she thinks is going to happen, but this doesn't seem the time to pepper her with questions.

"I'll leave you alone," I promise, "but please let me know if there's anything you need. I'm happy to talk whenever you're ready."

"Thank you."

Eliza disappears, and I go to take a shower. I think I need time to get my head around this as well. I can't believe her father would ask that of her. I've never wanted to marry. My parents' dysfunctional relationship made it obvious that marriages don't work, even when you go into them with the best intentions. Entering one under false pretenses is a recipe for disaster.

When my shower is complete, there's still no sign of Eliza, so I pace in my bedroom, somehow trying to stay out of her way. It feels wrong to leave her — to go out with friends or something — but she's asked to be alone, and I have to honor that.

I order some takeout and eat in front of the TV, hoping perhaps she'll come join me, but she never appears. Eventually, I go to bed, alone, and spend a restless night wondering what my role is here.

When the sun breaks, I vow to check in with her and encourage her to let me help somehow, even if it's just listening. But when I go to her room, it's empty. The bed is neatly made, probably not even slept in. She must have left at some point last night. But where would she go?

Something like panic grips me as I realize I don't have any idea where she might be. Is her condo at The Butterfly ready? I really hate that she's gone.

It's only when I return to my room that I see a note lying on the floor. My heart races. I pick it up and read with a mix of hope and fear.

> *My dearest Steven,*
>
> *Thank you for the time we've spent together, and thank you for everything you were willing to do to support my dream. I hope you know that I care about you very deeply, and because of that, I won't impose on you any longer. I wish you nothing but the best, always.*

Yours, Eliza

My emotions cycle through me. How could she just leave? Maybe our fake relationship is done, but that doesn't mean there's nothing between us. Or does it?

I sit down heavily on my bed. Without that framework to guide our actions, I realize I have no idea what we are…or how she really feels.

How do I really feel? I've not had to worry much about that, since I had a safe, temporary future with Eliza firmly in place until yesterday. And nothing has changed now that wasn't eventually going to be this way anyway, right? I haven't lost anything because it was never mine in the first place. I'm free. I'm ready to get back out there and have some fun. So why don't I want to?

Instead, I feel empty. I miss Eliza. I need to figure out what that means.

Chapter 29

Eliza

It's been five days since I moved out of Steve's place, and I still feel like I'm barely keeping my head above water. I also feel a little weird that I essentially left in the middle of the night, but I have to be practical at this point. There was no need to continue the charade with him, and once I realized that, I could not stand one more minute of trying to contort my life into looking a certain way to please my father. I'm frustrated that I ever tried in the first place, and I'm determined to change that now.

Anyway, I didn't want Steve to feel any pressure to be something he's not while I was falling apart. In the short time we spent together, I grew to love having him to talk to. But Steve never wants to marry. He's been honest with me from the beginning, and while my feelings for him, against my better judgment, have grown, it doesn't change who he is or what he wants for his life. So my only choice—because I care about him and because I need to move forward on my own terms — was to step away.

And not just from Steve. There's something else I have to do, which is what brings me to Dad's office at the stadium this morning. He's done with his cancer treatments for now, so he's taking a more active role with the team again. Still, he's looking thin and gaunt as I wait for him to finish his call. I sit across from him, listening to what sounds like a conversation about the engineering company he bought last year. My heart is heavy with sadness and resignation. I love him, but I know now what I have to do next, even if it breaks my heart.

Finally, he finishes and puts the phone down, looking up at me. "So, what did you want to meet about? Are you and Steve engaged?" He looks down at my left hand.

Unbelievable. He really does seem to think he can issue commands and that's just how things work. I shake my head. "No, Dad. In fact, we're not together any longer."

"I thought you wanted the team."

"Dad," I say, my voice quiet but firm. "You are not seeing me or hearing me. I do want the team. I have wanted it my whole life, and I have worked hard to make myself ready to handle it effectively. I believe I am ready. But I also have to live with myself. I understand that you want what you think is best for me, but I have to tell you, that isn't your call. I need to make choices I can feel good about, and manipulating the people in my life to fit a mold you've decided is correct doesn't work for me. I won't marry just so I can inherit the team. If I choose to marry, I want to do it once, and I want to marry because I'm in love, not because you require it. The Tigers mean everything to me, but I won't sacrifice my happiness or anyone else's, just to hold on to them."

My father looks at me, his face a mix of surprise and admiration. "Elizabeth, I'm proud of you," he says, his voice thick with emotion. "I know how much the Tigers mean to you, but your integrity and your heart are even more important. It sounds like you're the one who broke up with Steve."

I ignore that. I don't want him to see the heartbreak on my face. "I've moved into a temporary apartment. My condo isn't ready, and I can't stay at Mom's with Antonio living with her. They walk around partially undressed all the time. They're entitled to privacy."

Dad smiles. "I'm sorry you've moved out of Steve's home. Relationships are hard. Your mother put up with a lot from me."

"Yes, she did, and even though you were married, you didn't have balance in your life, so it didn't solve the problem you seem to think getting married will solve for me. Honestly, I don't understand why you think any marriage would last if I'm forced into it."

He looks over at the family picture that doesn't include me. "But I see you here at the stadium all the time. You need a life. I'm sorry you broke it off with Steve. If he's the right man for you, he'll fight for you. And if not, well, okay. We'll sell the team."

I shake my head, my heart aching with the weight of my decision. But I know I've done the right thing. I may want the team, but not at any price. I slide the envelope across the table at him. "Here is my letter of resignation."

My father's eyes widen. It isn't easy to surprise him, but I've just done it. "Why are you resigning?"

"For the same reason I ended things with Steve. I want to run my own life without you dictating the terms. If I'm going to date someone and fall in love, I want it to be because we like each other and want to spend time together. And if you can't accept that I am the best person to run the team, you need to sell it to Donnie Cochran and see what happens then." I can't resist that tiny little barb at the end. Donnie Cochran will be a disaster for the Tigers.

My father crosses his arms. "I have eighteen other companies. Which one are you going to run?"

I cross my arms right back. "None of them. As you pointed out, I have my own money. I don't need to worry about an income, so I don't have to take a job that doesn't interest me. That is all thanks to you, and I am grateful. But I'm going to stick with what I'm passionate about and start my own company. I will build it from the ground up."

"But what about my legacy? If you're doing this so I'll change my mind, know that I won't be doing that."

I shrug. "I guess your legacy is your own concern. I'm not doing this for any reason other than for me and my goals. I've realized the Tigers are your company. You can do with it whatever you want. I'm forever grateful for what you've given to me, not only financial independence but also the introductions to people who can help me with my new adventure."

"What are you going to do?"

"I'm still working on my business plan," I tell him. "Once I have it figured out, I'll let you know."

As I stand and leave my father's office, I feel a sense of relief and freedom. I'm no longer tied to his expectations of my personal life. The Tigers may be what I thought I'd always wanted, but I know there can be something else. I have to pursue my own happiness, wherever it may lead.

I'll always be a Tiger at heart, but I think I'll look back on this as the day my life finally began.

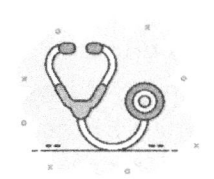

The next day, I don't go in to work, but Tanya and I meet mid-morning at a small café close to the stadium. I've just laid it all out for her—everything, from my dad changing his requirements for our deal and me reevaluating my life to letting Steve know he's not required to do anything for me anymore and resigning yesterday.

She shakes her head. "I can't believe you quit. You've done everything you can to prepare to run the team one day."

I nod. "I know. But my dad's requirements make it impossible. I can't let him run my life, no matter what I've dreamed of."

Tanya nods sympathetically, and I know she understands. "You did the right thing," she adds after a moment.

"I'll miss working with you every day," I tell her. "That's another thing that sucks about this."

"Have you decided what you're going to do?"

"I have a plan to start a sports marketing company. I want to put sponsors and athletes together. The big brands have people who do that, but the mid-sized brands don't. And I can start with Canadian companies, some that are interested in the U.S. market, and I can work with U.S. companies that want more visibility in Canada."

Tanya takes a sip of her tea. "I think that's a great idea. You will excel at this."

I smile. "Thanks. I'm working on attending an event in a couple weeks to help get things started. I've never considered life without the Tigers, but it's time to try, right?"

"What does your mother say?"

"She's a little overwhelmed by all the changes, and she's not thrilled that I might be working more instead of less if I start this new venture. She disagrees with Dad's methods, and she's fine with me not running the Tigers, but she wants me to have a life too. I'm sure she's chewed Dad out, but only because I know her. She'd never tell me that."

"What about Steve? Have you talked to him?"

I take a sip of my tea. "No. I need some space. I tried not to get my heart involved, but he's a great guy, and he did so much for me that of course I did." I pause, putting my head in my hands for a moment. "I miss him, but what we had together wasn't real. I needed him to know he doesn't owe me anything.

He's not a relationship guy, so I don't know where to go from here."

"Are you sure you know how he feels about this? About you?"

I ignore her question. I can't put anything else on my plate right now. I just have to move forward. "What's going on with you and Jun?" I ask, wanting to move past the upheaval in my life for a moment.

"Evidently, he's getting serious with some girl. His parents are going to have a fit. She's a redhead."

"Why do they care about her hair color?"

"She's not Chinese."

I sit back. "Ahh. How do you feel about it?"

Tanya takes another sip of her tea. "I'm actually really glad for him. I hope they'll be happy. And I met a nice guy at the grocery store last week."

"At the grocery store?"

"He was in the produce section, staring at a durian."

My face scrunches up in disgust. Those things smell like raw sewage and rotting flesh. "Why was he thinking about a durian?"

"He likes to be adventurous. He just moved here from Regina."

"So he went to an Asian market to pick up a durian. Is he for real?"

"His interest in durians aside, he works for Amazon as a developer."

I nod slowly. "Okay. And what did you suggest in place of the durian?"

"Dragonfruit."

"Smart move. Much better smelling and tasting. Are you going to go out sometime?"

"We've talked each night, and we're going out on Saturday. I thought I'd give him a tour of the best Chinese restaurants."

"He's in for a treat. How adventurous do you really

think he is? Will you order off the Chinese menu or the English menu?"

"I'm not sure yet," she says.

"Well, I want to hear all about it."

She promises a full report, and then she has to get back to the office. I appreciate her always making time for me, and it's an odd feeling when she runs off and I'm left sitting here with no real place I have to be. I know I need to learn to embrace that, but it just makes me miss Steve. My dad is right about one thing. My life was more fun when I had someone to share it with.

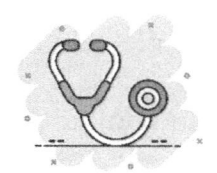

I've been moping a bit, even as I have some percolating excitement about my new business venture, but Tanya refuses to let me wallow too much. She's taken me to dinner and out to coffee this week, and this morning she called again, determined to get me out of the house for Saturday afternoon. I've been furiously working on my new business plan for this event I'm going to with Vince in San Diego next weekend, and now — as Tanya helpfully pointed out — I have just a week to find the perfect dress.

We've already hit the mall, Simon's downtown, and Hudson Bay, and now, we're at a boutique in West Van that Tanya has seen advertised on the society pages.

"Are you going to get together with Vince?" Tanya asks, trying to seem casual as she examines dress after dress on a department store rack of formal wear.

I search through the opposite rack, but I'm not seeing anything I like. I don't want to go too high-end. This event I'm attending is a fundraiser, and I want the people I meet to be interested in doing business with me, not think that I'm doing this as a hobby because of my trust fund.

I roll my eyes. I feel like I've been over this with her before. "Nope, that ship has sailed. Back in the day, he dumped me to date a cheerleader, and he's only interested now because that didn't pan out. This is professional. I've told him about my business idea, and he's agreed to introduce me to some of the Pelicans' sponsors at this fundraiser."

"And what's going on with Steve? I haven't been asking you about that, but I know it's on your mind."

I shake my head. "I haven't really talked to him. He sent me a text the other night, but nothing's changed. I can't stand the thought of him dating someone else, so I don't know how to be friends."

"Have you told him you quit the team?" Tanya surveys the dress in front of her and shakes her head.

"Didn't my dad send a notification to everyone?"

"If he did, I didn't get it."

I look at her, surprised. "Does he think no one's going to notice? Does he think I'm coming back?" I shake my head. I don't know what to make of that, and I don't have the energy to speculate. I guess I should at least let Steve know that. I pick up a black sequined full-length dress. "What about this?"

Tanya shakes her head. "That's something a lounge singer would wear."

I roll my eyes and throw it over my arm because it's a real possibility, no matter what she says. "What time is your date tonight?"

"We're meeting at the restaurant at six." Tanya pulls out a pink silk dress and looks at me.

It's as close as you can get to neon without being neon. I shake my head. "What are you going to do after dinner?"

"What I want to do and what I will do are two different things."

"Meaning?" I pull out a navy silk dress with a boat-neck

collar and put it on my arm. It has some rhinestone bows I'm not sure about, but worth a try.

A saleswoman approaches. "Can I get you a dressing room?"

"Please." She takes the stack of dresses I've collected, leaving me to pick more.

Tanya holds up a dress with a tulle skirt. It looks like I should wear ballet slippers with it. I shake my head.

"I want to take him back to my place and ride him like a pony," she informs me.

I laugh. "What's stopping you?"

"He's a nice guy," she says with a sigh. "A little shy, and he's looking for adventure, but not that kind of adventure."

"Are you sure about that?"

She rolls her eyes. "Well, I like him, and I want to go slow." Tanya pulls out an emerald-green dress. "What about this? It's Pelican color."

I tilt my head. "It may have too much cleavage."

"There's double-sided tape for that."

"What if I sweat? That would be awful."

She giggles. "Then Vince will have something to beat off to later that night."

My jaw drops. "You're feisty today."

She shrugs. "Unless you want him to peel you out of it."

"No. Definitely not."

"Go try it on."

Might as well. I walk back to the changing room. I have eight dresses, and I'm not sure about any of them. I start with the black sequined number, and it's about as basic as you can get. I understand why Tanya called it a lounge-singer dress.

I try on the navy one, but I don't care for the shoulder décor, so I take it off.

Next up is the green silk dress Tanya found. I struggle to figure out which is the front and which is the back, but finally I slip it on. The front dips low, but it's backless and skims the curve of my ass.

"Do any of them work?" Tanya calls.

I open the door and walk out to the mirrors where she's waiting for me. "This one fits…" I pick up the skirt. "But I would need at least a three-inch heel."

"Oh my God." I hear from behind me. I turn to see Paisley and Nadine waving and heading this way.

"You look fantastic," Nadine says, giving me a hug.

"I wish I could wear that dress," Paisley says, making a sizzling sound.

Tanya clears her throat.

"Ladies, this is my best friend, Tanya Wei," I tell them. "And Tanya, this is Paisley and Nadine. They're the wives of two of Steve's closest friends."

They exchange pleasantries, and then Nadine squeezes my arm. "We've missed you," she says. "Where are you going in that dress? Steve's going to love it."

Paisley elbows Nadine.

"Well, Steve and I aren't seeing each other any longer," I explain.

"He told us," Paisley says. "Davis says he's really struggling."

Is he? I manage a smile. "I resigned from the team, so I don't have much chance to see him."

"You quit the Tigers?" Paisley asks.

I nod. "It's not what I wanted, but it was the right thing to do. I'm not sure if Steve told you, but my dad changed the agreement we had in place that was going to allow me to take over the team. He wanted more control of my personal life than I was willing to give up, so I'm going to start my own thing."

"Does Steve know you quit?" Nadine asks.

"I'm not sure. Evidently, my dad hasn't announced it like I expected him to. I needed some space as I reevaluate, so I haven't really been talking with Steve."

"I can't imagine how the Tigers are going to get along without you," Nadine says.

"Well, my dad has an offer from someone to buy the

team. I'm expecting he's going to sell."

"Wow, that's huge," Paisley says.

I nod. I don't know what to say. It's not like I want to rehash this whole mess here outside the dressing room.

"Anyway, where are you going with that stunner of a dress?" Paisley asks.

"I have a friend who works for the San Diego Pelicans, and they have a big fundraiser I'm going to fly down for next weekend. I'm hoping I can jumpstart some work in sports marketing for myself."

Paisley nods. "That sounds like fun."

"I'm so impressed by your strength and resilience," Nadine says. "I may not understand all the details, but I respect and support you no matter what."

"Right? She's a rock star," Tanya jumps in.

I smile at them. "That's very kind of you."

"We need to get together for drinks soon," Paisley suggests. "Whether you're with Steve or not, we can be friends. You too, Tanya."

"I'd love that."

"Me too," Tanya says.

We talk a few minutes more, and Tanya suddenly snaps her fingers. "Wait a minute! You're the famous artist."

Paisley looks like a deer in headlights for a moment, and then she looks around to make sure no one heard Tanya's declaration. "I'm an artist, yes."

Nadine rolls her eyes. "The richest people in the world are on waitlists for her work."

Paisley turns crimson.

"I'm sorry," Tanya says. "I didn't mean to embarrass you. I've never seen any of your work up close."

"Yes, you have," I correct. "Steve has one of her driftwood-dipped-in-silver pieces."

Paisley laughs. "You know, that one caught on fire in the dipping process. I thought I was going to burn the building down."

Tanya lights up. "I should have looked more closely when I was there. Now, I want to go see it."

"I have an art exhibit going up at the gallery that gave me my start early next month," Paisley says. "I'll make sure you're on the list."

"Thank you." Tanya nods. "I'd love that."

As Tanya and I say goodbye to Paisley and Nadine, we agree to see each other soon. I'm still not sure about this green dress, and I may not know what the future holds, but I'm so grateful for the support of my friends. I know I can face whatever comes my way. Eventually, I'll stop missing Steve, right? I'm going to be okay.

Chapter 30

Steve

It's a Saturday night, and I'm sitting at a black-tie fundraiser dinner for the Vancouver Symphony, watching as my friends mingle with their partners, laughing and chatting the night away. I'm the only one of us without a date, and while my friends are doing their best to make me feel included, I'm still the odd man out.

I glance around the room, searching for a familiar face, and that's when I see her—or so I think. For a moment, I could've sworn Eliza was walking toward me, her long hair cascading down her back in loose waves. But as the woman gets closer, I realize it's not her. My heart sinks, and I'm hit with a surge of disappointment. I should have asked Eliza to come with me tonight. Though I'm not sure she would have said yes. She's not responding to my texts and messages, other than to tell me she resigned from the Tigers. I knew she was serious about not letting her dad control her life, and I guess he knows she's serious now too. I hope things work out for her... I don't know what else to do.

I try to shake off the feeling of regret and turn my attention back to my friends, but it's hard to ignore the nagging sensation that I'm missing something — or someone — important.

Over dinner, Paisley and Nadine regale me with the story of running into Eliza at a dress store last weekend. Evidently, she was buying something to wear for a Pelicans fundraiser in San Diego. That's where she is now, and I know exactly who she's there with. Vince Harding was aggressive enough when I was standing right next to her. The thought of Eliza going to an event with him is unbearable, especially when I have no idea what's going on with her.

I know she has to be devastated by what's happened, but I don't know why she's shutting me out. Our relationship wasn't real, but I thought our friendship and connection were. Could I have done something more to support her? Does she think I don't want to be in contact anymore? I truly have no idea, and I don't know how to fix that. I don't even know where she's living, or I'd stop by.

I stew about this a little while longer as the meal concludes and my friends get up to mingle again. I'm completely ignoring everything around me, lost in my own world, and then I realize how different this is. I'm the guy who kept women at arm's length, always. I never needed a date, much less a partner, to feel complete or included. Why is Eliza different?

I look up and see Davis and Paisley laughing together across the room. Then my eye catches on Michael swooping Nadine into some sort of crazy ballroom dance as the orchestra plays. I want that. I miss Eliza. I want her to be part of my life.

I'm in love with her.

Time slows for a moment as that sinks in, but admitting it to myself doesn't scare me as I expected it would. It just seems obvious. She's so strong, so determined, and yet she's playful and fun at the same time. I miss the way her eyes sparkle when she's passionate about something. For a moment, I'm grateful to her dad and his ridiculous plan for her life because I think it gave both of us reason to take a chance on something we never would have otherwise. Now, I just need to show her that that plan has nothing to do with how I've come to feel about her, and I don't need a goal or a fake relationship to have a reason to be with her. For the first time, I want to pursue a relationship just because…it's actually what I want. Eliza is my one and only, and I need to get her back.

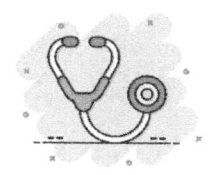

When I wake up the next day, I'm ready to spring into action, but I still have the basic problem of not knowing where Eliza is — probably still in San Diego right now — and no way to get her to communicate with me. This seems like a lot to send in a text. But giving up is not an option, and I have to believe I can show her how much she means to me, to remind her of the connection we have. I'm determined to win her over, no matter what it takes.

I decide to work from the stadium today. I know Eliza resigned from the team, but that means her dad's in charge, and maybe she'll have reason to come by. When I arrive, her office is dark, but then I spot her friend Tanya headed down the hall.

"Tanya!" I call, probably sounding like a crazy person.

She stops and turns back, giving me an odd look. "Are you looking for Eliza?"

"Yes, do you know when she's due back?"

Her brow furrows. "Well, she's not working here anymore."

I nod. "Yes, she told me, but she hasn't told me much of anything else. I don't know how to find her, and she's not returning my calls."

"Why are you calling her?" Tanya asks.

I take a breath. If I say it out loud, there's no taking it back. But deep down, I know I don't want to. "When she gave up on trying to meet her dad's requirements, she ended our relationship. I think she thought she was doing me a favor, but she wasn't." I look Tanya in the eye. "I want to be with her, no matter what. I need her to understand that. Can you help me get in touch with her?"

Tanya smiles, but she still doesn't seem willing to divulge any information.

"I'm in love with her, and I want her in my life. Where can I find her?"

She finally seems satisfied that I'm serious. "She rented a furnished place down on Hastings, but she's still out of town right now." She writes the address down and hands it to me.

"When is she due back?"

"Tonight."

"Thank you."

This paper feels like gold in my hands. I consider going to the airport to try to meet her flight, but the chances of missing her are too great. Instead, I go to her building and wait for her across the street at a coffee shop, my heart pounding with anticipation. After a couple hours, I've had four coffees, and she's still not here. I'm about to give up when a cab finally pulls up, and I see her get out.

Thank God! I race over, desperate to have her in my life again. "Hi," I say as I approach her on the sidewalk.

She jumps and hurries toward the door until she recognizes me. "Steve? What are you doing here?"

"I miss you," I blurt, the words tumbling out of my mouth. "I don't like it that you've erased yourself from my life."

Her eyes search my face, and I can tell she's unsure.

"Could we just talk about this for a minute? Please?" I

beg.

She pulls her bag up farther on her shoulder. "Come on," she says. "Follow me."

She leads me inside and into the elevator. "What is it you want?" she asks. She looks tired. It's not a jetlag tired, but more a long-term exhaustion.

I take a deep breath. "I miss you. I understand that you don't need me as your fake boyfriend anymore, but do you not need me at all? Don't we have something real underneath all the other stuff? I am in awe of your strength and determination, and I'm so proud of you for taking a stand against your father. But do you have to throw all of this away? My house is empty without you. I can smell your shampoo and perfume on my pillows. Watching TSN isn't the same without you yelling at the sportscasters when they oversimplify things."

The elevator doors open at her floor, and she walks out. I'm left to follow her down the hall like a lost puppy, which I am.

She waves a key fob over the door, and we walk into a utilitarian apartment. The view is beautiful as it looks at the bright yellow piles of sulfur across Coal Harbor on the north shore.

"Look, I want us to be friends, but I don't know how to do that right—" she starts.

"Why not?" I yell in frustration. I take a moment to collect myself. "I know your life must feel turned upside down. But just like you decided what your dad wants doesn't matter anymore, I've decided that too. I want to be with you, and not because I'm helping you reach a goal. Just because I want to. And I don't want to date anyone else. I should make that clear. I want to date you. Let's start over and see where we end up."

She was staring out the window, but now, her eyes are riveted to mine. "What?"

Can she really have had no idea how I felt? "No matter why we started doing this, I really enjoy hanging out with you, and I'd like to see where this goes. That's not usually how I feel about women I spend time with, but I can't get you out of my mind. I want to date you."

"Dating?" She looks a little shellshocked.

"Well, that was my thought until I realized where you're living. This neighborhood has not quite made it. Maybe you can move back into my guest room, and we'll date from there."

She shakes her head and crosses her arms, but something in her eyes is different now. "The building is safe, and I have parking, so I drive to work. It's fine."

"I'm not going to argue about where you live," I tell her, sensing victory. "We should argue about where we're going to dinner."

She finally smiles. "Do you mind if we order in? I've been flying today, and I'm tired."

"We can do whatever you'd like."

Chapter 31

Eliza

Just a few days later as Steve and I walk into my mother's home, nerves wash over me, though they're a different sort than I would have expected. This is the first time Mom is meeting Steve, and I just really want her to like him, not because I need her approval or because it's part of any kind of plan, but just because.

Her apartment is dark. I look around, confused. "I spoke with her this afternoon. I know I didn't get the time wrong." I look in the kitchen, and there isn't anything prepared, but Mom is more likely to have something delivered anyway.

"Mom?" I yell into her apartment.

I hear some rustling, and it takes a few minutes, but Mom finally comes out in a silk bathrobe. "Sorry, sweetheart. The afternoon got away from us."

I roll my eyes, and I'm a little grossed out because I can absolutely tell that we interrupted Antonio and Mom's afternoon delight. "Would you like us to come back or meet you somewhere later?"

She waves that away. "Nonsense. I'm sure, sometime, I'll do the same to you." Her eyes twinkle. She rushes over and pulls me into a hug. "Who is this handsome devil you've brought with you?"

She really is too much. "Mom, I'd like you to meet Steve McCormick."

"You're the one who stole my little girl's heart. I'm so happy to meet you." She surrounds Steve in a hug as well.

And yes, she's only wearing a bathrobe.

"Steve, this is my mother, Nicolette."

She ushers us into her living room, and Antonio joins us, wearing jeans and a disheveled T-shirt.

"Mom, feel free to go get dressed," I say, more direction than suggestion.

"I don't know how you ended up so puritanical. Your father and I—"

I hold up my hand as I interrupt her. "I don't want to know about you and Dad. Please get dressed."

I introduce Antonio and Steve. Antonio nods at Steve and once again picks up my hand to kiss my knuckles. It gives me shivers, and I can tell Steve is not happy.

Antonio flips on the television, and I leave him and Steve to discuss the nuances of soccer and football as I go in search of Mom. I find her wearing a maxi dress and brushing her hair in her bedroom.

"Have you already ordered dinner?" I ask.

"Not yet. I figured we could decide what we want together. What are you thinking?"

"Steve and I are pretty easy to please on that front."

"How about Moroccan? Greek?"

"I'm sure either would be just fine."

"Steve's very handsome."

I nod. "Agreed. He doesn't have a hard time picking up women."

She looks at me with her brow raised.

"I'm just trying to keep my expectations under control."

She stops brushing her hair. "I thought you were getting serious."

"We are, but there's a little voice in the back of my head that reminds me we started as a one-night stand. This isn't anything I was expecting, so it's still hard to wrap my mind around sometimes."

"Some men are meant to be placeholders until the next one comes along. Only you can decide if Steve is the one who's going to stick around."

"Well, if he's going to sleep with other women, that's his decision not mine."

"I see how he looks at you. Trust me. It's up to you."

We walk back out, and the guys have decided on paella from a Spanish restaurant not too far from here.

Mom sits so close to Antonio she's practically on his lap. "That is perfect."

Mom and Antonio are engrossed in one another, their eyes sparkling with joy. I look at Steve and roll my eyes. He puts his arm around me and kisses my temple.

We make small talk while we wait for dinner. "What kind of work do you do?" I ask Antonio.

"I am a sculptor. I saw your mother wandering the town I was visiting, and I wanted to create her in marble. I spent many hours drawing her, and that led to many hours of making love."

"Wow. That's really great," I say, not sure of the appropriate response to that.

"I love a woman's body—the roundness of her hips and the fullness of her breasts." Antonio looks at me carefully. "I would love to sculpt you too."

"Not a chance," Steve says before I can respond.

Thankfully, the buzzer sounds.

"Steve, can you help me get the food downstairs?" I ask.

"I'd love to."

When we get in the elevator, Steve turns to me. "That guy is a little creepy."

"He seems like he's into my mom, and he makes her happy. That's all that matters."

Steve harrumphs.

When we return to Mom's with the huge bag of food, the table is set, and Antonio is pouring wine into Mom's glass as she sits at the table.

Antonio rushes over to pull out a chair for me, and Steve gives him a questioning look. "I've got this," Steve assures him.

"So, how did you two meet?" Mom asks as we distribute the food.

"We met at a Tigers party," Steve says. "Eliza was wearing this stunning red dress, and I couldn't take my eyes off of her. I didn't want to spend any time with anyone else but her that night."

I look at Steve with surprise. "I had no idea."

"Of course he did. You're a beautiful woman," Antonio says. "Just like your mother."

Mom reaches for his thigh, and I'm about ready to gag when Steve turns and looks at me with a silly grin. Once everyone is eating, the conversation flows easily.

Throughout the evening, Antonio keeps touching my mother, his gaze always lingering on hers for just a moment too long. I try to ignore them, but it's a constant reminder of their age difference.

Mom flirts with Steve, and it should bother me, but it doesn't. That's just her way, and I know she's happy that she's found love with Antonio.

After dinner, when we stand to say our goodbyes, Mom pulls me aside. "Steve's a real catch."

I look over at him, again talking to Antonio about soccer, and I smile. "I think so too."

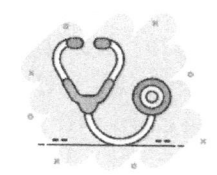

I change my sweater for the third time.

"You look great in dark green. Why are you changing? What you wore to your mom's this morning would be fine for tonight."

"Because I wore that to dinner at Paisley and Davis's house before. I can't wear the same thing twice," I explain as if he's a small child.

Steve rolls his eyes. "The gallery opening is in less than an hour, and we need to leave to get there on time."

I stop looking through my clothes. "Has something changed?"

"What do you mean?"

"We have a rideshare arriving at six thirty. It'll drop us off at the Aquabus, which will shuttle us across False Creek. We'll be there before the gallery even opens. The opening is invite only, so it's not like they won't let us in."

"I don't like being late."

I step in close. "Dr. McCormick, this is a side of you I've never seen before. Why are you so worried?"

"I want the good scotch tonight."

"Okay, I'll be ready. I promise. Go downstairs and wrap up the bouquet. I'll be right there."

Steve leaves, and I turn back to the closet. I should have bought something new. If the gallery gets too crowded, I could get hot. I don't want to get all shiny. I reach for a light green sweater set. It's conservative, and if I get too hot, I can take the outer layer off. I run lip gloss over my lips, and as I start down the stairs, I hear Steve call, "The rideshare is here."

I look at my watch. "It's early, and I'm on time."

We get in the back of the Subaru wagon, and we're off to the Aquabus. Granville Island is on the other side of False Creek, so rather than struggle with the traffic over a bridge and fight to get parking, we're doing this. I love it.

Steve still seems nervous. I've never seen him like this before.

When we arrive at the Aquabus, Nadine and Michael are getting out of their own rideshare.

"Great minds think alike," Michael announces. He wraps his arms around me. "If you get to the point that you want Nadine or me to distract him so you can get away, just let us know."

I smile and look at Steve. "He was very stressed about arriving on time."

Nadine links her arm with mine. "That's because within the first half hour, everything Paisley has on display will be sold."

I look at Steve. "Why didn't you tell me that?"

He turns a great shade of crimson and shrugs.

"I'm so glad you two are back together," Nadine whispers. Then she freezes. "You are back together, aren't you?"

I smile. "We are. For real this time."

"You two belong together," she says.

The trip across False Creek is less than ten minutes, and then we walk to the gallery. I adore Granville Island. It is an artists' enclave, so besides some hipster restaurants, there are shops that sell all sorts of art. My favorite is the washed wool boutique. She has the most beautiful sweaters and coats. I also love the jewelry sellers.

Steve laces his fingers with mine as we walk.

"What are you looking for this evening?" I ask.

"I don't know. Before long I won't be able to afford her work, so the group of us have been buying whatever strikes our fancy, knowing it's a great investment."

When we arrive, there's a line, and Tanya is already here

with her new boyfriend, Beau Compton. We take our places behind them, and Beau seems to get along well with Steve and his friends as we wait for the gallery to open.

When the doors open, we're checked in one couple at a time. When we get to the front, Steve gives the woman his name. She looks at the list. "I'm sorry. I don't have you down."

"What?" Steve says. "There must be some kind of mistake. McCormick—M-C-C-O-R-M-I-C-K."

She shakes her head. "I'm sorry. This is by invite only, and we're at capacity."

What could be happening? Steve and I step out of line.

Michael and Nadine step forward as Steve types frantically on his phone.

"Don't worry about it. There's a great brewery right around the corner," I suggest.

"I have a Nadine Khalili and a plus one," the woman announces into her walkie-talkie. She steps aside and lets them pass.

I think for a minute. "By chance do you have a reservation for Elizabeth or Eliza Rourke?"

Impatiently, she looks at her list. "Yes, I do have you, and a plus one."

I smile and grab Steve by the hand. "Come on. You're my guest tonight."

He rolls his eyes. "I'm going to kill Davis. I know that he did that on purpose."

I stop just as we get inside. The only light in the room comes from small pendant lamps and lights on the artwork. It takes my breath away.

Steve points to a watercolor of the Lions Gate Bridge. "What do you think?"

"I love it."

He walks over to the woman behind the desk. "I'd like the Lions Gate Bridge painting."

He plops down his credit card, and we continue to look. As she's getting the sale registered and paid for, two other people come up to ask about the painting. "I need to get the red dot on the card," she murmurs.

Nadine walks up. "We got a piece for Michael's parents for Christmas. After all they do for us, it's the least we can do."

Michael nods. "I like this one better than mine."

Allison joins the line to buy a piece and gives me a hug. "I was hoping I'd see you tonight. You saved my bacon. Since you couldn't go, I took Julia and Paisley with me to look at the MacLean Museum, and it was fantastic. With a generous donation, we'll be the first event hosted there, and we'll have the entire grounds to ourselves. Paisley did have to promise a piece for them to display when the museum opens though."

"I'm so glad! I love the drawings I saw of those gardens. I can't wait to see photos."

"Well, you'll be with us for the rehearsal dinner and wedding."

"I will?"

"Steve is one of Henry's groomsmen, so of course."

I hug her again. "I can't wait."

I'm thrilled to be here. I truly enjoy Steve's friends, and they've been so welcoming to me and supportive of our relationship.

After the gallery opening, the party moves upstairs to Paisley's loft space. She's invited only a small group of us to stay.

"Congratulations," Nadine tells her. "I heard someone complain that they arrived thirty minutes after the event opened, and there was nothing left to buy."

Paisley blushes. "I am the luckiest woman alive."

"I agree," Davis says. "You married me."

That leads us down a rabbit hole of weddings, and already Steve's friends want to know when we're going to get engaged.

I finally hold up my hand. "We've just begun dating again."

"We're just happy for you," Julia Martin says. "I saw

your mother the other day, and she seemed in good spirits."

"She's returned from Italy with a man younger than me," I tell her. "He seems to make her very happy."

"I think that's great," Julia gushes. "What do they call it when the woman is older than the man?"

"She's a cougar, I think?" Davis offers.

"I thought she was a MILF," Julia says.

Henry spits his drink, spraying us. "I'm so sorry," he says, coughing and cleaning us up.

"Mom, do you know what a MILF is?" Henry finally asks.

"Of course, I do. I watch television."

I really like Julia.

Chapter 32

Eliza

Two months later.

As Tanya and I make our way toward the stadium in Montreal, the excitement in the air is palpable. It's the Grey Cup, the biggest sporting event of the year, and I am lucky enough to be in attendance. More than that, the Tigers are lucky enough to be playing today.

Somehow, they ended the season with a winning record. Getting rid of the bad seeds made a real difference, and getting Hudson off the injured list helped as well. They came together to win their bracket and have surprised everyone by getting all the way here. Even before entering the stadium, I'm greeted by a sea of fans decked out in Tiger team colors, eagerly anticipating the day's festivities.

I've missed being at the stadium and overseeing all this

excitement, but I know it's what's right for me right now. Instead, I've spent the last couple of months working on my business plan and talking to a contact Vince connected me with who has given me a lot of great information. I'm excited about the possibilities for my marketing venture, and I even met with Dad last week to talk about it. He still doesn't fully grasp why I'm upset with him and why I've made this choice, but he's encouraging of my new venture and had some good ideas about how to get the CFL to buy into my ideas.

And Steve and I are finding our way as an actual couple, which is still amazing to me. I haven't seen him since the team left on Wednesday to go to Montreal, and I'm missing him. They've been practicing there all week.

As I enter the stadium, vendors walk around selling all sorts of Grey Cup merchandise, from hats and shirts to commemorative programs and souvenirs. The smell of popcorn and hot dogs fills the air, tempting me to indulge in some game-day snacks.

As I walk farther into the stadium, I'm a bit awed by the sheer size and grandeur of it all. Giant screens run highlights from past Grey Cups, and banners and flags of the competing teams hang from the rafters. Everywhere I look, there are signs of the pomp and circumstance that surround this grand event.

In the concourse, there are interactive exhibits and games set up for fans to enjoy. They even offer a chance to take a picture with the Grey Cup, the ultimate prize on this day.

I reach our box in time to watch as the Tigers and the Toronto Pirates warm up on the field below. I haven't been to a Tigers game since I resigned, and I've missed this.

Sandy Thompson, the owner of the Regina Royals, comes to stand next to me. "You did a great job with the team this year."

Warmth washes over me from his compliment. Sandy owns the most profitable franchise in the league. I smile and thank him. "I was only doing it while my dad was recovering."

"He's told all of us how much work you put into this."

"Thank you."

"He also mentioned that you've started a marketing company. Maybe in a few weeks we can meet up and talk about what you're doing."

I nod. "That would be great. I'm using my experience with the NFL to put some ideas together."

"I'm definitely interested."

I grin as we shake hands. If I can win Sandy over, the rest of the league will follow.

I return my attention to the field, where Marty Holloway leads the Tigers through their warmups. I know I should want the Tigers to win, but I really don't care. They made it to the Grey Cup, and I am thrilled with that.

Suddenly, there's a commotion on the field. Marty Holloway is on the ground, clutching his head in pain. Dread washes over me as he's helped up by Steve and the medical team. Even from the owners' box, I can see the concern etched on Steve's face as he examines the quarterback.

A golf cart drives onto the field, and they load Marty up and drive into the tunnels toward the locker room. My heart sinks. I'm okay if they don't win, but not if they get hammered today. I want them to have what they need to play their best.

I turn to go down to the locker room, and I'm stopped by two other owners on the way. They also want to hear about my new endeavor, and I promise to contact them in the coming weeks.

When I get downstairs, I can hear Marty arguing. "Doc, really I'm okay," he insists. "There's no concussion."

"Look at the light," someone tells him. That's not Steve's voice.

I come around the corner into the crowded room. Dad is there with Steve and the team neurologist, Dr. Gregori. Steve smiles at me, and my heart races.

"His eyes are not dilated, and all signs indicate that he can start the game," Dr. Gregori announces. "But if he takes another hit like that, we'll most likely need to pull him."

"Doc, I've worked my whole life for today," Marty says. "This is my dream to be here and take that trophy back to Vancouver. I want this. I know concussions are serious, but I was mostly just stunned to be knocked down in the warmup. I'm okay. I promise."

The weight of his words settles over me. Head injuries are dangerous, and the thought of anyone—even Marty himself—putting winning ahead of the care of our players as human beings fills me with anxiety.

After some additional examinations, they finally agree to let Marty start the game. He runs back out to the field with Steve and Dr. Gregori on his tail.

I turn to Dad. "I talked to Sandy and a few of the other owners upstairs. Thank you for putting in a good word for me."

Dad looks at me with warmth in his eyes. "I've only wanted what's best for you. You don't have to own a team to be influential in the league."

The subject is still sore. "I know."

After a few minutes, warmups are finished, and the team returns to the locker room. They're letting people into the stands now, and the intensity is only going to rise around here. In fact, I can hear the pre-game entertainment getting started. It sounds like a marching band is playing in the end zone, and the cheerleaders are pumping up the crowd.

Looking around the locker room, I'm relieved to see nothing but a great group of players. Coach Roy has done a good job rebuilding and resetting with the season already underway. It's too bad that we got off to such a rough start.

"Any word from Charles about how those difficult players made it onto our roster earlier this season?"

Dad nods, though his attention is already being pulled elsewhere. "It's not quite concluded, but we should talk. I think he'll be ready soon."

Coach Roy gathers the team. "I'm so proud of all of you. When a reporter asks you, who are the Vancouver Tigers? You don't say we're the team with the guy who had twelve sacks in a single game. You don't say we're the team with the guy who has fifteen-thousand yards rushing. You don't say we were the worst team in the first half of the season. You tell them we are the toughest, smartest, and best team in this league. We were eight and two going into Labor Day weekend, and we haven't looked back. You've gelled as a team, and you make me very proud to be your coach. I want you to go out there today and play hard, play fair, and show Canada why we invented football, and why it should be the country's number one sport. Right, guys?"

There's a lot of clapping and excitement, and my heart swells. This team has exceeded what I thought was possible for them. Dad steps back and signals me to follow him as he heads back to the elevator and our box.

"Why don't you and Steve come over for dinner this week?" he suggests.

I look at him, eyes narrowed. I'm never sure of his angle these days. "I'll have to check Steve's schedule. I believe it's changing as he transitions back to the hospital and his practice."

He shrugs. "We'll work around you."

I nod and decide to leave it at that. Maybe it's really just an invitation to spend time together.

As the game begins, conversation flows more easily for my father and me. This is our common ground. It always has been. It's been a long time since we've had a chance to catch up, and the excitement of the game makes it even more special. We strategize about the team's performance, the strengths and weaknesses of the players, and the techniques Coach Roy has been using to lead the team to success.

Then the topic shifts to the health of the players, and in particular, the importance of having top-notch medical staff to keep them safe on the field.

"I think we need to keep Steve as the chief medical officer," I say, my voice quiet but firm. "You need someone who is assessing the players as a whole. Obviously, we should keep Dr. Gregori on staff as a neurologist, but you should be prepared to argue with the league if they have a problem with it. We can't afford to take any chances with the players' health."

My father nods an agreement, a thoughtful expression on his face. "I couldn't agree more," he says. "We need to do everything we can to make sure the players are safe. No one's career is worth more than their health."

As we turn our attention back to the game, I feel a sense of satisfaction. It's good to know we're doing everything we can to support the team, both on and off the field. The Pirates score first, but the Tigers answer quickly, and it seems like they're going to keep it interesting. Regardless of who wins, the Tigers are playing with skill and determination, and I can't help but feel a sense of hope for the future, both in this game and beyond.

Chapter 33

Steve

From the moment of kickoff, this game has been intense, with both teams fiercely battling for every yard. Neither side has been able to gain a decisive advantage. That seems to be the norm for a Grey Cup match, and at halftime, the game is a nail biter with the score tied.

I finally make it up to the owners' box for the second half. I kiss Eliza on the cheek, and she wraps her arms around my waist. We're too anxious to sit in our seats and instead stand near the window as the second half gets underway.

The Pirates come out firing on all cylinders. They immediately score another touchdown, giving them a fourteen-to-seven lead. The crowd is on their feet, cheering. But the Tigers are not going down without a fight. They mount a furious comeback, scoring a touchdown of their own to tie the game once again. The tension in the stadium is palpable as fans of both teams nervously watch the clock tick down.

With just seconds left, the Tigers kick a field goal, taking a three-point lead. The Pirates have one last chance to win the game.

Eliza stands with her hands together as if in prayer, her eyes tracking every movement on the field. The Pirates drive the ball hard, and in three plays, they score the winning touchdown.

The final whistle blows, and the Pirates erupt in celebration. It was a hard-fought game, but in the end, the Pirates emerged victorious, winning the championship by four measly points.

"It wasn't a blowout, and given how the team started this year, they should be very proud of themselves," Eliza says, probably more to herself than me.

I give her a squeeze. "I agree, but let's not be too forgiving until maybe tomorrow. Let them stew and plan their revenge for next year."

We watch the ceremony on the field as the Pirates get the Grey Cup. Tom whispers something in Eliza's ear and she nods. "Steve and I will be there."

I look at her expectantly.

"Dad says Charles has an update. Would you like to join me when I meet with him?"

I nod. "Of course. But I have some things to do down in the locker room."

"That's fine. We'll meet later this afternoon. I want to go down and talk to Coach Roy and tell him how impressed I am."

"He may need to hear that today." I wink at her.

It takes nearly two hours to get everything done, including the press conferences, and then we have to deal with traffic to get back to our hotel.

"Did you at least have fun this weekend?" I ask as we take what feels like the longest elevator ride ever.

Eliza nods enthusiastically. "I did. I'm glad we were here together."

I kiss her softly. "Me too."

When Eliza knocks on her father's hotel suite door, Laura opens it with Minni and Logan right behind her. They look like they're heading out.

Eliza peels Minni from her leg. "Where are you going?"

"We're going to a play park that has lots of slides and trampolines," Minni says, bouncing up and down.

"They have a lot of energy, and I plan on running it out of them so we can sleep tonight," Laura explains.

Eliza hugs her. "Good luck."

As they step out, we move into the living room area. Tom is sitting in a leather chair with a drink in his hand. Charles is standing, looking out the window at the Montreal skyline.

"You brought Steve," Tom states.

"As I told you I would," Eliza replies. "He was part of this when we first talked to Charles, and he has insight into the team."

Charles hands each of us a stack of papers that have been bound together. "We found four issues at least loosely related to the three players added to the roster erroneously, and each of them impeded the team's success this year."

Eliza gasps. "Four?"

Charles nods. "We believe that there were games thrown to guarantee losses, you had a doping scandal, and there were issues with your travel and leaks to the press."

I have so many questions, but I sit back and listen.

"Can you break this down?" Tom asks.

"First, the losses. We found a money trail to Sean Rhymes. After each loss, he received a deposit of fifty-thousand dollars."

"What?" Eliza screeches. "Where did the money come from?"

"An offshore account."

"Do you know who sent it?" Tom asks.

"We do," Charles says. "But I'd like to go through everything first. Can you hold that thought?"

Tom nods and takes a sip of his drink.

"Sean Rhymes often fumbled catches he should have completed. Granted, these issues could have been legitimate, but the payments seem to indicate otherwise."

"But we continued to lose after he left," I point out.

Charles smiles. "We did. The other part of bringing on those three was to impact team morale, and that continued to contribute to the losses."

"Why would anyone do this?" Eliza asks, shaking her head.

"Then we had a doping scandal." Charles turns to look at me. "You were a suspect, Dr. McCormick."

I sit up straight. "I was? Why?"

"You were the only one who had control of the samples. But you pushed for a retest at an independent lab before it got out to the press, which then removed you from our list."

That's good news, I think. "Where did the money land on that one?" I ask.

"That was the hardest to find," Charles cautions. "But we did find it. More on that in a minute." He flips to the next page. "Travel was greatly disrupted this year."

"How did I not realize that?" Eliza questions.

"Because the team has a strong travel coordinator who had contingencies upon contingencies. But we found that there were buses canceled and a four-hours-late departure because the plane didn't get fueled like it was supposed to."

I remember that one. "That was a tight arrival," I point out. "We ended up getting to Yellowknife at midnight. Didn't make for easy going the next morning. At least we still won."

"It was the semi-final game," Tom adds, looking at Eliza.

She nods understanding. She'd quit the team by then.

"The head of travel got a ten-thousand-dollar kickback each time the team had a transportation problem, with the money coming from the same off-shore account."

Tom clears his throat. "And the leaks?"

"Rumors are normal when a team is struggling," Charles begins. "But because we found the offshore account, we were able to identify deposits that seemed to coincide with the drama going on within the team."

We all look at Charles expectantly.

"We were watching the entire team—the coaching staff, front office staff, and all the trainers and therapists, and anyone else associated."

"Including me?" Eliza asks.

"Yes, and your father."

Tom raises a brow. Charles ignores him.

"Assistant Coach Jimmy Majors was the person behind the leaks," Charles announces.

"That's a violation of his contract," Dad announces. "He'll be fired immediately."

"Why would he take money to destroy the team?" Eliza asks.

Charles looks out at the sun setting behind the Notre-Dame Basilica. "We believe he was promised the job as head coach."

"He wouldn't be my first choice," Tom says.

"I don't believe that's a concern for him." Charles begins to pace. "The offshore account was hidden behind over a dozen shell companies from around the world. The payments totaled nearly a half million dollars."

"Who's so angry at me that they'd spend that kind of money to torpedo my team?" Tom asks. "It isn't another owner. We respect each other too much for that."

Charles nods. "It was not any of the other owners, but we looked for that. With some finagling, we traced the offshore account back to Cochran Limited."

Tom sets his drink heavily on the table.

"No wonder he was holding out for the Tigers, despite the other two teams for sale," Eliza says. "He'd invested money. But what value would the team have for him if he gutted it in the process?"

The corners of Charles' mouth turn up. "One might estimate that the half million he spent would reduce the value of the team by more than five million. The contract he submitted stated he could revalue the team before purchase. That's very common, so it was overlooked."

Tom laughs. "If it had worked, it would have been a good investment."

"True. But he didn't expect that Elizabeth would be working for the team this year, and she probably brought me in much earlier than you would have—if at all."

"I would have brought you in sooner if I hadn't been out of commission," Tom retorts.

"Donnie Cochran set this plan in motion before he made an offer on the team," Charles says. "He made initial payments to five members of the Tigers' staff."

"They're all fired," Tom rants. "I want security to lock them out of the practice space and the offices. I will not tolerate this kind of behavior."

Eliza holds up her hand, and Charles looks at her. "But how did he get Rhymes, Pelletier, and Cotton on the team?"

"The push for them came from Coach Roy's email."

"Is he one of the five?" Eliza asks. "Is he involved too?"

"We don't think so. We found a copy of the email on the server, but it had been deleted from his sent box. Our theory is that Jimmy Majors snuck into his office, sent it, and then deleted the send notice."

"Why don't you think it was Coach Roy?" I ask.

"Because Roy would be fired. Why would anyone sink their career like that?" Charles replies.

Tom still looks shellshocked.

"What are the next steps?" Eliza asks.

"We'll turn over the espionage evidence to the police, and I expect they will pursue this under federal racketeering laws. People will go to jail. We have proof of who was involved, so we should terminate everyone who received payments. We'll also notify the league so they're aware of what happened. The report you're looking at is ready for their eyes. It doesn't mention anyone who is not involved—so none of our research is included."

"This is going to make the papers," Eliza says. "We should also engage our public relations team and possibly a crisis public relations team."

"I'm not going to sell the team," Tom announces suddenly. "I told Elizabeth she could have the team if she married and had kids. I'll plan on holding on to it until then."

Eliza looks at him. "What if my sports marketing company is so successful that I don't want the team? What if I don't want to be part of any agreement that puts demands on my personal life? I know you love me, but my life is mine. I need you to see that."

Tom is quiet a moment, looking steadily at Eliza. "If you don't want it, I'll sell it to someone else when the time is right. But for now, I want you to go and succeed with your own company. That will bring value to the league. I have no problem championing you and your skills. And if you never decide to marry and have kids, my will will grant you the ability to manage the team however you please once I'm gone."

Eliza's shoulders fall. "You know, you could have saved me a lot of heartache if you'd said that at the beginning."

He shrugs. "I love you, and I know you don't agree with my methods, but I'm pleased with the progress you've made. I'm enjoying you having a life outside of your work, and I think you are as well."

Chapter 34

Steve

I wake up early on the day we're leaving for Belize too excited to sleep any longer. This trip is going to be monumental for Eliza and me.

Her condo at The Butterfly is finally complete now, and she's moved in. We've spent most every night together at one place or the other in the two months since the Grey Cup, but I'm looking forward to being alone with Eliza, all on our own and without any football-related agenda.

I get out of bed and head to the kitchen to make coffee and boil water for Eliza's tea. As I wait, I glance at the suitcases sitting by the door. They're packed and ready, filled with everything we need for our week-long vacation. We've been planning this trip for weeks, and I have been secretly planning my proposal for just as long.

I want Eliza to be rested and ready for the long day of travel ahead of us, so I sip my coffee and try to relax as I wait for her to wake.

This is a shorter trip than I wanted, but with football done for now, I'm back to spending one hundred percent of my time working at my orthopedic practice and doing surgery at Mercy Hospital. My patients have waited for me, and things are busy.

"Good morning," Eliza says, wrapping her arms around my waist from behind. "How long have you been up?"

"I didn't sleep well last night. I kept dreaming we were going to miss the rideshare."

"Did I snore and keep you up?" she asks.

She did snore, but I don't care. She's even beautiful when she snores. "Nope. I'm just ready for some sunny, warm weather."

"Me too." She stretches, exposing her midriff, and suddenly, I'm not worried about the rideshare at all. I'd like to take her right back upstairs.

She looks over at the clock. "Can you believe that by dinner time we'll be on the beach in Belize?"

I pull her close. "I wouldn't care if we were going to see the polar bears in the Artic Circle."

Her eyes light up. "We totally need to do that. I've seen these monster vans that drive around on stilt things, and the polar bears can look you in the eye."

"That does sound fun, maybe we'll do that next."

She nods. "The car arrives in forty-five minutes. I'll be ready."

I doctor her tea the way she likes it and send her on her way. When I hear the shower running, I pull out the engagement ring I bought her. It's a four-carat oval solitaire with a platinum eternity band. The wedding band will match. It's elegant, just like she is. I tuck it into the bag that won't be out of my sight.

The rideshare arrives on time, and Eliza is almost giddy. She's been looking forward to this trip as much as I have. The ride across town is as expected, and we get our bags checked and we're through security without a hitch. Once we've boarded the plane, I breathe a little easier, though as we take off, my nerves begin to build. I can't believe I'm actually doing this.

While we wait for them to close the doors, I look at my phone. It's littered with text messages from the guys.

Davis: Have a great time on your much needed vacation.

Michael: Where are you staying? Nadine and I were thinking of coming down.

Jack: Normally, I'd tell you not to do what you're planning, but Eliza is perfect for you, and you're perfect for her. Let us know when you do it.

Davis: Yes! And we'll plan a celebration at your house when you get back.

Michael: Sounds fun. And if she says no, we'll be there to hold your hand.
Michael: This is Nadine. She's not going to decline. Good luck, and I'm going for a walk and leaving Michael with the twins. Ignore all posts from him for the next three hours.

Michael: She's going on a three-hour walk? What did I do?

I smile. I love my friends. They're generous to a fault and support me in every way.

"What are the guys up to today?" Eliza asks.

I quickly close the message program. "Sounds like Nadine is leaving the twins with Michael for a few hours."

Eliza laughs. "She's a sneaky one, that's for sure."

We snuggle up and the flight is long, but we have plenty of distractions to keep us occupied. We watch movies, listen to music, and play plenty of cribbage. Eliza kills me every time.

When we finally arrive in Belize, the heat and humidity slap us in the face as soon as the door to the plane opens. This is the most temperate time to visit, but it's still a lot different from the cool rain and gray skies at home.

We collect our bags and make our way to the car that will take us to our resort. Along the way, we pass palm trees and vibrant flowers, and we can smell the salt water of the Pacific. The driver talks the entire way, telling us all about the places he can take us and the things we can do. We nod along. That might work later in the week, but initially, I want nothing more than to relax with Eliza by the pool or in our bed.

The resort is even more beautiful than I had imagined. We're greeted with cold rum punch and smiling faces, and we're shown quickly to our room. It's spacious and modern, with a balcony that overlooks the ocean. Eliza is thrilled, and I know this is going to be a week we will never forget.

Over the next few days, we explore Belize. We go snorkeling in the crystal-clear waters, hike through the jungle, and visit ancient ruins. We eat delicious food and drink tropical cocktails, and we laugh and talk like we always do.

But the whole time, I'm carrying a secret. I keep the ring with me at all times, tucked away in my pocket. Every moment feels like it's the right moment, and yet none of them do. I don't want to rush or force it, so I wait, not so patiently, for the perfect time.

And then, on the fourth day of our trip, it arrives. We're sitting on the beach, watching the sunset. The sky is a riot of oranges and pinks, and the ocean is calm and peaceful. Eliza leans her head on my shoulder, and I can feel her warmth and love.

I take a deep breath and reach into my pocket. Eliza looks up at me, curious as I take her hand. "Eliza, I love you more than anything in this world. You're my best friend, my partner, and my soulmate. I never thought marriage would be in my future until I met you. I want to spend the rest of my life with you. Will you marry me?"

Tears fill her eyes, and she gasps. "Yes," she says, her voice choked with emotion. "Yes, of course I'll marry you."

I slip the ring onto her finger, and we hug each other tightly. "It's perfect," she murmurs in my shoulder. "Just like you."

We spend the rest of the evening on the beach, talking about our future together. Falling in love with Eliza was the easiest thing I've ever done, once I got over my hang-ups, I suppose. We watch the stars come out and listen to the sound of the waves licking against the shore.

"Let's go upstairs and celebrate," she whispers.

We meander back to our room, our fingers laced together.

"I never expected you to propose," she tells me.

"I never thought I would marry until I met you. My parents are the worst example when it comes to love, but I want to be different." I wave the key card over the lock, and it opens.

"We will be." Eliza softly kisses me. "All that matters is that we're together."

I lead her to the bed, stripping off her sundress and peeling away her underwear before I lay her down and quickly lose my shorts and T-shirt.

"I get to look at this view for the rest of my life," she says.

My cock is hard, and I stroke it as she watches. "It's yours and only yours."

Straddling her, I lean down and kiss her passionately, overwhelmed by a feeling of content, something I never knew was missing. I pull away. "Fuck, I love you so much!"

Eliza pulls me back to her, her hips looking for friction. "Then prove it, you stud."

I chuckle. "Fine. I'll show you how much I love you."

I move down her body and my tongue swirls, my teeth nip, and my lips touch her skin everywhere. Her eyes, clouded with desire, watch me. "You're so beautiful when you're so ready."

"I am ready," she pants.

The view is possibly the sexiest thing I've ever seen. Her nude figure stretched out, desire filling her eyes. "Let's start with a warm-up." I lie beside her, my hand wandering slowly. I circle each of her nipples as I lave them, bringing them to diamond points.

"Fuck me," she moans.

"You like this, don't you?"

"Yessssss."

My cock pushes into her hip, and it's weeping. I part her legs, and she's so wet. She shivers as I circle her bud. "That's one," she sighs.

"That was too small to count. I want the whole hotel to hear your climax."

Eliza moans, and her breathing increases as she makes happy noises and moans while guiding my actions. "Oh, yeah. Right there... Faster!"

Her pussy contracts around my fingers, and Eliza grips my arm as she goes over the cliff. "You're so beautiful when you come," I murmur. "That's your first orgasm of the night. Are you ready for more?"

Our lips connect, and our tongues interact playfully. "I never realized I could love you more than I already did," she says.

"I know," I tease. "My sexual prowess is legendary."

"Yeah, that's why." Eliza rolls onto her stomach. "No, it's knowing that it will be us together forever."

I lean down and kiss her shoulder. "Yes, it will be, and maybe a few rugrats too."

She smiles. "I'd like that."

I pull her to her knees and line myself up to take her from behind. After her orgasm, she's even tighter than usual.

She drops her head. "Give me a minute to adjust."

I lean down and kiss her shoulder. "Take as long as you

need."

She pulls away and pushes back into me. "I'm ready."

"Then let's go," I growl. I move my hips firmly, thrusting in and out, and quickly gain speed. I reach around and pull on her nipple, then start to strum her clit.

She groans my name as her channel grips my cock, which only pushes my own climax higher. After my release, I slump onto her soft body, and we collapse on the bed. For a blurry second, we exist in pure bliss, our sweaty bodies intertwined, panting breaths coming side by side.

"That was fucking amazing," Eliza says.

"Hell yeah, it was."

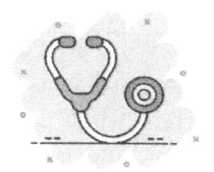

The rest of our vacation is even more special as we enjoy it as a newly engaged couple. We take long walks on the beach, holding hands and talking about our plans for the future. We eat romantic dinners and even have a couples massage.

As our trip ends, we both are sad to be leaving Belize. It's been such an incredible adventure, and it's hard to say goodbye to the beautiful scenery and friendly people. However, we're also excited to get home.

We sleep the entire plane ride home, and when we walk out of the airport into the Vancouver afternoon, the cool air and rain immediately produce goose bumps.

Eliza pulls her coat tighter. "We can go hide in Belize, but it only makes winter seem drearier and wetter when we return."

I wrap my arm around her, and we fire up our phones once we've settled in the car service. We haven't checked email the entire time we were gone. I'm not worried about work, but my friends have been active. No surprise there.

"We need to go see my dad," Eliza says after a moment.

"Today? Is everything okay?"

"Yes, I'm just excited to share our news. What do you think about having Dad, Laura, and the kids over with Mom and Antonio?"

"As long as you order in."

She thinks a moment. "Maybe we include your parents and your sister too. We can tell them all at the same time."

I kiss her forehead. "Sweetheart, I told your dad I was going to propose to you before the Grey Cup."

She scoots away from me and stares. "You mean everyone knew except me?"

I try not to laugh. "Yes, but if you'd said no, they would have circled the wagons around you and not me."

"What about your friends?" she challenges.

"Davis and Paisley knew, but they were under strict orders to keep it under wraps. But they told Michael, who told everyone. And I got Tanya's buy-in on the ring."

"I can't believe so many people kept your secret."

I smile, feeling proud of myself.

When the driver turns onto my street, I kiss Eliza on the neck. "Let's go upstairs and fool around a little and get some sleep. I'm completely wasted."

Eliza nods. "That sounds perfect."

But when I open my front door, suddenly, it's chaos. "Surprise!" rings in our ears from many voices.

Eliza holds onto her heart, and she nearly jumps into my arms.

"What are you doing here?" she marvels, looking around.

"Congratulations!" Tanya yells.

We're surrounded by our friends and family. Today is positively perfect. I've found the one woman on this Earth who is yin to my yang, and I couldn't be any happier.

Do you want more of Steve and Eliza? Check out the bonus content here. https://dl.bookfunnel.com/3xhrlgri8e

Books by Grace Maxwell

Doctor of the Heart
Paisley and Davis

Doctor of Women
Nadine and Michael

Doctor of Sports
Eliza and Steve

Doctor of Beauty
coming September 2023

Printed in Great Britain
by Amazon